Mahoud ig
pushing th
aside

His resistance was futile as the group rushed to meet him, beating him to his knees with rifle butts and barrels, the brutal blows driving him down, blood streaking his face.

Bolan had his own weapon snatched from his hands. He was searched for any other weapons, but all that was found was the GPS unit and Bolan's cell phone. He watched as they were thrown to the cave floor and crushed under heavy boots.

"They will not be of use to you any longer, American. You are in the hands of the Taliban now. We will give the orders."

Bolan looked him in the eye. "I'll try to remember that."

The Taliban leader laughed. "Be certain, American. You *will* remember. I promise you."

*Other titles available in
this series:*

Renegade Force
Retribution
Initiation
Cloud of Death
Termination Point
Hellfire Strike
Code of Conflict
Vengeance
Executive Action
Killsport
Conflagration
Storm Front
War Season
Evil Alliance
Scorched Earth
Deception
Destiny's Hour
Power of the Lance
A Dying Evil
Deep Treachery
War Load
Sworn Enemies
Dark Truth
Breakaway
Blood and Sand
Caged
Sleepers
Strike and Retrieve
Age of War
Line of Control
Breached
Retaliation
Pressure Point
Silent Running
Stolen Arrows

Zero Option
Predator Paradise
Circle of Deception
Devil's Bargain
False Front
Lethal Tribute
Season of Slaughter
Point of Betrayal
Ballistic Force
Renegade
Survival Reflex
Path to War
Blood Dynasty
Ultimate Stakes
State of Evil
Force Lines
Contagion Option
Hellfire Code
War Drums
Ripple Effect
Devil's Playground
The Killing Rule
Patriot Play
Appointment in Baghdad
Havana Five
The Judas Project
Plains of Fire
Colony of Evil
Hard Passage
Interception
Cold War Reprise
Mission: Apocalypse
Altered State
Killing Game
Diplomacy Directive

Don Pendleton's Mack Bolan®

Betrayed

A GOLD EAGLE BOOK FROM

WORLDWIDE®

TORONTO • NEW YORK • LONDON
AMSTERDAM • PARIS • SYDNEY • HAMBURG
STOCKHOLM • ATHENS • TOKYO • MILAN
MADRID • WARSAW • BUDAPEST • AUCKLAND

Recycling programs
for this product may
not exist in your area.

First edition March 2010

ISBN-13: 978-0-373-61535-3

Special thanks and acknowledgment to
Mike Linaker for his contribution to this work.

BETRAYED

Printed in U.S.A.

Have the courage to say no. Have the courage to face the truth. Do the right thing because it is right. These are the magic keys to living your life with integrity.
—W. Clement Stone,
1902–2002

A person who steps forward to do the right thing must be protected. I'll stand my ground and offer whatever support I can give, no matter what the consequences.
—Mack Bolan

For the peacemakers

They tracked Jamal Mehet to Paris, caught up with him when he emerged from a Métro station, followed him until he was alone on a quiet side street, grabbed him and bundled him into the rear of a Citroen delivery truck. Even as the vehicle was pulling away from the curb, a hypo needle was jabbed into Mehet's neck. It held a liberal dose of a powerful drug that rendered him unconscious. By the time he woke up he was far away from the city, locked in a room that had a mattress on the bare floor and nothing else. When he regained consciousness he was violently ill, emptying what little food his stomach held on to the floorboards. The aftereffects of the drug weren't pleasant, and he spent most of the day curled up on the mattress, drifting in and out of sleep. When his senses allowed him to focus he tried to work out how long he had been in the room.

A day?

Two?

He couldn't be sure. His watch was missing, so he had to judge the time of day by the passage of light he could see through the grubby window set in the roof over his head. It had already started to grow dark when he heard a key rattle in the lock and the door was flung open wide, banging against the inner wall with hard force.

Mehet rolled over so he could see the doorway. He had to blink his eyes to sharpen the image, and that was when he made out two figures stepping into the room. Beyond them he saw a third. Someone stood watch. The three figures separated and he could see them in detail now. The man just outside the door was holding a weapon. The two inside the room he didn't recognize. They were unknown to him. Both wore expensive, well-cut suits, complete with shirts and ties. He even found himself looking down at their polished shoes.

When he looked into their faces his first impression was they were business executives. Everything about them spoke of wealth. And they were Westerners with their light-colored, clean-shaved skin and benign expressions.

One of the pair moved farther into the room, his actions controlled and precise. He stopped at the foot of the bed, his hands crossed in front of him. Mehet noticed the man's fingernails. Neat and well manicured. Odd details that seemed very important to Mehet at that moment.

"We know who you are, Jamal Mehet," the man said. "We know all about your connections to Sharif Mahoud. We know he trusts you more than any man alive. That he trusts you with his life. I'm sure you will realize by now why you are here and what we want."

Mehet did realize what this was all about even as the man mouthed the words. He had been taken because of his intimate knowledge of Sharif Mahoud. These men, whoever they were, wanted the knowledge he carried inside his head. He also realized they were Mahoud's enemies. They wanted to locate Mahoud and not for any good reason.

If they found his friend, they would most likely kill him.

A small realization pushed into Mehet's mind at that moment.

The man speaking to him had an American accent. Quiet, refined almost, but most definitely American.

"You have had enough time to think over what I've just said, so I'll tell you what happens next. I'm going to ask you a simple question. I will ask it once, and you will have the opportunity to answer. Give me what I want or I walk out of here and place you in the hands of my associates who are waiting in the cellar below. In the end you *will* deliver your friend Sharif Mahoud to us. Choose the second option, and you will live longer but the experience will not be pleasant. I believe I have explained everything clearly." The man paused for a short time. "You know the current whereabouts of Mahoud. I need that location. Will you tell me where he is?"

Mehet felt his stomach churn. He understood the threat the man had posed, and he knew his refusal to answer would condemn him to pain and suffering. Two things he did not even want to imagine. He would give the man an answer, the only one he could.

"No," Mehet said, "I will not."

True to his word the man accepted Mehet's reply. He simply turned away, followed by his companion. They walked out of the room. The guard at the door leaned in and pulled it shut.

Mehet lay back, staring at the patch of light beyond the skylight. He saw the clouds drifting by, watched the gloom deepen, and knew darkness would soon fall and he would be lost in that darkness.

No more than ten minutes passed before they came for him, took him from the room and led him to the cellar beneath the house.

It became Mehet's final refuge. He spent almost three days in the place, days of terrible suffering as his captors worked on him, using every crude method of torture they could think of. There was little finesse in their actions. They believed in physical brutality of the worst kind. The intention was to inflict severe pain and mutilation to extract the information they needed. Mehet's pitiful screams echoed through the vaulted bleakness of the cellar, never reaching beyond the thick stone walls.

On the third day there was little more that could be done to make him suffer. Barely an inch of his body had not been violated, and it was a surprise even to Mehet's torturers that he was still alive.

An additional surprise they received was when he spoke for the first time since they had brought him to the cellar. They had to lean close to understand the words that whispered from his bleeding lips, sliding over toothless gums where his teeth had been torn free. He had gestured them to come closer by jerking the raw stumps of severed fingers at them.

And he had finally told them where they could find Sharif Mahoud, then begged them to put him out of his misery.

The chief torturer sent one of his men to relay the information upstairs and then put two 9 mm bullets into Mehet's head.

TWO NIGHTS LATER a strike force of three men, dressed from head to foot in black, splashed through the waves and came ashore from a small boat onto a beach in Northern Algeria. Behind them lay the Mediterranean Sea. In front the low profile of the isolated villa that was their target.

Intelligence had told them there were four armed guards patrolling the villa and surrounding terrain. Two more and the subject inside. The black-clad trio understood the patrol parameters that had been passed to them, providing them with the movements of the security team, so they were able to move in quickly. Using Heckler & Koch MP-5s fitted with suppressors, they were well equipped for what lay ahead.

The first guard was taken down by the lead shooter, his body crumpling under the impact of the suppressed 9 mm slugs. Skirting the perimeter of the villa, the strike team closed on the other guards, making their kills quickly and with a minimum of fuss.

With four guards down, the team crossed the tiled courtyard, skirted the circular stone fountain and approached the open archway that gave access to the interior of the villa.

Their information about the two bodyguards inside the villa, protecting Sharif Mahoud, was correct. As the strike team burst into the room, covering the occupants, the pair of guards sprang up from their seats, weapons sliding from holsters. They were too slow and went down in a hail of 9 mm bullets, their bodies torn and bloodied.

The robed figure seated with his back to the strike team rose slowly to his feet, turning to meet them. As light fell across his face, alarm showed in his eyes.

"What is going on? Who are you people and what do you want?" He stared down at the bodies on the floor. "This is not what I agreed to. It was only to be an impersonation for a few days."

The lead shooter took a long look at the robed figure, shaking his head in frustration.

"This is *not* Sharif Mahoud. We have been deceived. Mehet gave us false information."

The impersonator realizing his position was untenable turned back and forth in desperation. Now he understood, and in understanding he panicked. He turned his back on the strike team, wailing in terror as he ran for the door on the far side of the room.

Three SMGs fired simultaneously, riddling his body with 9 mm slugs. Cloth was shredded, flesh punctured and bloody gouts erupted from his back. When a number of the slugs tore his spinal column apart, the man dropped to the tiled floor. He sprawled across the smooth tiles, blood starting to seep from beneath him in rich red fingers.

The head shooter took out a sat phone and punched in a number. He waited until pickup.

"We were tricked," he said simply. "Mahoud is not here. Only a look-alike decoy. While we have been searching for him, he has probably moved on to a new location. By God, if that jackal Mehet could be brought back to life I would kill him all over again."

The American voice on the other end of the call maintained a calmness that was all the more chilling due to the circumstances.

"Leave the villa. Return to the landing zone and get back to the ship. We will rendezvous as soon as possible and review. I don't care where he has gone. We will keep looking until we find Mahoud, take the information he possesses, and then we will kill him. Him and his whole damn family."

CHAPTER ONE

The motor yacht *Crescent Moon* coasted sedately along the Corsican coastline, heading north toward Monaco. It was a half-day out, plowing gracefully through the Mediterranean Sea. Outwardly it looked like one of the many expensive pleasure crafts cruising the blue waters. Inside, however, the talk was far from casual.

The three men sitting around the large table in the ship's main cabin had more on their minds than the current trends in Monaco.

"We need to make a decision," Daniel Hartman said. "Rolling ideas back and forth is all very well, but it doesn't advance us one little bit."

His cultured tones, never raised above conversational level, drew everyone's eyes toward him. His importance in the group was enough to command its undivided attention. He had a policy of seldom repeating himself. And when he gave an ultimatum he never, ever, went back on it.

Hartman had been the man who had allowed Jamal Mehet his one chance to answer the question concerning Sharif Mahoud. The man's refusal had condemned him to the torturers waiting in the cellars and ultimately his death. His false information had drawn the three-man strike team to the villa on the Algerian coast. When Hartman had learned Mahoud hadn't been at the villa his calm exterior showed nothing of how he felt inside. He had simply called the strike team back and the team leader to this gathering to decide on their next move.

The quiet American looked around the table. His exceptional patience was often mistaken for indifference. It made him appear cold and distant even to those who knew him. Almost passive. Yet behind the facade was a sharp, incisive mind capable of intellectual keenness and an ability to make unpleasant decisions without a moment's hesitation.

The leader of the strike team, Ali Asadi, said, "Whatever else we decide, I think it is time to put the California operation into action. Everything is in place. At least that would give us something to fall back on."

Hartman nodded in agreement.

"I agree." He turned to the man on his left. "Make the call, Roger. Tell Marino to go. Once they have the Mahoud boy secure, Marino can advise us."

Roger Dane stood and crossed to a sat phone. He picked up the receiver and tapped in a number, waiting as the connection was made.

"Marino, this is Dane. You're on. Do it and advise us on completion."

"Good," Hartman said as Dane resumed his seat. "Let's continue. We have to accept that even if we succeed and get our hands on Mahoud's son there's no guarantee it will bring Mahoud himself into the open, or even force him to do what we ask. So we still need to follow this through ourselves. One thing is in our favor. Mahoud must have heard by now that Mehet has disappeared, that we took his bait and went for his decoy. No matter how dedicated the man is, losing someone like Mehet must unnerve him. He wouldn't have expected that to happen. Having his decoy killed will also make him realize he can't hide from us forever. Those two elements are likely to force him into doing something that might leave a trace. So we double our efforts. Increase the bounty and make sure that every informant available to us is fully aware that Sharif Mahoud is the most important name on their lists."

"He must be found. And eliminated," Asadi said, unable to keep his emotion under control. "The man is a traitor to everything he ever believed in. He defiles the very air he breathes, and his words are blasphemy each time he speaks."

"That may well be so, Ali," Hartman said, "but we can't ignore the fact that he is held in great respect by many men of influence throughout your region and beyond. Sharif Mahoud is a force to be reckoned with. No doubt because of his popularity he has many followers willing to hide him and throw off anyone looking for him. Why do you think we've had so much difficulty locating the man?"

Asadi's face darkened as he listened to the American. The knuckles of his clenched fists cracked under the tension.

"Should I begin to suspect that maybe your passion against Sharif Mahoud is not as strong as it should be? Perhaps our collaboration is not such a good idea after all."

"That is not—"

Hartman raised a hand to silence Dane.

"Please, Ali, you must not take what I said as praise for Mahoud. I'm merely attempting to explain that the man has great standing among his supporters. Not me. Or you. Or the people behind both of us. Our joint aim is to find and eliminate Sharif Mahoud. Be in no doubt as to that. But to help us in our search we have to look at the man as others see him.

"Mahoud has a gift. One we must never overlook. That gift is his ability to communicate. To be able to sit down with men from opposing cultures and religions. To talk with politicians of all persuasions. Even to bring together those who have fought bitterly for many years. Mahoud does this through his communication skills. It's a rare quality, and it makes our task that much more difficult because we'll receive very little help overall. Ali, we may not like how the world perceives Mahoud, but we can't ignore it."

Asadi digested what Hartman said, not liking what he was implying because it only added to Mahoud's mystique. He couldn't deny the effect Mahoud had over many he came into contact with. Secretly he envied the man's power to sway a crowd with his words. The ease at which he drew people to him and seemed able to calm their fear and suspicion. Asadi might only ever admit to himself that it was that very persuasiveness that generated his distrust of Mahoud. In his eyes it was not normal. As if Mahoud possessed some otherworldly spirituality above that of normal men. That was what created the hostility against him.

That and of course the more mundane fact that Mahoud's interference in the region's business might tip the balance of power within certain political-religious factions. Bringing them together might appear a miracle cure for the region's ills, but many were violently opposed to such maneuvering.

Roger Dane cleared his throat, one hand nervously touching the buff folder he had brought to the meeting.

"There is also the matter of the information Mahoud

has in his possession concerning the identification and af-filiation of a number of important figures within the various breakaway factions."

"Thank you, Roger. We can't ignore that detail," Hartman said. "Mahoud's zeal for his righteous crusade well may bring down these notable figures. Singly and collectively these individuals have great influence within various radical groups. If they were compromised, even killed, the effect could be serious. Cut off the head of a snake and the body may well still thrash around, but it will have lost its purpose and in doing that, its effectiveness."

AN HOUR LATER Roger Dane found Hartman relaxing on deck, a chilled drink in his hand. Watching his assistant approaching, Hartman peered over the top of his dark glasses, allowing a thin smile to curl his lips.

Dane, he knew, was a worrier. He always found the weak spot in any argument, the chink in armor, something to fret about. The look on the man's lean face spoke volumes.

"All right, Roger, spit it out. I always know when you have something to say."

"I just got off the phone with Wazir Homani. The word is out on Mahoud, but Homani told me he has heard that Mahoud has a deal being set up. He's on the verge of ac-cepting. Homani doesn't have all the details yet, but he'll inform us when he has more."

Hartman tool a long swallow from his glass. "And?"

"From what Homani has found out, Mahoud will make his commitment to broker the talks if he can be guaran-teed safe passage to a secret location for them. He has made a nonnegotiable demand that his family is to be brought out, as well. Homani believes his source had also verified this deal is being made by the U.S. President himself. He's going to send in someone *he* vouches for. Someone he trusts to do the job. The President, Daniel, of the United States, is getting personally involved."

Dane turned and helped himself to a large drink, swallowing it back in a single gulp.

"Am I missing something here?" Hartman asked.

"Only that the American Commander in Chief is dealing himself in. Our own President."

"Well, hell, Roger, let's stand up and salute the flag. We didn't expect it to be an easy ride. Don't wet your pants over this. Look on it as a sign they're taking things seriously. Nothing changes. We carry on as we have been. This might work in our favor. We have contacts in Washington. If the administration has thrown its cap into the ring, it presents us with a possible chance to pick up scuttlebutt. Jesus, Roger, the D.C. circuit has more holes than a leaky sieve. This could make life a lot easier for us. You get back on your phone and rouse everyone we know in Washington. Call in favors. Make threats. Do what the hell is needed, but see if you can get the info we need."

Alone again Hartman topped up his own drink and turned to stare out across the blue expanse of the Mediterranean. The unexpected news Dane had delivered added a new angle to the affair. He wouldn't have admitted it to Dane, but the emergence of the U.S. President sanctioning an operation to assist Sharif Mahoud had two sides. The probability of clashing with the American administration was something that needed consideration, though it was small compared with the positive benefits. If they could connect with whoever the President was sending in, their job could be made easier. All in all, it wasn't too bad a deal, and Daniel Hartman had never been one to back off from a reasonable gamble.

Now all they needed to do was to find out the identity of the man the President was putting forward and give him enough leeway to guide them to Mahoud himself.

CHAPTER TWO

"The guy in the picture is—*was*—Jamal Mehet. That was how the French police found him in the cellar of a house outside of Paris," Hal Brognola, director of the Sensitive Operations Group at Stony Man Farm, said. "The house had been rented by some guy who walked into the Paris office of the selling agent. Said he worked for a movie company and they just needed to shoot some interiors for a production. They only needed it for a few days. Guy paid cash. The agent figured it an easy deal because the old place was showing no signs of being bought. It was only when the keys weren't returned and the agent drove out to check that he found the body. The medical examiner worked out that the body had been in the cellar for at least four days. Before he died Mehet had been subject to some pretty horrendous torture. On top of everything else both his legs had been broken. Fingers on both hands amputated. His teeth torn from his gums. He finally died from a double tap of 9 mm slugs to the back of his skull."

Mack Bolan looked over the copies of the official police photographs. They were far from pleasant viewing. The fact that he had seen similar images many times over didn't make any difference. The sight of what had once been a living, breathing human reduced to a shrunken and battered corpse always affected him. The idea that a human could do this to another, for whatever reason, saddened him.

He placed the photographs on the table, pushing them away.

"Not exactly family snapshots," Brognola remarked. "Whoever did that to Mehet wanted something from him. Badly enough to torture him, then execute him when he was no more use to them."

"And do you believe they did get something?"

"All we do know is that a couple of days later a hit team breached a villa on the Algerian coast after taking out the four-man security force. Once inside they also killed the two bodyguards, then cut down the guy they had been led to believe was Dr. Sharif Mahoud. Only it wasn't Mahoud. Guy was a decoy being employed as a diversion while the real Sharif Mahoud was moving to a new location in Afghanistan."

"Doesn't look as if it worked the way Mahoud wanted."

"His opponents found out he was in Afghanistan and broke up his trip. Mahoud and his family were separated, if that's what you mean. Now the guy needs our help, Mack."

"If Mahoud can be helped."

"The President feels we should at least give Dr. Mahoud the benefit of the doubt. We should give the guy his chance. The President believes the man could make a difference."

Bolan didn't answer as quickly as Brognola expected, and his silence threw the big Fed slightly off balance.

"Or don't you agree?" Brognola asked, trying to elicit some kind of response.

"Hal, I understand exactly what you're pitching on the President's behalf."

"I happen to go along with him, Mack. His argument for backing Mahoud makes sense. If the guy can offer something—anything—out there we should be backing him. Hell, the Middle East, the whole region, is in a mess. I'm the first to hold up my hand to that. If someone comes along willing to put himself up as a mediator and without any kind of agenda other than looking for peace…"

Silence again as Bolan considered his friend's words. He respected Hal Brognola more than any other man he could name. The big Fed was open, without guile, and he would be ahead of the list to cheer if Stony Man had to stand down because universal peace broke out. Brognola carried no death wish on his broad shoulders. He wanted a world where the eradication of violent conflict became the norm, but he also understood the likelihood of such a condition wasn't in the cards. Greed, ignorance, political and religious desires were simply not going to vanish overnight. So the need for units such as Stony Man remained, and would for a long time.

As much as he might regret that need, Hal Brognola would use Stony Man to continue the fight. He would also reach out for any glimmer of hope, no matter how fragile.

"If you go for it, Hal, I'm in."

"Son of a bitch," Brognola muttered good-naturedly. "You enjoy seeing me squirm?"

He understood Bolan's need to have the nature of a mission clarified, the reason behind it placed before him. The mission had to fit in with Bolan's own agenda before he would put himself on the firing line.

"Mahoud believes he can bring various factions together, draw them to future meetings with opposing parties long enough to make serious inroads?"

"The man has that ability, Striker. You only have to check back over previous successes, the way he negotiated a cease-fire in one area of Afghanistan. He sat opposing warlords down at the table to talk and finally got them to agree to stop killing each other and cooperate. That was six months ago and the peace has held in that region. Don't ask me how the guy does it. People have called him a messiah, a holy man. That he has the touch. And that comes from any region across the spectrum. Mention Dr. Sharif Mahoud and you've said the magic words."

"What about the other side of the coin, Hal? He must have enemies. A man with that set of skills has to have upset a lot of people."

Brognola nodded.

"Damn right. When it comes down to it, Mahoud has the premium. Mullahs. Clerics. Out-and-out hard-liners. They put out calls for his death routinely. He's been accused of everything from being a false prophet to a blasphemer. His detractors accuse him of trying to weaken the beliefs of those who trust in God. The moderates accuse the hard-liners of being afraid of one man who only wishes to bring about peace across the region."

"Do we know where Mahoud is right now?"

"Increased threats are forcing him to keep changing locations. He's trying to stay one step ahead. When his message got through to the President he said he would make his whereabouts known only if the Man promised to bring him to safety."

"And where would *safety* be?"

Brognola shrugged. "That's open to debate. We're working on it. First we need to get Mahoud and his family free and clear from Afghanistan."

"Odds are that could be tricky. Bringing one man out from hostile territory isn't going to be an easy trip."

"Correction, Stricker. Not one man. Mahoud made a strict stipulation. He'll fulfill his role as mediator for as long as it takes. But only if his wife and two children are also brought out with him."

"Four people. An extraction from unfriendly territory. No backup."

Bolan's statement wasn't a question or an exclamation of surprise. It was simply a confirmation of the cold, hard facts.

He leaned back in his seat, gently tapping the file on the table in front of him. Brognola recognized the signs. Bolan working the facts over in his mind, agilely creating and dismissing operational scenarios until he brought the number down to one.

"Five," Brognola said.

"Say again."

"Mahoud has a son, Rafiq, who just turned eighteen. He's a student at Southern Cal, and according to information the kid is a high achiever."

"In that case I'm going to need an assist. Even I can't stretch myself between Afghanistan and California."

"Yeah, I figured you'd say that so I pulled Carl's name out of the hat. He's on standing down at the moment, visiting a friend in Oregon. That puts him the closest to California. I'll contact him."

"So when do I get my flight plan?"

"I'm waiting for the President to pass me details," Brognola replied. "When Mahoud spoke with him, he said one man would be waiting to guide you in to where Mahoud is in hiding. One of the few of his countrymen Mahoud trusts not to betray him."

"Kind of putting his head into the lion's jaws, isn't it? What if this guy isn't as loyal as Mahoud believes?"

"Mahoud does trust this guy. Enough to put his life in

his hands. He'll take you to Mahoud, then it's down to you to make sure the man and his family gets safely to the U.S. base for his extract. You bring him out and stay with him until the conference. Stony Man will provide backup and whatever you need. President's orders. You have full control on this mission."

Bolan raised the file. "Time for me to read up on Mahoud and his family."

CHAPTER THREE

Greg Marino checked the temperature and humidity of the Spanish cedarwood humidor. Satisfied it was steady at the required sixty-five degrees and seventy percent humidity, he removed one of the nine-inch Grand Corona cigars. He returned to his leather recliner and proceeded to cut the tip from the thick cigar, then took his time lighting it with a wooden match. He took a slow draw, allowing the mellow aroma to suffuse the length of the cigar, relaxing as the tendrils of tobacco smoke wreathed around him. Next to great sex, what he got from the cigar was the closest to perfection he could imagine.

Reaching for the phone, he hit a speed-dial number and waited for pickup. He recognized the subdued voice instantly.

"Grover, I just had the call from Dane," Marino said. "We're up. Let's do it, buddy."

"Okay. I'll call Kate and have her push the kid's buttons." He chuckled. "The sap won't know what's hit him til it's too late."

"Keep me posted," Marino said. "I'll be leaving for the cabin in a couple of hours, so use my cell number."

"Will do."

Marino ended the call. He leaned back in the recliner, deciding to finish the cigar before he left. After all, he decided, good things should never be rushed. The deal was under way. His team would make it work, so he had nothing to concern himself with for a while.

RAFIQ MAHOUD SPOTTED the young woman the moment he stepped out of the science building. He weaved his way between the other exiting students and made directly for her. As far as Rafiq was concerned, she could have been the only other person on campus. His full attention was focused on her.

His Callie. Blond and blue-eyed. A toned, supple figure. Clad in pale blue shorts, extremely short, and an equally skimpy stretch T-shirt. She was, as far as Rafiq was concerned, the ideal California girl.

His girl.

She made sure he understood that at every opportunity, and especially when they were alone. Just thinking about those times made him blush.

Callie waved as he caught her eye, her smile bright and caring. He might not have spoken it out loud, but Rafiq's emotions were in a turmoil. They always were when he was in her presence. In a word, she captivated him. From the first day he had met her, the delightful blonde had him wrapped around her little finger, and he loved every moment.

"Hi," she said when Rafiq reached her side.

"Hi, yourself. I almost didn't get clear. Some of the guys wanted to get together and chill. Took me a while to break away."

"Last thing I want is you chilling out." She laughed. "I want you hot." She kissed him on the cheek. "Very hot. Especially for this weekend. Or had you forgotten?"

As they moved along the sidewalk, heading for the parking area and Rafiq's two-year-old SUV, he shook his head.

"My stuff is already in the truck. What about you?"

Callie showed him the backpack over her left shoulder. "Everything I need is in here."

"It doesn't look like much."

"Enough for what we're going to be doing."

"You are a terrible woman."

"It's why you like me."

"Yeah? And for a few other things."

When they reached his vehicle, Rafiq unlocked it and Carrie threw her backpack on the rear seat alongside his own. She climbed in and waited as he joined her. He started the engine and reversed out of the slot, raising a hand to a passing group of students. Then he drove out of the lot and negotiated his way along the feeder road until they were on the highway.

"Let's go, cowboy," Carrie said, reaching to click on the radio.

Rafiq pushed down on the gas pedal and boosted the SUV up a notch.

He was feeling good. It was a beautiful day. The weekend was coming up and he was alone with the most fantastic woman he had ever known. Things couldn't get any better.

CHAPTER FOUR

The Air Force plane touched down late afternoon and Mack Bolan stepped back onto Afghanistan soil. Already dressed in military combat fatigues and boots, he slung his backpack over his shoulder, picked up his heavy hold all, and crossed the dusty field to meet the Hummer speeding out to pick him up.

Beyond the military base the inhospitable Afghanistan landscape glowered beneath an empty sky. There were few clouds. It was hot and dusty, with the ever present dry wind soughing down off the higher hills. Underfoot the ground was hard and stony, with little vegetation other than isolated clumps of brittle grass.

The Hummer rolled to a stop a few feet away. The uniformed figure stepping out from behind the wheel nodded at Bolan. The guy was young, Bolan's height. Lean and burned brown from the sun.

"Mr. Cooper."

"I'll be out of your hair ASAP, Lieutenant Pearson," Bolan said, reading the man's uniform name tag.

He understood the sometimes reluctance of the military to have to nursemaid civilians in their midst. They had enough on their hands, and Mack Bolan had no desire to add to their problems.

The officer smiled, said, "I don't suppose you want to be here either."

"I can think of more pleasant surroundings."

They climbed into the Hummer. Bolan stowed his rucksack and weapons hold-all. Pearson turned the Hummer and headed in the direction of the collection of tents and huts that made up the base. It all looked familiar to Bolan, bringing back memories of his own service time, when he had lived and operated out of such places. It made him aware once more of the privations and the danger the men and women placed themselves in when they became part of the operation. Here, in this foreign environment, thousands of miles from family and country, they daily put themselves in harm's way, exposing themselves to the ever present threat of violence. There were no guarantees out here. No promises of uneventful tours. Only the reality of sudden and brutal action.

"I was told to expect you, do whatever was needed to facilitate your mission, and not ask questions. I was told a local would be showing up to meet you. Something about him walking you into hostile territory, so I guess you're not here to sightsee."

"You've got that right, LT."

Pearson threw him a quick glance, smiling.

"Now that's not a civilian speaking. I'd say you've served your time."

"And then some," Bolan answered.

He didn't expand and Pearson didn't probe. The soldier might have been surprised if he learned about Bolan's own private war, waged for many years against enemies who might not have worn regular uniforms but who were certainly combatants. It might have been waged against a different backdrop in some instances, but by any definition it was still war.

They reached the main camp, Pearson rolling the Hummer to a stop outside one of the smaller huts.

"Your guy is there," the soldier said. He waited until Bolan had claimed his gear. "Anything you might need, give me a shout. I was told you might need assistance with an extract?"

"If I do, I'll call."

"We'll be around if you need us."

"Good to know."

Pearson raised a hand, then gunned the Hummer and drove away.

Bolan pushed his way through the hut's door and went inside. It was sparsely furnished, functional.

It was empty except for a single occupant.

A tall, lean Afghan turned at Bolan's entrance. He wore a mix of traditional Afghan and Western clothing. A long sheepskin coat covered a colorful shirt, and U.S.-style combat pants were tucked into sturdy leather boots. He wore a *lungee*, the turban's long scarf hanging almost to his waist. A broad leather belt circled his hips, supporting a canvas holster that held a modern autopistol. On the opposite hip was a sheathed knife. Leaning against a table was an AK-47. The Afghan eyed the big American while he continued to drink from a tin mug. Finally he lowered the mug. He wore a trimmed dark beard.

"You are Cooper?" When Bolan nodded, the man said, "I am Rahim Azal. You know why I am here?"

"Yes."

"It is too late to go today. We will leave in the morning. Early." Azal indicated a steaming pot sitting on a butane gas stove. "Tea?"

Bolan nodded. "Sure."

The tin mug Azal handed Bolan was hot, the strong tea scalding. Bolan tasted it, nodding his approval.

"I can see why the Afghans are good fighters," he said. "If you can drink this, you can face anyone."

Azal laughed.

"I think I might like you, Cooper." He looked Bolan over. "Are you a warrior? Dressing as one does not make it so."

Bolan picked up his hold-all and dropped it on the table. He opened it to show Azal his ordnance. The Afghan peered at the contents of the bag.

Azal raised his mug. "Defeat to our enemies."

THEY WERE on the move at first light. The air was still chilled from the cold night as Bolan and Azal finished their breakfast and readied themselves. The soldier took out his weapons and strapped on the webbing belt that would carry his Beretta 93-R in a hip holster. He had an MP-5 SMG, and a Cold Steel Tanto knife sheathed on his left side. A combat harness held extra magazines for both his weapons and Bolan added a few fragmentation grenades. From his backpack he took a black baseball cap and an olive-drab cotton scarf. The long scarf wound around his neck could be used to wipe away dust and sweat from his face; it could also prevent dust entering his mouth. Azal watched as Bolan put on the scarf, a smile curling his lips as he observed.

"Now I know you have been here before," he said. "Once the dust of Afghan has been tasted, no man wants to repeat the experience if he can avoid it."

Bolan swung his backpack into place and adjusted the straps. He checked his filled canteen and clipped it to his web belt.

Lieutenant Pearson drove up in his Hummer. He had

been assigned to drive Bolan and Azal for the initial part of their journey, where he would leave them in the foothills. The lieutenant was fully armed, and a second soldier sat in the seat beside him.

The trip took them a couple of hours, over rugged terrain that offered little relief from the ever present heat and the restless, drifting breeze. Serrated, undulating, the Afghan landscape had little to recommend itself. This was a savage and unwelcoming place, and Bolan knew that there might easily be armed figures waiting behind any one of a dozen boulders, or concealed in shallow ravines. Maybe he was in someone's sights at that very moment. It was an unsettling thought, one he had experienced many times, so he accepted the fact because there wasn't a damn thing he could do about it.

Pearson slowed the Hummer, swinging the vehicle in a half circle at Azal's instruction. When he came to a full stop the Afghan leaned forward and tapped him on the shoulder.

"This is the place. We go on foot from here."

Pearson waited until Bolan and the Afghan climbed out.

"Good luck, Cooper. Don't forget the ride home when you need it."

Bolan nodded. "Thanks for the assist, LT. Take it easy on your way back."

The Hummer sped away, leaving Bolan and his guide alone. Dust drifted in the Hummer's wake. Azal turned to check the way ahead.

"You enjoy walking, Cooper?"

"Yeah. Let's move out."

They followed a faint track that led directly into the rugged hills. After a couple of miles even the thin trail vanished. Azal didn't hesitate. He moved with great agility, ignoring the steep angle of the slopes. Azal glanced back a few times, smiling to himself when he saw the American keeping pace with him.

It was noon straight up when Azal called a halt. He guided Bolan to a wide overhang of rock that shielded them from the sun. From his pack the Afghan produced a loaf of bread and a wedge of goat's cheese. He divided the meal, handing half to Bolan. The bread was coarse, the cheese strong. They ate in silence, washing the food down with water from their canteens.

"There is a small spring ahead," Azal said. "We can refill the canteens."

"You've known Mahoud a long time?" Bolan asked.

Azal nodded. "We were born and raised in the same village. We grew up together. Both our families were as one. Our fathers and grandfathers fought against the Russians. We both lost people in the war." Azal shrugged. "As far as I can remember there has always been some kind of fighting going on. But we survived. We were never wealthy but life could be good."

"Mahoud wanted more?" Bolan said.

"Even as a young man he was unhappy with the fighting, though there were times he had to use a gun to defend what was his. The tribal squabbling saddened him. He wanted changes. Everyone told him it could never happen. Sharif refused to accept that. He started to speak at village councils and traveled all over talking to people. He had a way with words. He sat and discussed matters with politicians and religious leaders. People trusted him. He settled local differences. It was good for him, but he was restless for more change and in the end he went away for almost three years. When he returned, he was different. Still passionate about making things better, but he said staying here wouldn't allow him to do that. He had been accepted to a place of learning in France, where he could understand the ways of higher learning. It was all too complicated for me to understand. Sharif was away for seven years and the next time he came to the village he brought his wife and children with him."

"Was he different then?"

"Yes, and no," Azal said. "He was Sharif of the village, but he was also Dr. Sharif Mahoud, a man of the world. A learned man building his reputation as a negotiator. He had written books and articles for magazines. His qualifications allowed him to mix with powerful men and took him around the country and to far places in the Middle East. When he sat in his parents' house he was one of us again. Everyone was so proud of Sharif. They took to his beautiful wife and their children. But when I watched his face, I knew he would not be staying for long. He had his path to follow and it was not just to be in Afghanistan. When we talked alone, he told me how he needed to travel to other places to do what he could for other oppressed people. To try and bring enemies together and settled differences.

"From his wife we learned of their other life. An apartment in Paris. Their visits to America and London. The important people they met. His work with government organizations. Sharif has gone far. Has helped many. His friends are all over the world." Azal raised his hands. "But so are his enemies. He has disturbed many people who are angry at his attempts to make solid peace. For many reasons, Cooper. Money. Power. Religious intolerance. He knows this, but all he does is shrug and say it is something he has to bear."

"These enemies are the ones who want him dead?"

Azal nodded. "Yes. The ones who murdered Jamal Mehet. The same ones who killed the man acting as a decoy. The same ones who tried to disrupt his meetings and forced his wife and children into hiding while Sharif had to seek sanctuary elsewhere."

He leaned back, closing his eyes, and rested.

"We will reach our next place before dark," he said. "A village I used to know well. It is empty now. You will see what the Taliban is doing to our life."

THE VILLAGE had been empty for some time. Azal explained how the Taliban had driven out the occupants, forcing them to clear the village or be wiped out.

"They wanted to make an example to show how they were in charge. All around here the Taliban has been forcing people to do as they say. Anyone who defies them is either killed or beaten until they are crippled. This is the way the Taliban works. Fear. Violence. Their fighters wage war on women and children, and force the young men to join them, or watch their families be slaughtered. These villagers are poor. They have nothing, no power, so they can be exploited."

"So where do they go?"

Azal shrugged. "Look around, Cooper. Where is there for them to go? Many of them simply vanish into the hills. They hide. Starve. If they are lucky, they make their way to the refugee camps many miles away. Some die on the way there. The Taliban is ripping out the heart of my country because so many refuse to bow to their demands." The Afghan faced Bolan. "Now ask me why I believe in Sharif Mahoud. Because he is the one man who is prepared to face up to the truths about these people. He is willing stand up to them. Talk with the moderates and face the enemies of Afghanistan. I am simple man, Cooper. Not clever with words, but I would give my life so Sharif Mahoud can speak for me."

"For a man who claims he is not clever with words, Rahim, you make your point well."

Azal shook his head, smiling briefly.

"I will make tea. We will rest here overnight." He turned to indicate the rising wall of the rocky hills behind the village. "Then we have that to climb. And no clever words will make that any easier."

"Let's check out the area. Make sure we have a way to get clear if needed. Too late if we find ourselves boxed in."

"Yes. I will show you something I found once before when I was here. It will serve us well."

THEY WERE PREPARING to leave a couple of hours after dawn when Bolan picked up the distant sound of a vehicle engine powering its way up the incline leading into the village. The narrow track he and Azal had used bore faint tire impressions, showing past usage by motorized transport. The Afghan was inside one of the empty huts, packing away the gear they had been using.

"Azal."

The Afghan joined him, nodding. "I hear it."

"Taliban?"

"Could be. But the fighters would be less likely to allow themselves be heard in such a way. A vehicle cannot go farther than this place. Your military would only use helicopters if they were coming here."

"Wait inside the hut," Bolan said. "Cover me from there."

Azal backed away and stood inside the doorway, hidden in the shadows, while Bolan edged around the corner of the hut.

The vehicle turned out to be a battered 4WD Land Rover. Bolan couldn't have guessed how old it was. Despite the outward appearance, the mechanics of the vehicle seemed to be in good shape. It rocked into view over the final rise in the trail and came to a stop near the edge of the steep drop-off. The beat of the engine faded.

The passenger door opened and a man climbed out, one hand raised to shade his eyes from the glare of the sun. He was of medium height, heavy build, with beefy shoulders. He wore crumpled chinos and a short-sleeved bush shirt. The moment he stepped from the Land Rover the man locked eyes with Bolan, staring at him with a hard gaze. His eyes were shadowed under thick brows, deep set in a lined, unshaved brown face, and he made no attempt to hide his aggressive manner.

"You guys are off the beaten track," he said, which was more of an accusation than a query.

Bolan ignored him. That seemed to annoy the man even more.

"You hear me?"

"They can probably hear you in Pakistan," Bolan said. He hadn't missed the man's reference to Bolan not being on his own.

You guys.

Whoever he was, the newcomer was sharp. Or he knew more than was apparent.

"You want something or are you passing through?" Bolan asked.

"Could be we're both looking for the same thing."

"You think so?"

"How many Afghans are there in these hills who go by the name of Sharif Mahoud?" the newcomer queried.

"You're the one with all the answers," Bolan said. "I haven't a clue what you're talking about."

"The hell you don't." The man turned and waved to the Land Rover's driver to join him.

When the guy stepped into view, Bolan saw he was

carrying a professional video camera. He hoisted it on his shoulder and trained it on the soldier.

"Hey," Bolan called. "You carry life insurance?"

The cameraman frowned, then said, "What's that mean?"

"It means turn that thing away from me or you'll find out if your policy pays off."

"Anja, don't listen to him. We can film whatever we want."

"It isn't you he has that gun pointing at."

"Don't be a chicken-shit." The guy turned back to Bolan. "You know who I am?"

"Why don't you tell me."

"Kris Shehan."

Bolan's face didn't flicker with recognition.

"Look at that," he said. "You didn't surprise me. Should I have heard of you?" he asked.

"I'm starting not to like you, pal," Shehan stated.

"One, I don't give a damn about that. Two, I'm not your pal. And I think it's time you backed off."

Bolan turned to stare at the cameraman, who had turned his lens back in Bolan's direction. Shehan's voice interrupted him.

"I'm getting tired of you playing the hard guy. Why don't you move your ass out of my way? My assignment is to meet up with Mahoud and get his story. What are you going to do? Shoot me?"

"The thought had occurred to me."

"Go ahead. Anja will get it all on tape. Hell, I could make you famous." Shehan was smiling now, enjoying himself. "I could sell you all over the Middle East. Maybe even get it picked up by CBS or Fox News. You know how the great American public likes its violence."

Bolan blocked Shehan's way.

"You leave it right there," he said. "Take your cameraman and turn around. Get clear of this village and stay out of my sight."

Shehan glanced at his cameraman, a knowing grin crossing his face. When he faced Bolan again that smile had gone.

"You know who I am? Who I represent?"

"I know you believe you have the right to push your way into people's lives. Put them at risk just so you get your thirty seconds on some cheap TV news program."

"Fuck you, mister. I've brought home more important reports than you could imagine. I put my life on the edge to get my stories. You think American networks are the only ones allowed to tell what is happening here? Ha. My news is for the real people of Afghanistan. Sharif Mahoud is a story. I'm going after an exclusive. Who the hell are you to try to stop me?"

This time it was Bolan who gave a weary smile.

"Correction, Shehan. It won't be *try* to stop you. I will stop you if you get in my way."

"Hard man now, huh? Listen, friend, I've faced off with real warlords in my time. Some cheap merc isn't making me back down."

"Having to keep correcting you is becoming a habit. If I *was* a merc, I wouldn't be cheap."

Bolan shouldered the man aside as he crossed to the cameraman who had been videoing the confrontation.

"Do you have a backup camera?" he asked.

"Yeah. In the Rover. Why?"

"You're going to need it," Bolan told him.

He reached out and wrenched the vidcam from the man's hands. Ignoring Shehan's yell of protest, Bolan walked to the trail's edge and hurled the vidcam into space. It spun in a downward spiral to smash on the sun-bleached rocks far below.

"You bastard," Shehan screamed. "Do you know how much that cost?"

"Rough country out here," Bolan said. "Stuff gets smashed all the time."

"You'll regret this. I'll fucking well sue you for every cent you have."

Bolan shrugged. "Good luck. Remember I'm just a cheap merc. Your own words."

Shehan's face flushed with righteous anger. He turned to the cameraman, thrusting a finger as he yelled, "Go and get the other vidcam." Anja simply stared back at him. "I said, get the other fu… What the hell is wrong with you?"

Bolan sensed the cameraman's agitation. He turned to check out what the man was looking at and saw armed figures emerging from the rocks beyond the village. The soldier picked up a familiar, rising sound. His gaze rose and he spotted the thin trail, curving and pale against the hard blue sky.

A mortar shell.

"Incoming," he yelled.

The mortar hit even as he called the warning. The solid thump of the explosion was followed by the geyser of dirt and rock. It mushroomed across the clearing, yards from Shehan's Land Rover. The force of the blast rocked the vehicle and flying debris took out the side windows.

"Azal," Bolan called.

"I am here," the Afghan said. He appeared at Bolan's side, shaking his head. "They will be Taliban. This is bad."

"Tell me about it."

A second and third shell landed. Number three was close enough to lift the Land Rover and flip it onto its side, one rear wheel torn from the axle. Smoke swirled, caught by the hot wind.

With the truck disabled the armed figures Bolan had

seen started to move in, opening fire with the AKs they were carrying.

"Get us out of here," Shehan yelled, lunging at Bolan, his fingers clutching at Bolan's shirt. "They hit my truck."

Bolan ignored him.

With the smoke clearing he had just seen the cameraman, flat down on the ground, his back a ragged wound from neck to hips. Bone and flesh had been shredded by the blast from one of the mortar rounds. Little remained of the man's rear skull and neck.

"Let's move, Azal," Bolan said, brushing off Shehan's hands. "We're leaving. Shehan, come with us or sit and wait for the people you most likely led here."

The lead attacker pounded across the path that snaked into the village from the rocky slope above, Kalashnikov crackling. Slugs whined off the stony ground. Bolan leaned around the edge of the hut wall, his MP-5 rising. He led the rushing figure and waited, then triggered a short burst, slamming the guy to the ground in a flurry of dust and bloody spray. Close by, Azal was using his own weapon to good effect, putting down two more of the agile figures as they bounded across the open ground leading into the village.

With three of their number suddenly down, the attack faltered. The armed figures retreated into cover.

"They are eager but not bloody foolish." Azal grinned at Bolan.

"I doubt they're ready to quit, either," the soldier said.

As he spoke he was checking out the area, recalling the lay of the land around the village. He had checked it out even as he had walked in, selecting possible back door escape routes in case of emergencies.

He lifted his head as he heard more incoming, mortars sizzling in from deep cover. The attackers could bide their time, laying down a solid wall of shells that would saturate the area. While the defenders were forced to maintain cover, the attackers could start to close in while maintaining their own safety. The hard thump of explosions, lifting more dirt and rock, created clouds of acrid dust that swirled back and forth across the village. Bolan crouched with his back to the wall, figuring that by the law of averages the hut they were using was going to take a hit.

"Azal, if we sit here too long…"

"I know. We should leave quickly before they regroup and come for us again."

Then as swiftly as it had started the mortar attack ceased. Someone shouted in the distance. Shadowy figures began to emerge from the dispersing clouds of dust. More of the armed attackers. They came from two directions, opening up with hard autofire that threw streams of 7.62 mm slugs across the area. Bolan could hear the solid thwack as they ripped into the dry earth, the harsher sound as they struck rock, some whining off into the air. The rattle of autofire continued without let up.

"Let's go," Bolan snapped at Azal.

The Afghan moved without a word, crossing the hut and exiting through the rear window, dropping out of sight. Bolan followed.

"What about me?" Shehan demanded, his tone losing none of its arrogance.

Bolan paused, throwing a hard look across his shoulder. "Follow or stay. Your choice. I don't care." Then he was gone, clearing the frame.

CHAPTER FIVE

As Bolan's boots hit the dusty ground at the rear of the hut, he picked up Azal's moving figure. The Afghan was moving fast, weaving his way through the scattered rocks and brush, and heading for the jagged defile snaking away from the village. It was the best way out. Bolan and Azal had picked it during their early recon. He checked the immediate area and saw that it was clear—for the moment at least. Bolan didn't expect it to remain that way. The autofire was still crackling and now Bolan picked up raised voices. The attackers were getting closer, probably wondering why there was no further resistance.

He took off after Azal.

"Hey…"

Looking back Bolan saw Shehan tumbling through the window. He fell as he hit the ground, luck favoring him as a burst of autofire chewed at the wooden frame, splintering wood and filling the air with splinters. Bolan was tempted to keep moving, leaving the obnoxious journalist behind. Something held him back and he spun on his heel, sending a long burst from the MP-5 in through the shadowed window. He was rewarded by a brief shriek as his bullets found a target.

"Move, Shehan. Get your ass over here and head for that defile up ahead, or so help me I'll shoot you myself."

Bolan plucked a grenade from his harness and pulled the pin. He let the lever pop free, held the grenade for a count, then hurled it in the direction of the window. The projectile sailed through the gap. As Shehan passed him, and Bolan followed, the grenade detonated with a solid crash of sound, smoke gushing from the window. The impact of the explosion shifted some of the wall stones.

Hard on Shehan's heels Bolan sprinted for the defile. As the journalist vanished down the gap leading into the defile, Bolan dropped and rolled, taking up a defensive position, giving the others time to move deeper into the fissure. He exchanged the almost empty MP-5 magazine for a fresh one, slipping the ejected mag into a pouch. He freed a second grenade, took out the pin and waited.

His wait was a short one. Gunners began to move around the side of the hut. Bolan counted at least four of them. They clustered together, uncertain which way to move. They hadn't yet seen the defile, but Bolan knew they would spot it quickly enough. He wasn't about to allow them that luxury. He let the lever go, raised himself and threw the grenade hard. It hit the ground only feet from the hesitant group and they began to scatter. The lethal blast from the grenade caught them on the run, the white-hot fragments ripping into flesh and sending the enemy sprawling.

Before they could regroup Bolan slid down into the defile and raced after Azal and Shehan.

They needed to clear the area, to move out of range of the locals. The Taliban would offer little in the way of mercy if they got their hands on him and his companions.

Like it or not, Bolan was saddled with Shehan, at least for the moment. Despite his reservations concerning the morals of the man's business, Bolan couldn't simply leave him alone in enemy territory. So until he could deliver him into friendly hands he was stuck with the guy. Bolan decided he wasn't going to allow Shehan an easy ride. If the soldier was going to have to devote some of his energy and skill toward keeping Shehan alive, the man would earn his keep.

As he hit the base of the defile, feeling the rocky sides close around him, Bolan spotted Shehan and Azal directly ahead. He pressed on, closing in, calling for them to keep moving.

He almost missed the sound of an incoming mortar. The shell struck the upper rim of the defile, and though it was yards behind, the explosion threw thick clods of earth and a shower of stone fragments into the ravine. The opposition was not giving in easily. Bolan understood that the cards were all falling into their hands. This was their territory, and they would know it intimately. Every rock and patch of brush. Every place where a man could hide. All Bolan had was his desire to survive and not let himself fall into the hands of the Taliban.

A second mortar blew more debris over them. This time it was closer, the blast rocking them on their feet. Yards ahead Shehan stumbled and fell, shredding his hands on the flinty rocks.

"Christ, my hands!"

"On your feet, mister," Bolan ordered. "Sooner or later those mortars are going to be ranged in, and whining about your grazed fingers isn't going to be much help. Now get up and keep moving."

Shehan dragged himself upright, wiping his bloody hands down his shirt. The look he threw at Bolan was mur-

derous, but it had no effect on the soldier. Bolan understood the situation they were in. They had no time to
discuss the finer points of battlefield etiquette. They were
in a race for their lives and one slip, one miscalculation,
would allow the enemy to close in and end it.

The rattle of small-arms fire echoed the length of the
defile. Slugs struck rock, splinters flying. As Bolan followed the natural curve of the land he plucked a grenade
from his harness, yanked out the pin and let the lever go.
Ignoring the small insistent voice urging him to throw the
projectile, he waited, then turned and lobbed the grenade
around the curve. The detonation was close, but the sweep
of the bend protected Bolan from the blast. He heard a
couple of harsh screams as the pursuers were caught, their
luck running out.

Moving on, Bolan caught the flicker of moving figures
at the top of the defile, heard the crackle of fire as they
angled their weapons into the gap. Slugs pounded the dry
earth, kicking up dusty gouts. Bolan flattened against the
wall, turning his weapon up at the gunners. He triggered
a burst that dragged dirt from the defile feet below his
target, using it as a guide for his second burst. His next
shots caught one guy in the lower legs, blowing out gouts
of red. The Taliban fighter stumbled to his knees, missed
his balance and plunged headfirst into the defile, slamming into the ground only yards from Bolan, his skull
shattering on impact. The second shooter shouted something unintelligible, firing even as he uttered the yell. His
slugs tore at the defile wall above Bolan's head, showering him with dirt and stone chips. The soldier returned fire
and caught the guy center mass, tossing him back out of
sight.

Running hard, Bolan caught up with Azal and Shehan.
The Afghan was ushering the journalist into a shadowed

gap where the defile merged with the rock face that ended it.

"Quickly," Azal said. "This will take us to other side of the hills."

Pausing at the entrance, Bolan asked, "You sure?"

Azal grinned. "I remember from many years ago. We played in here when I was a child. It goes all the way through the hills. Would I be so foolish as to walk into a trap myself?"

"Guess not," Bolan said.

Azal led the way deeper into the passage. The farther they walked, the less the light penetrated. After a few hundred yards they were stumbling along in near darkness. The air was hot and stale. The walls curved and hollowed out as they progressed along the rough ground. At one point the ceiling overhead swooped down to shoulder height, and they had to hunch forward to avoid cracking their heads on the unyielding rock. Water glistened in the pale light, sliding down the rock face from some unseen source, creating shallow pools they had to walk through.

Bolan took time to backtrack a few yards, listening to the silence behind them. He waited, his ears straining to pick up any sound of their pursuers. He was almost ready to move on when he caught the merest whisper of boot leather sliding over rock. As the sound increased, Bolan judged there had to be at least five, possibly six. They were still following, but staying well back after the last encounter with the grenade. The soldier idly fingered one of the remaining two grenades clipped to his harness, then decided to hold them back. He moved to the opposite side of the defile, back pressed against the rock wall.

Shapes emerged from the rock-strewn backdrop, and Bolan opened fire instantly. Two went down. He kept up his rate of fire, driving the others back. Angling the MP-5's muzzle, the Executioner raked the angle of the rock wall, hearing the slugs ricochet. He was hoping some of the slugs might bounce off and cause some extra confusion for the enemy. Anything to make them stay back. He emptied the magazine and quickly snapped in a fresh one, then turned and picked up the pace.

The way ahead widened, the rock ceiling rising to a great height; light was starting to penetrate. Bolan picked out Azal and Shehan way ahead of him, crossing a wide, smooth table of stone that angled upward. As he hit the table he felt warm sun on him. Glancing up he saw sections of the ceiling were open to the sky. Reaching the peak of the table, Bolan saw the high cavern give way to exposed ground, a massed jumble of massive boulders, water tumbling in a narrow fall from some greater height and splashing onto the bleached stone below where it spilled from a naturally formed rock pan to create a runoff.

"Come quickly," Azal called, gesturing with his arm.

Bolan saw Shehan close by the Afghan. There was a moment when the journalist seemed to be pulling at his crumpled shirt. Then Shehan suddenly pulled a long-bladed knife from under his shirt. He swung it hard at Azal's back, stabbing down into the Afghan's body. Azal gasped, his lean body twisting in agony as Shehan yanked out the glittering steel blade and raised it to strike a second time, plunging it deep into Azal's flesh.

Bolan had raised the MP-5 by this time, and he hit Shehan with a burst. The slugs clawed at the journalist's right side, splintering ribs and gouging flesh. The man stumbled, shock etched across his face. He went down on one knee, the knife slipping from his fingers and his head turned toward Bolan. The soldier was moving fast, powering his way across the open rock, and the expression on his face warned Shehan not to expect any leeway. The journalist had showed his hand at the wrong moment. Bolan fired again, this time going for a kill shot, placing his 9 mm slugs into Shehan's chest. The man fell backward, slamming down hard, the rear of his skull striking the rock. He was still conscious when Bolan's shadow fell across him. Shehan stared up at him, his eyes blazing with a righteous fervor, spitting blood as he tried to speak.

"You won't succeed. We will still get to Mahoud and he *will* die."

Bolan ignored him, knowing the man would bleed out in seconds.

Azal was hunched over on his knees, his head almost touching the rock. As Bolan bent over him, he noted the spreading blood patch extending down the Afghan's back from the knife wounds. Azal turned his head so he could see Shehan sprawled on the rock only feet away.

"Was it something I said?" he whispered, managing a wisp of a laugh. Then, "Cooper, you need to go. If you stay you will be caught. Then Mahoud *will* lose his chance."

"I'm supposed to leave you?"

"You are a good man, Cooper. Be a wise one. I'm not going any farther. Shehan saw to that." When Azal slowly raised his head, Bolan saw blood dribbling from his mouth. "Whatever else he was, Shehan knew where to place his blade."

"Azal…"

"Here." Azal slid his hand inside his long coat and pulled out a slim six-by-four item that he thrust at Bolan. "GPS unit. A backup in case I failed. I believe this is what Shehan wanted from me. Mahoud's location is keyed in. He is due east from where we are. In the higher country." Azal's free hand gripped Bolan. "Get him out, Cooper, and he will do what he has promised. Now pass me my weapon."

At Azal's urging Bolan eased the Afghan into a sitting position, his bloody back pressed to the curve of a large boulder. He placed the AK-47 in the man's hands. Azal gestured at the two grenades on Bolan's harness, and he handed them to him.

"Now go before those bloody Taliban jackals show their ugly faces. Go now, Cooper. I will cover your back."

Bolan found himself hesitating, torn between his mission and the fate of the man in front of him.

"What good if we both die here? Mahoud promises at least some measure of success and, however small, it must be allowed its chance."

Bolan laid his hand on Azal's shoulder. Nothing more spoken passed between them, but the Afghan's words made him aware of why he was here and what he had to do. He turned away and cut across to the east and the forbidding, craggy slopes. As he moved he slid the GPS unit into a pocket for safety.

The terrain was harsh and unforgiving. Bolan kept up as fast a pace as he could, slinging the MP-5 to free both hands as he hauled himself over jagged outcroppings and eroded ledges of dusty rock.

He picked up the chatter of autofire coming from behind him. There was a pause, then more rapid fire followed by the sharp blast of a detonating grenade. Azal was making good use of his limited ordnance. The second grenade blew. The Taliban would know who they were facing—a single man, yes, but an Afghan warrior from a long line of warriors who had fought invaders before and had never been truly defeated.

The sound of battle faded. Bolan's way was becoming steeper, the ground beneath his feet less firm. Afghanistan refused to treat anyone with any kind of favor. Its lofty slopes presented obstacles at every turn, demanding that anyone bold enough to confront it did so at a high cost. Many had tried and failed. This time the inhospitable met the undefeatable. Mack Bolan never gave up, no matter what the odds. Afghanistan was about to find that out.

Something played on his mind: Shehan, a paid mercenary or a believer in the cause?

Bolan could accept either, but it seemed illogical for someone like Shehan to kill Bolan's guide *before* he led him to Mahoud. It was a counterproductive move. If the intention was to get to Mahoud, why eliminate Azal now? Bolan saw no sense in the act. Unless Shehan had known about the GPS unit and decided to step up his mission by taking out Azal and gaining possession of the unit himself. Anything was possible. Maybe Bolan had been next on Shehan's list. If it had been his intention Shehan had shown his hand too quickly. His unexpected action, the savage attack on Azal, the man directing Bolan to Mahoud's whereabouts, had played out his hand. There didn't appear to be any kind of logic in his desire to kill the Afghan—unless Shehan had been in the pay of Mahoud's enemies, working covertly until the moment arrived when he could strike at Azal and remove him, leaving Bolan without his guide, alone in enemy territory with little way of knowing where Mahoud was waiting. It was likely, now that he considered Shehan's risky move, that the man had panicked because of the Taliban attack. He had been just as surprised as Bolan when they had showed up. Fearing his chance slipping away Shehan had gone for the GPS unit, hoping he could lose Bolan and go after Mahoud himself.

He hadn't thought his plan through. Maybe he panicked when he realized Bolan had almost wiped out the unexpected Taliban group and he, Shehan, was on his own. Whichever way, it forced Bolan to carry on his mission solo. Not the first time he had been left to his own devices.

Bolan secured his backpack, drawing the straps tight. He did the same with the MP-5. The last thing he needed was the subgun swinging loose as he made his climb. With his equipment seen to, the soldier ran a final check from the GPS unit, establishing his line of travel before he began his ascent.

It wasn't exactly a vertical climb, but the slopes were some of the steepest Bolan had faced for a long time. The outcroppings weren't solid, often breaking away when he put weight on them. It forced him to move slowly, testing each section as he moved across it. That wasn't a bad thing, Bolan decided. Better late than no show.

Despite his caution, he twice found a handhold giving way. The second time he found himself slipping down the slope. It took a few stomach-clenching moments before he arrested his fall, digging for footholds and flattening himself against the rocks until his breathing settled. Bolan felt warm blood oozing from grazes on the palm of one hand, and he wiped it across his jacket.

Moving on, he negotiated the fragile surface and pushed himself another fifty feet before he was able to take a break on a dusty ledge. He allowed himself some water, pressing himself back against the rocks. The temperature was high on this exposed slope. Bolan looked out across the empty landscape. It was all sky. Cloudless. He picked out contrails showing against the blue, wondering who the jets belonged to. Bolan knew there were allied aircraft operating high overhead. U.S.? British? There was no way he could determine which at their great height. Were they on their way to initiate an armed strike, or on their way back to base at the conclusion of their mission?

CHAPTER SIX

Four hours in and Bolan was making progress, albeit slow. Reaching a comparatively level section, he rolled into the scant shade of an overhang, placing his back against the hot rock wall. He took his water bottle from its webbing and used a small amount of the warm liquid to moisten his lips. He spit the dusty taste from his mouth and took a couple of sips, just enough to ease his dry throat. Bolan put away the bottle and took the GPS unit from the pocket he'd stored it in. He checked his position and found he had drifted slightly off course. Not by much, but every deviation from the satellite track simply added to his journey time. Bolan figured he could pull himself back on line without too much effort. It was worth a great deal to him right now. He was starting to feel the effects of his climb. Not so much that it would hold him back, but enough to warn him to maintain his steady pace. He used the scarf around his neck to wipe his face, then pulled off his baseball cap and ran a hand through his damp hair. He allowed himself a full ten minutes of rest before pushing to his feet and moving off again.

Once he built up to his steady pace again he kept a

regular check of the GPS and after a half hour he was back on track. He estimated that if he kept up this pace he would reach his destination just before dark.

The heights Bolan scaled gave way to what was level terrain for Afghanistan—a jumbled maze of baked and dusty rock and brittle vegetation. Bolan had the MP-5 back in his hands as he made his way, according to the GPS, in a direct line for Sharif Mahoud's location.

That high up the wind was constant, the fine dust it stirred scratching at his skin. Bolan pulled his scarf across his mouth so he didn't have to breathe in so much of the fine grit. He kept his MP-5 close to his body, the muzzle angled down and away from the drifting dust.

His last GPS reading had indicated he was close to his destination. The soldier made his way along a dry stream-bed, the earth underfoot cracked and broken. There hadn't been water here for a long time.

The whisper of sound might easily have been lost in the wind, but Bolan picked it up. To his left and just behind. He turned the MP-5, snapping into position and locating its target as the newcomer mirrored Bolan's move.

They faced off, neither man willing to back down, weapons trained on each other, fingers laid against triggers. The only movement the restless flap of the other man's loose garb, caught by the wind. Bolan saw traditional Afghan dress—sturdy, coarse clothing, a wrapped robe and headdress; strong boots for comfortable travel across the harsh terrain; a belt around the man's waist with a holstered, modern autopistol and a curved knife; in his strong brown hands an AK-47. Above the neatly bearded face keen eyes surveyed Bolan with unblinking calm.

Bolan knew the face from the photographs he had seen in Brognola's files.

Dr. Sharif Mahoud, the man he had come to meet. But not dressed the way his photograph had shown him.

It was Mahoud who broke the silence.

"Tell me how you see the Koran."

"It presents the true believer with the peaceful path he should walk. Not as a handbook of war and injustice."

The password phrase Mahoud and the U.S. President had decided on.

Mahoud's eyes remained steady. His gaze penetrated the outer man, looking down into Bolan's soul. The moment passed. The muzzle of the AK lowered a fraction and Mahoud's shoulders relaxed.

"You are Cooper?"

"Yes, Dr. Mahoud."

"Where is Azal?"

"Most likely dead. We were betrayed by a man named Shehan. He must have been in the pay of your enemies. We had been attacked by a roving group of Taliban and had to retreat. Azal took us through the hills and we lost the Taliban, but Shehan turned on Azal and stabbed him before I could stop him. Azal knew he couldn't keep up with me, so he chose to hold off any Taliban. He stayed behind to give me time."

"Azal was a good friend. Then how did you find me, Cooper?"

Bolan showed the GPS unit.

"Azal gave me this. Told me it would lead me to you."

"This man Shehan?"

"He won't be killing anyone else."

Mahoud turned, beckoning Bolan to follow him. They walked along the dry bed for a couple hundred yards before Mahoud turned abruptly and led Bolan through tangled scrub, emerging at what looked very much like a narrow slit in the dry streambed. He pushed his way through, Bolan close behind, and after a few feet they emerged in a small clearing with a cave entrance on one side.

Inside, the head-high cave proved to be surprisingly expansive. Mahoud was equipped with relatively few belongings: a bedroll and blankets, a few cooking items, a sturdy backpack.

"As you see, I travel light."

"Makes it easy to move on."

"Dangerous times force us to desperate measures."

Bolan eyed the AK-47 in Mahoud's grasp.

"So I see."

"I am not by nature a violent man, Mr. Cooper. By the same token I am also not stupid. If someone makes an attempt to harm me, or a member of my family, I will defend myself." Mahoud made a vague gesture with the AK. "To the extent of using this." He smiled wistfully. "So much for the man of peace."

"Denying yourself the right to live is no answer," Bolan said. "It benefits no one."

"Except my enemy." Mahoud smiled, a weary expression that betrayed his sadness, his dismay at how the region and its people were trapped in the mire of religious and political intolerance. It was a state that had kept the country at war, struggling through years of deprivation and suffering, violence and mistrust. "Afghanistan is once again the prize that others struggle over. Its people are the real victims. Pushed back and forth by the different groups, each working its own agenda. Then the foreign powers who come here and tell us they will liberate us. Make us free so we can plan our own destiny. The destiny of Afghanistan lies in the hands of our invaders. It has been this way for so many decades it is hard to remember when the country was its own master.

"Tell me, Mr. Cooper, how will Afghanistan ever break free from the imposition of those who come here and decide our fate? Who say one year that this group are their allies, and the next declare them to be terrorists? First they arm them, give them great supplies of weapons, and then find those very same groups have turned against the Afghan people and are slaughtering them."

"I have no answer, Dr. Mahoud. I'm just a soldier sent to protect you and take you to safety. I'm told you are the man who might be able to bring some sanity to this madness. That you have the skills to bring opposing factions to the conference table and get them talking. If that's true, then it's worth the risk to enable you to do just that. Someone has to try."

Mahoud smiled, nodding as he said, "Your President told me he would send me a man I could trust with my life." He leaned forward to stare at Bolan's face, looking deep into the American's eyes. Bolan held his stare, unblinking, aware that Mahoud's scrutiny might make the difference between acceptance or rejection. "I see no guile. No deceit. But I do see honesty. I see a man who has endured a great deal of adversity and who has learned to overcome. Perhaps together we can confront whatever lies before us and reach sanctuary together."

Mahoud leaned his rifle against the cave wall beside his makeshift bed. He squatted in front of his cooking stove, a small butane-fueled unit. He set water on to boil.

"Azal's death serves to show how determined my enemies are to reach me. I hope you realize how much danger you have placed yourself in, Mr. Cooper."

"Let's concern ourselves with *your* safety, Dr. Mahoud."

"On one condition. We may be together for some time. Too long for you to keep calling me Dr. Mahoud. Call me Reef. Please."

Bolan nodded. "Matt."

"I will prepare food, then. While we eat we can talk."

At the cave entrance Bolan took time to check out the terrain. From this high position he could see for a long way. The Afghan landscape was stark, empty, simply endless miles of bleak rock formations. Serrated and steep-sided, it gave the impression it went on forever. At this higher elevation the wind held constant and Bolan knew once darkness fell the temperature would drop. As the days were hot, the nights were bitter. It wasn't Bolan's first time in the country. He had tramped the inhospitable hills and dusty plains on a number of occasions, and he had seen blood spilled. The country had seen its share of bloody war, oppression and divided loyalties. The Afghan people were a resilient breed, a proud warrior class that refused to bend beneath the heel of the invader. It was nothing new. Afghanistan resisted, survived and watched its enemies withdraw.

Squatting in the dust, Bolan took out compact but powerful binoculars from his backpack and spent long minutes scanning the area. His meticulous surveillance told him there were no insurgents around. Even so Bolan maintained a cautious attitude. It was too easy to let himself be convinced the enemy was nowhere around. That kind of thinking could get a man killed. Just because he couldn't see anyone didn't mean gunners weren't out there somewhere. He stayed where he was until Mahoud called him in for the meal.

"This is the last of the food I have with me," Mahoud explained. "I brought it from the last village I was in. Many Afghan people have helped me as I traveled. Often at possible great risk to themselves. If the local Taliban learned they had been aiding me…" There was no need for him to finish. "They gave me some food at each place, even though they had little. This is all I have left. Rice. Some lamb and onion. Spices." He smiled at something. "You know, in Paris this would cost a great deal of money in a restaurant. It is a traditional dish. Qorma. Not very fancy but tasty."

He filled bowls and passed one to Bolan. From a satchel he produced rolled wheat Afghan bread. They broke it and used it to scoop up the spicy stew, eating in silence for a while.

"This makes me appreciate the expensive meals I've eaten in Paris restaurants," Mahoud said. He studied Bolan's face. "And why then, you wonder, does the man exile himself to a cave in the middle of nowhere, dressed this way?"

"I'd say you're less likely to get yourself shot than walking around in an Armani suit."

"Perhaps. But how could I get the locals to take my word seriously from the comparative safety of Paris. Or London. Or New York. I promise them I will plead their case for peace. Should I expect them to believe me if I refuse to walk into their village while I drive through Washington in a bulletproof automobile? Matt, these are men who live and fight in this country. They build their homes from the materials they find around them. They trust someone who will talk to them face-to-face, who will eat what they eat, a man who would walk ten miles to help a neighbor. I will do what I can to try to bring some kind of order here. There is mistrust here, religious intolerance, bigotry, tribal disputes. Expand that across the borders and you will find the same in Iran and Iraq. All across the Middle East." Mahoud leaned back against the cave wall. "I want to help. I *must* help. While I am able, I have to try. Does that sound naive to you? Be truthful—am I deluding myself? Am I a lone voice in the wilderness, unheard, ignored?"

Mack Bolan understood Mahoud's dilemma. The man's cause mirrored his own struggles against evil. Bolan, too, did what he could because he was able to. If he stood by and allowed evil to flourish, those who were too weak, incapable of fighting back, would simply suffer and perish. Bolan was a warrior trained in the art of war. His unique perspective of the machinery of savagery had placed in his hands and in his heart the will and the ability to fight the battles on behalf of the beleaguered. Bolan did what he did because he was able and he felt himself allied with Mahoud.

"I'd say the opposite. If your cause is having no effect, why are so many out to stop you? Why are there people desperate to silence you?"

Mahoud filled tin mugs with hot bitter coffee, thoughtful as he returned the tin pot to the stove.

"You will have heard about my good friend Jamal Mehet being murdered. And the decoy in Algeria. They were brave men who willingly stood alone so I can make my bid for peace. And now my dear friend Rahim Azal. They have all died because they believed in what I try to do. And I put my family at risk by bringing them here. All that because there are those who are still determined to kill me."

"Do you have any idea who these enemies are?" Bolan asked.

"Believe me, Matt, I know who they are. Some are from Afghanistan. Those who want me out of the way because I threaten their grip on positions of power. If my particular brand of peace becomes accepted, then there are those who will see their control fade away. Add to them the entrenched religious zealots who use the written words in twisted versions, forcing the ordinary people to bend to their will. They terrorize. Cajole. Turn brother against brother because they refuse to look beyond carved-in-stone obedience to rigid laws. They want me dead. Of that I have no doubt. And there are others from your own country, men who see coming peace as a tragedy because it will weaken their hold on the region. They encourage the radicals, the rabble-rousers, the hotheads so full of rage against the U.S.A. These are their customers. They buy the arms these people offer. They make deals for oil. For long-term agitation. These hyenas feed off the despair of the Middle East. They foment confrontation because it is worth millions of dollars to them. War is big business, Matt. And these men are powerful. Their organizations are worldwide. They have the power to influence the policies of nations, to manipulate and direct governments. They want conflict to continue to maintain their markets. If my upcoming negotiations help to pacify the regions, these men will see their dealings dwindle." Mahoud paused, smiling at Bolan. "Do I talk too much? I am afraid it is one of my failings."

"Reef, we need more men who can talk enough to bring adversaries together. Talking is easy, but the kind you bring to the table is special. As long as you are able keep that going, you keep right on speaking. If we don't talk our way to some kind of accord, the Middle East is going to stay on the path that will simply eat away at all the good."

Mahoud refilled the coffee mugs. He placed the pot down, thoughtful, then looked directly at Bolan.

"Is my son safe? Is he being protected in America?"

"One of my most trusted people is guarding him."

"Yes?"

"I'd put myself in his hands if my life was at risk. Whatever happens, he won't let you down."

"Well, your President said he would send me a man *I* should trust. He must think of you very highly."

Bolan smiled. "We have an understanding. We would never betray each other, or break our word."

"I wish trust was as easy to gain in my world," Mahoud said. "Unfortunately it is not. Among those who oppose me betrayal is the watchword. I have little reason to trust anyone."

"Things are that bad?"

"The reason is simple," Mahoud said. "I know many of the ones who may attend the meeting are not who they seem. They pretend to be peacemakers, but truly they are in league with the hard-line radicals. And they know if I attend and stand in front of them I will point the finger and expose them. Over the past couple of years I have made it part of my mission to gain a great amount of data on the betrayals and the deceit.

"Deals are made behind closed doors. Money and favors are bartered for loyalty. Matt, if the talks are to offer any chance of reconciliation, no matter how small, then the ones who want to wreck the conference have to be exposed for what they are."

"And that's why they seem set on pulling your family apart, to silence you? To make it impossible for you to offer your solutions?"

"These people are desperate. And they will resist me to the last breath."

"Who controls them?"

"The one with power here in Afghanistan is Mullah Homani. We have been declared enemies for many years. He has denounced the peace accord as nothing more than blasphemy. He condemns it every chance he gets, to anyone who will listen. My sources tell me that many are tired of his radical posturing, the way he urges his followers to make every sacrifice in order to crush my initiative." Mahoud smiled. "He sends out his followers, convinced they are on missions for God, and that their sacrifices will be rewarded with a wonderful afterlife. This man sits in comparative safety, issuing death sentences, and never once places himself in any kind of danger. His hypocrisy staggers me. He denounces everything that is not of our religion as evil, as corrupting, but orders the deaths of men and women and even children if, in his words, they contribute a threat to God. The sad thing is he will never run short of those who he can bend to his will. He calls *himself* a peacemaker. Yet he refuses to even discuss that very thing, and is willing to urge hundreds to follow his calling."

"In reality I guess any leader with influence employs similar actions," Bolan said. "They all have to call on their people to go to war while they sit in the safety of their offices."

"An astute observation, and in a way you are correct. But the reasoning behind the call differs here. Homani is urging slaughter. He wants his believers to go out and create rivers of blood, to destroy Western culture, to wipe out Israel. He even wages his Holy War against other Muslims, those who see things differently. The man openly declares he will spread his campaigns across the Middle East. I cannot in all honesty sit back and allow his poison to be spread.

"Homani condemns the West to his followers but also deals with the consortium of Americans whose aim is to bolster his plans, to make him stronger. They promise him weapons and backing to keep the Middle East in a state of war. They profit from the concessions he and his own partners across the region offer—contracts for construction, for rebuilding, minerals, oil, of course. These powerful groups comprise businessmen and politicians, even the military. To them it is a great game that will bring them more power and wealth. They manipulate policy, playing the region as if it is a chess game, seeking the advantage, setting one regime against another."

"And it's the people who suffer," Bolan said. "They become the losers, the refugees, and are dispossessed in their own countries. They lose every time."

"Now you see why I must carry on. Why I have to try."

Bolan dropped his coffee mug, reaching for his MP-5. He pushed to his feet and headed for the cave entrance.

"What is it?" Mahoud asked, snatching up his own weapon. "Did you hear something?"

Bolan didn't get a chance to reply. Shadows loomed large as gunmen rushed the cave entrance, crowding in. Their weapons were up and ready, covering Bolan and Mahoud as they pushed forward. Bolan counted at least seven, maybe eight. He had no chance to tackle them. There were too many.

The superior force failed to stop Mahoud. He rushed at the interlopers, his weapon rising.

"Mahoud, don't give them the chance…" Bolan yelled.

Mahoud ignored him, pushing the American aside.

His resistance was futile as the group rushed to meet him, someone knocking aside Mahoud's AK-47. His finger jerked against the trigger, sending a single shot into the cave wall. And then Mahoud was beaten to his knees with rifle butts and barrels, the brutal blows driving him down, blood streaking his face.

Bolan had his own weapon snatched from his hands. Others took his Beretta and his sheathed knife. He was searched for any other weapons, but all that was found was the GPS unit and Bolan's triband cell phone. He watched as they were thrown to the cave floor and crushed under heavy boots.

One of the attackers scattered the crushed items across the cave.

"They will not be of use to you any longer, American. You are in our hands now. We are the Taliban. We will give the orders."

Bolan looked him in the eye. "I'll try to remember that."

The Taliban fighter laughed. He spoke to his men in the local dialect. His words seemed to humor them. The leader turned back to Bolan.

"Be certain, American. You *will* remember. I promise you."

"So will I," Bolan said.

And he meant it.

CHAPTER SEVEN

The journey lasted at least a couple of hours. The vehicle drove over some of the worst tracks Bolan had ever experienced. The old truck had worn springs, or no springs at all. The fact he was bound hand and foot and had been thrown on the wooden floor did little to ease Bolan's condition. His body ached from the continuous bouncing as the truck wheels hit every pothole and crevice.

Mahoud lay a couple of feet away, his back to Bolan. He was bound in a similar fashion, his body rocked and jarred by the truck's passage.

Five armed rebels sat on the side benches, watching over their captives, endlessly talking, and occasionally aiming hard kicks at the prisoners.

Bolan blinked away sweat that ran into his eyes. Inside the canvas-topped truck the heat and the cloying odor from unwashed bodies made the air rank. From the angle of the truck floor, they were climbing. He had no idea where they were. Not that it mattered. Bolan's only thoughts were centered around how he and Mahoud were going to get free.

It was going to happen. Bolan was convinced of that.

He would never allow himself to accept defeat. It wasn't in his glossary of words. He had always erred on the side of optimism. Until the final breath was taken it didn't matter how hopeless the situation. There was always a chance to reverse things, to turn a less than positive predicament into success. So while he lay on the truck floor Bolan was looking forward to the moment, and that was all he needed, when he would reverse the way things were now and take control on his terms.

The truck made a final lurch over stony ground and swung in a half circle before coming to a stop.

Rough hands dragged Bolan and Mahoud over the tailgate. The ropes around their wrists and ankles were cut away, and they were marched in the direction of a huddle of crude huts. The village had been cleared and was now being used by the local rebels. The door to one hut was dragged open across the village square and Mahoud was hustled off toward it.

A dusty Toyota 4x4 had been driving ahead of the truck, leading the way. Bolan watched it circle the area and vanish behind one of the huts.

The soldier was hauled off to one of the other huts. His eyes scanned the area, picking out points of interest and seeking possible escape routes. The hut door swung open and Bolan was unceremoniously thrust inside. The door banged shut behind him. He moved to the facing wall and peered through cracks in the stonework where mortar had crumbled and dropped out.

He was able to look across the central area and could see Mahoud's hut. To the right was a stack of fuel drums. Some yards farther back was the hut where the 4x4 was now parked.

Bolan saw three armed men heading for his hut. He moved to the rear, back to the wall as the door was kicked open and the trio stepped inside. One remained by the door, his AK-47 trained on Bolan. The man in charge of the group was one of Bolan's visitors.

"What are you doing in Afghanistan?" he asked.

"They told me it's a nice country for a vacation."

The butt of an AK-47 swept up and cracked against the side of Bolan's head. The pain stunned him momentarily. The Taliban rebel planted a big hand against Bolan's chest and pushed him against the wall.

"Choose what you say with care, American. Your death is of no consequence to me." He stepped back. "Why are you helping Sharif Mahoud, the blasphemer? He is a traitor to his own people. He has sold his soul to the West."

"Is that what Homani tells you?"

"Do not defile his name or I will have your tongue torn from your mouth."

"All Mahoud is doing is trying to bring peace. Isn't it worth seeing what he has to offer? Or perhaps you don't want peace."

The Afghan shook his fist at Bolan.

"I am Ashid Khan. I rule these hills and the people in them. What do you know about my country? Nothing, like all Westerners. You come here and make war on us. The Russians tried and went home like whipped dogs. Now it is the turn of the Americans, Canadians and the British. We will send you *all* home in coffins." Khan stepped close, staring deeply into Bolan's eyes. "For those of my men you have killed, American, I will make sure you remember them up until the moment you die screaming."

Bolan worked his aching jaw, watching as the leader turned and spoke to the man beside him. He couldn't hear what was being said, but he understood the message when the butt of the AK-47 was slammed into his stomach. A hard fist clubbed him behind the ear and Bolan stumbled and fell to his knees, dazed by the sheer power behind the blow. When the mist cleared, he was alone again.

On his feet Bolan took another look through the fractured wall. The village looked all but deserted. Only a couple of armed men standing watch.

The violent visitations would occur again. Bolan figured Mahoud was probably being treated in a similar fashion. Most likely worse. The Taliban fighters would be doing their best to gain information from him, and no matter how courageous, Mahoud would talk eventually.

Bolan didn't want that to happen. He wanted them to make their bid for freedom while they were still physically able. That meant they needed to get out now.

A half hour later Bolan saw two of the Afghans approaching his hut again. That cut down the odds for him.

The hut door opened and one man stepped inside, the second standing just outside. Bolan recognized his visitor as the man who had used his gun butt and fist on him.

Bolan stood, his head lowered, open hands at his sides. He watched the Afghan cross the dirt floor. He snapped out a command, but Bolan didn't move. The words were shouted this time and the man moved closer, reaching out to shake him. His AK-47 was in his left hand, muzzle down. Over the guy's shoulder Bolan could see the second Afghan. He had his rifle partially raised, but Bolan was blocked from his sight by the bulk of the man standing in front of him.

The Afghan's fingers brushed Bolan's shirt.

Before the man could take hold Bolan erupted into action. He slammed his knee up between the Afghan's thighs, a brutal, well-aimed blow that struck with crippling force. The Afghan screamed in agony. He would have dropped the AK-47 but Bolan was already reaching for it, turning it in his grip. He kept his eye on the second guy, arcing the rifle around and bracing it against the injured Afghan's hip. Bolan's finger squeezed back on the trigger. The Russian combat rifle crackling viciously, sending a burst of 7.62 mm rounds at his target. They cored in through his chest and spun him away from the door. He hit the ground on his back, twisting in pain as his body responded to the internal damage.

Bolan hooked his free arm around the neck of his moaning Afghan and dragged him to the door. The Executioner took a quick look across the square, fixing on the hut where Mahoud had been imprisoned. He could see a couple of armed rebels turning in his direction and started to count down the numbers.

The injured Afghan was wearing a U.S. style harness over his thick coat. Bolan saw a fragmentation grenade on one of the straps. He jerked it free and pushed it into one of the deep pockets in his combat pants. He grabbed his 9 mm Beretta pistol, which had been jammed behind the man's leather belt. Bolan slammed the Afghan's head against the stone wall hard enough to crack his skull. As the man slumped to the floor, Bolan's eyes picked up an armed man running across the square.

The gunner opened fire as he spotted Bolan. Slugs peppered the stone wall near the open door. The Executioner took a couple of steps to clear the door, then launched himself in a full dive toward the ground.

Landing on his left shoulder, he used his forward momentum to keep him moving, then got to his knees, the AK-47 already tracking the movement of the rebel. Bolan triggered a burst, caught the guy in the left thigh, then adjusted his aim and fired again. The Afghan went down, still yelling, as other gunners exited the other huts. Once on his feet Bolan turned, powered forward and slammed up against the first of the stacked fuel drums. Behind him he could hear the yells of anger as his pursuers saw where he was. It didn't stop Bolan. He raised the AK-47 and snapped a shot at the closest rebel. His burst caught the guy in the jaw, tearing out an ugly chunk of flesh and muscle. The Afghan gave a shriek of pain, dropping his rifle and clutching at the shattered jaw, blood spurting through his fingers. His companions hesitated, a couple of them grabbing the groaning casualty and dragging him away.

Bolan used the break in the action to move himself along the line of drums and out of sight. His reprieve would be short-lived, he knew, and he wanted to make the most of it. As he moved around the end of the row, the soldier heard a raised shout. His time was already up and the Taliban rebels were closing in. He pulled the grenade from his pocket. Pulling the pin, he sprang the lever and dropped the grenade under the closest drum. From the far side of the stacked metal containers he heard the shuffle of feet and the rattle of weapons.

The soldier ducked around the end of the closest hut, wanting to clear the immediate area before the grenade went off.

The sharp sound of the blast preceded the heavier explosion as the volatile fuel blew, a ripple effect as the first explosion scattered shards of metal into the next drum and down the line. The vapor inside the containers ignited, expanding and sending sheets of blazing fuel up and out. The sudden screams of those caught in the surges of burning fuel were quickly lost. Bolan felt the ground underfoot shiver from the blast. The backlash lifted the rear of the standing truck inches off the ground and debris whistled overhead, keen-edged fragments of steel from the ruptured fuel drums.

The moment he was clear of the truck Bolan cut off at

an angle, heading directly for the hut that imprisoned Mahoud. He flattened against a stack of timber, leaning out to check the guard. The man was craning his neck, attempting to see what had happened but his position denied him a clear image. All he could see were the rising coils of flame and smoke, the storage shed blocking his view.

Bolan stepped around to the rear of the timber, leaning out with the AK-47 in both hands. He tracked in and held his target, stroked the trigger and saw the guard go down, his skull shattered by the burst. Pushing clear Bolan crossed the open space.

With the knowledge that he was still working against the clock the soldier didn't hesitate. He moved to the wooden door, raised a booted foot and kicked it open. The force slammed it back against the inner wall, tearing it from one hinge so it sagged crookedly. Bolan followed it in. A robed figure sprang up from a seat, reaching for the AK leaning against the wall. Bolan hit him with a burst that ripped into his chest and tumbled the guy back across the open fire burning in the corner.

There was only one door in front of Bolan. He yanked back the iron bolt and pushed the door open. Mahoud stood in the center of the room, a small wooden stool held in both hands, ready to protect himself.

"Relax, Reef, it's me."

Mahoud glanced at the stool, then tossed it aside. "I thought you were never coming." Then his bloody, battered face split into a smile.

Bolan led the way from the cell, pointing to the AK-47 leaning against the wall. Mahoud snatched it up. Spare magazines sat on a wooden table. The soldier checked them and found they were full. He handed a couple to Mahoud and took the others himself. At the open door Bolan checked the area. The raging blaze had spread to the storage building. Coils of smoke drifted across the area, constantly moved by the persistent Afghan wind. The smoke would give them temporary cover.

"Around the rear," Bolan said as he exited the hut, Mahoud close behind.

Overhead the midday sky was darkening. Bolan could already feel the drop in temperature. Before they had gone many yards the first drops of rain fell.

Someone began to shout. The cry was taken up, and Bolan spotted half a dozen gunners breaking into full view from around the side of burning storage buildings. Raised weapons began to chatter, slugs whipping up chunks of hard earth.

"Keep moving," Bolan said.

He turned abruptly, cradling his AK, and opened fire on the advancing Taliban fighters. His first burst caught the lead rebel. The guy went down with both legs shattered, his blood staining the sand as he wriggled in agony. Bolan stood his ground, his weapon firing in short, controlled bursts. Two more gunners were slammed to the ground before the others pulled back. Bolan allowed them no leeway. His autorifle crackling steadily and one more of the Taliban rebels was hit, the guy tumbling awkwardly from the 7.62 mm slugs.

Mahoud skidded around the line of huts, calling out, "We have transport."

It was the Toyota 4x4 that had accompanied the truck bringing them to the village.

"Let's go," Bolan urged.

They sprinted toward the vehicle, Bolan hoping the keys were still in the ignition, and assuming the Taliban's sense of security within their own territory would allow them that confidence. He yanked open the driver's door and almost gave a whoop of pleasure when he saw the key in place. On the far side of the Toyota, Mahoud hauled the passenger door open, then turned aside, bringing up his AK. Bolan saw an armed rebel burst into view from the gap between huts. Mahoud's autorifle hammered out a long burst, 7.62 mm slugs, ripping stone shards from the hut wall and flesh from the Taliban gunner. The man fell back with a sharp cry, his body blossoming red as he absorbed the scything burst. As Bolan turned the key and the Toyota's engine roared to life, Mahoud rolled into the cab, slamming his door shut.

Bolan slammed the vehicle into gear and released the handbrake. The powerful drive threw the 4x4 forward, tires slipping on the wet surface, the vehicle bouncing over the rough ground as the wheels finally gripped. Bolan searched for and switched on the wipers. The first few strokes smeared dust in greasy streaks across the glass, but the increasing downpour quickly cleared that. The 4x4's power steering helped Bolan control the erratic course as he swung the vehicle across the open camp, heading it in the direction of the rough trail that had brought them to the deserted village.

As they cleared the main section of the village, Bolan yanking on the wheel to line the Toyota up with the sloping trail, a gunman ran into view from his guard position. Bolan stamped on the gas, sending the 4x4 at the guy. The front of the Toyota hit the Taliban fighter head-on, flipping the screaming man up over the hood. There was a split second when the man's face was visible through the windshield, then he slid up the glass and bounced across the roof. Twisting, Mahoud was in time to see the broken body slam to the hard ground.

At the first sharp bend in the trail Bolan hugged the wheel, guiding the speeding vehicle as the heavy tread tires slid on the rain-slick surface. The edge of the trail came disturbingly close before he hauled the Toyota back on line.

Instinct made Bolan check the rearview mirror. What he saw, in a jerking image, was one of the Taliban gunmen standing at the head of the trail. The Afghan rebel had an object in his hands that Bolan recognized even at that distance—a Russian RPG-7 rocket launcher.

The rebel shouldered the launcher, tracking the movement of the Toyota as it followed the trail. At the apex of the bend the vehicle was parallel to the head of the trail. Bolan saw the blue-gray coil of smoke as the rocket left the launcher, the missile swooping across the open distance. The RPG wasn't acknowledged to be entirely accurate over longer distances, but it missed the Toyota by only a few feet. It slammed into the far side of the trail and exploded in a burst of flame, showering the 4x4 with clods of earth and rock. The detonation rocked the Toyota. Bolan felt the rear slide away from him as he fought the wheel.

"Not good," he heard Mahoud say.

Bolan might have agreed if he hadn't been busy.

A second missile struck a few yards behind. The force of the blast lifted the rear of the Toyota. For a few heart-stopping seconds the vehicle hung suspended, then it fell back to earth with a hard slam. Mahoud lost his grip on the AK-47 and it dropped into the foot well. He made no attempt to pick it up. He was gripping the sides of his seat, staring out through the windshield.

Bolan saw the trail veering to the left. If they could reach that point they would be shielded from further attack. He pushed down on the pedal and the 4x4 barreled forward. He could feel the slippery trail surface under the wheels as they hurtled toward the bend. He teased the wheel gently now, easing the vehicle into the curve. As they slid around the bend a third missile detonated, falling short but expending enough energy to push the rear of the 4x4 toward the open side of the trail. A heavy chunk of debris slammed into the rear, catapulting the Toyota forward. That halted the slide. Bolan felt the tires bite, giving him more control. He took them clear around the curve in the trail and straightened the vehicle. He eased off the gas and made careful use of the brake, feeling the Toyota reduce speed.

"A drive in the country will never have the same appeal again," Mahoud said.

Within the next half hour two things happened to affect their situation.

The rain stopped and so did the Toyota. When Bolan checked, he saw the fuel gauge showing empty. He stepped out of the vehicle and could smell gasoline. A quick look under the 4x4 revealed a split in the fuel tank.

"Looks like we're back on foot," Bolan said.

Mahoud's shrug expressed his feelings. "At least we have good weather for it."

"Until it gets dark."

Bolan was aware of the temperature drop that would accompany the oncoming night. And that cold would be severe.

Mahoud took some time checking their position. He seemed to be familiar with the area. Bolan saw little difference in the terrain. To him it was all the same. Featureless and far from user-friendly.

"We should go that way," Mahoud said, indicating a tapering ridge that led off to the south and west. "It will take us down off the hills." He checked the sky. "If we move fast enough, we should be able to cover a good distance before dark."

Bolan let Mahoud move ahead, falling in behind the

man so he could maintain a watch on their back trail. He felt sure they hadn't seen the last of the Taliban. The rebels weren't going to let Mahoud slip away so easily. Not after all the trouble to capture him in the first instance.

A couple of miles on and they had descended some distance. Mahoud moved with the assurance of a man who knew the terrain well. His knowledge of the area was gaining them ground.

But not enough.

A bullet gouged a slab of stone only feet away, the whip crack of sound following, echoing around the stony hills.

A quick glance back showed armed figures emerging from the higher slopes.

Taliban, weapons up and firing.

CHAPTER EIGHT

Bolan reached out and pushed Mahoud forward, sending the man stumbling out of harm's way. Mahoud dropped into a shallow depression, turning so he could see up the slope.

As more shots clattered from the enemy weapons Bolan stood his ground, tracking his AK-47 on the moving rebels. His finger eased back on the trigger and he sent a searching burst at the Taliban fighter closest to his position. The man jerked aside as 7.62 mm slugs punched into his chest. He fell hard. Losing his grip on his rifle and following it down the uneven rocky slope, his momentum increased until he was bouncing and rolling in the loose-limbed way that only came with death.

"Get down," Mahoud shouted, using his AK-47 to cover Bolan.

Heeding the advice, Bolan scrambled behind a crumbling slab of rock, slugs slamming into the hard surface an instant after he slid into cover. He about-faced, reaching over the top of the slab to pick out another target, sending a second man sprawling as the rebel reached a close position but refused to take cover himself. The man was screaming in Pashto, the language native to Afghanistan. Bolan knew only a few words and the way the man was yelling he couldn't make them out. The guy's rant ceased the moment he took Bolan's slugs.

Mahoud's AK was firing single shots steadily, well placed to keep the rebels off balance.

Bolan worked his way alongside Mahoud. He checked out the surrounding terrain, following the run of the depression, which sloped down away from their present position. He turned to look toward the western horizon where the sun was already sinking.

"It'll be dark soon," he said. "We'll have good cover then. If we take this route, we can maybe lose those guys."

Mahoud nodded. "Whatever you decide."

"Hit them with some hard fire to make them keep their heads down, then we go. You ready?"

"Yes."

The AK-47s cracked on full-auto as Bolan and Mahoud expended their magazines, firing in the general direction of the Taliban. The sustained fire threw 7.62 mm slugs in deadly streams. The harsh bursts hammered against rock and earth, filling the air with debris, the effect forcing the rebels to stay under cover for the duration.

The moment their weapons locked on empty Bolan slapped Mahoud on the shoulder. "Go," he said simply.

They turned and headed along the depression, ejecting empty magazines and replacing them, ignoring caution now as they distanced themselves from the enemy who would soon be following. Bolan knew they had a thin window in which to get themselves clear. However narrow, they had to make the most of it.

Shadows were starting to lengthen. The light was fading quickly around them, and darkness would apply dual problems. The rebels would find their tracking abilities restricted, but at the same time Bolan and Mahoud would have their own rate of travel reduced.

Reaching the edge of the depression, Bolan saw the slope fall away in a sheer incline. Even in the fading light he could see the surface was loose, covered in stretches of eroded rock. Checking left and right he saw the incline spread in both directions. He sensed Mahoud close by, and by the look of the man's face they were both reaching the same conclusion.

"No choice," Mahoud said.

Both men slung his AK-47, stepped onto the incline and began their descent, feeling the loose surface move beneath their feet almost immediately. The rattle of disturbed shale underfoot would carry for a long way in the thinner air, so the pursuing Taliban would be drawn to the spot. There was nothing Bolan or Mahoud could do to prevent that, so they made no attempt. They simply moved as fast as the shifting incline would allow. Dust began to rise from their passage, clouding the air. When Bolan checked the base of the long incline, he was unable to make it out. The shadows were spreading quickly now as the daylight faded.

Even though he heard the angry cries above him, Bolan kept moving. He couldn't know how well the rebels could see him and Mahoud, and he had no desire to find out. The abrupt crackle of shots from above told him the Taliban head reached the top of the incline. The shots that came were off target, slamming into the slope around Bolan and Mahoud. The sharp whine of ricochets spun off into the encroaching darkness.

The soldier felt a section of the incline start to slide and heard a startled cry from Mahoud. When he turned toward the man he was barely able to see him. The slide began to pick up speed. More dust rose, making Bolan cough even though he had wrapped his scarf across his mouth, and the gritty feel stung his eyes. He struggled to keep his balance, lost it, and felt his legs sinking deeper into the soft mass of the collapsing slope. It gripped him, dragging him down the incline at an expanding rate.

Bolan lost the struggle. He was pulled down into the darkness, losing his balance. He slammed facedown, feeling the overwhelming mass of loose stones covering him. There was a roaring sound in his ears as the fall tumbled and rolled him, bruising his body as he was swept away like a drowning man in a flood.

CHAPTER NINE

A weight was pressing down on Bolan, pinning him the full length of his aching body. Darkness surrounded him when he opened his eyes, and it took a moment for him to recall what had happened—the Taliban following him and Mahoud; he and Mahoud plunging down the steep incline; the struggle against the shifting surface that had dragged them into the utter darkness at the bottom…

Bolan drew a deep breath, tasted the dust in his mouth. He flexed his limbs. Nothing appeared to be broken, but every muscle screamed for release from the weight pressing down on them. He moved, felt the rocks above him shift.

"The hell with this," Bolan said softly.

He worked his hands beneath him, found some semblance of support and pushed up hard, feeling shards of stone fall away as he continued his efforts. Bolan's aching body demanded he stop. His abused muscles screamed for release from the extra strain he was putting them through. Bolan closed his mind to the pain, aware that if he quit now he literally might lay down and die. He was far from ready to do that. This temporary setback needed to be overcome. He managed to pull his legs into a kneeling position, which helped to give him more leverage. Bolan paused long enough to gather strength, then heaved again, the sound of tumbling rock like thunder in his ears. Only now could he taste blood in his mouth from a cut on the inside of his cheek. That at least told him he was still alive. His head broke free, cold air hitting him like a slap in the face. It had never felt more welcome. A final push and he was on his knees, free of the restricting weight.

Bolan sucked in the chill air, feeling the burn in his aching lungs. When he raised a hand to his aching head, he felt the warm slick of blood from cuts and grazes. He stayed on his knees, staring around him. Overhead a pale moon gleamed through scudding clouds. Faint light showed him the spread of the rockslide, which was substantial. It seemed he and Mahoud had disturbed half the Afghan landscape.

The soldier lurched to his feet, hauling his AK-47 from his back, awareness returning with a vengeance.

Where was Mahoud?

Was the Taliban still around, waiting?

He stared into the semidark, attempting to break shadow into substance. Bolan saw nothing except the spread of fallen stones. Beyond the range of his vision there was the Afghan night. Empty and cold. He realized just *how* cold it was. The wind that had brought constant heat during daylight hours now blew in and enveloped him in its icy grip. He could hear the low moan as it sifted through the rocky terrain. Bolan braced himself against the chill, lowering his gaze to the loose surface at his feet.

He had to locate Mahoud.

He recalled the man had been on his right as they first negotiated the incline. But which way had they both fallen as the tide of rock had swept them to the deep base of the long slope? Bolan had been swept along himself, turned back and forth, end over end, and by the time he'd reached the base of the slope he had no idea where he had been deposited. Mahoud had obviously undergone similar treatment. He could be anywhere within a wide radius. Maybe buried deeper than Bolan. Unconscious.

Dead.

Bolan refused to accept that. Until he saw Mahoud's body, the man was alive.

The sound came from his left, yards away, the stirring of loose stone disturbed by some unseen source. As Bolan turned in that direction, he heard the rattle increase, and he moved in on the source.

And as Bolan bore down on the location he picked up the soft muttering of someone not too happy at being buried beneath a mass of sharp rocks.

Sharif Mahoud rose out of the rockslide like something from a horror movie, pushing to his feet with a loud gasp drawing fresh air into his starved lungs. He swayed on his feet, turning in Bolan's direction when he heard his approach.

"It's me," Bolan said.

"I have lost my weapon," Mahoud replied. He patted his clothing. "But I still have extra magazines."

"You hang on to them," Bolan said. "I have a feeling we may still need them."

"Why? Is the Taliban still here?"

"I don't think so. Too dark to see much. So I suggest we move out in case they're still close by."

"You are right. We should go."

"Are you hurt? Any broken bones?"

"I'm cut and bruised all over. My head aches. This damned dust does not get to taste any better, either."

"We were lucky," Bolan said.

Mahoud laughed sharply. "Lucky? Matt, let me know when things get bad and I'll quietly leave."

"Let's move out. The more distance we can make, the better I'll feel."

"As soon as it is light, they will be back."

CHAPTER TEN

In the first couple of hours of the new day Bolan and Mahoud were crossing a dusty section of the plateau. They had little choice. Staying out in the open was forced on them by the fact there was little real cover where they were.

They had barely slept during the night, preferring to keep moving so the cold didn't engulf them. Dusty and bruised from their rockslide, they moved slowly across the inhospitable landscape, watching, checking all around them in case the Taliban tried different options.

Bolan heard the first distant sound and came to a dead stop, scanning the sky. The sound faded, then returned. Each time it came back it was louder.

"That's all we need," he said.

"Is that what I think it is?" Mahoud asked.

Bolan had already identified the sound. It was a helicopter. But the configuration didn't sound like any military chopper. It was lighter, suggesting a civilian helicopter. That gave him further concern.

Mahoud touched his arm. "Over there."

Bolan followed his finger and saw a pair of Taliban

rebels on a nearby ridge. One was holding a transceiver to his ear as he spoke rapidly. His right arm was signaling, indicating Bolan and Mahoud's position.

"He's guiding the chopper in," Bolan said.

As the words were spoken, the helicopter hove into view, sweeping up out of a low depression, moving fast. It was a sleek machine, dark blue and black, with a narrow orange stripe angling across the fuselage. Light bounced off the tinted canopy.

Bolan reached out and caught a handful of Mahoud's robe, hauling the man to him, then pushed hard. The roar of the rotors filled his ears as the dark bulk of the chopper loomed large.

The sharp crackle of autofire canceled out any other sounds. A line of heavy slugs hammered the ground, kicking up debris.

At the last moment Bolan yanked Mahoud off balance, almost throwing the man into the cover of a canted boulder the size of a small house. His move caught the chopper's pilot off balance and the machine overshot. Bolan knew they would have only a short respite before the pilot swung around and came for them again. And if the gunner fixed them in his sights…

He saw there was a gap at the base of the boulder, wide and high enough for a man to take cover.

"In there, Reef, and don't make a fuss."

Bolan could hear the chopper turning around, the beat of the rotors rising and falling as it repositioned itself. He heard the steadying pulse as the aircraft made its run. The soldier stayed low, pushing himself tight against the base of the boulder so it would be harder for the pilot and gunner to pick him out. His dust-coated clothing helped him merge in with the ground. The Executioner had his AK-47 set to automatic fire, with a full magazine in place, and now he waited.

The chopper cast a large, dark shadow on the parched, dusty earth as it coasted in. The pilot had throttled back to allow the gunner to identify his target.

Peering out from his ground-level position, Bolan watched the silhouette of the helicopter. He could barely see the pilot through the tinted canopy; he was just a dark shape working the controls. As the chopper slid by, Bolan spotted the opened rear slide door. A 7.62 mm M-60 machine gun was swivel-mounted on a swing-arm pintle, enabling the gunner solid control over the weapon. On the balanced rig the big gun could be swung back and forth with comparative ease. The machine gun looked out of place in the civilian helicopter. Bolan thought that but also knew the placement wouldn't reduce the devastating power of the weapon.

The rotor wash was kicking up swirls of dust, denying the gunner a clear vision of his intended target. The chopper had dropped to within twenty feet of the ground, almost at a hover. Bolan saw he was not going to get a better opportunity. Before the dust obscured *his* vision, he angled up the AK-47 and triggered a long burst aimed directly at the gunner in his open hatch. He heard slugs slap against the fuselage to the right of the hatch and quickly adjusted his aim, sending a further burst that screamed into the gap.

As the chopper powered up and away Bolan saw the gunner fall back, letting go of the M-60 as he hung suspended in his safety rig. The chopper gained height quickly. Bolan emptied his magazine into the underside of the fuselage, then ejected the empty magazine and clicked in a fresh one. The chopper yawed to the side, swinging away to a safe distance, then hung in the air. Bolan saw a dark figure drag the gunner back inside the chopper's cabin and take his place at the 7.62 mm machine gun.

Leaning out from cover, Bolan checked out the guy who had been signaling the chopper in. A third figure had joined the original two, and they were racing down off the ridge, moving purposely in Bolan's direction.

The helicopter remained in its stationary position. The 7.62 mm machine gun had a greater range than Bolan's Kalashnikov. As long as it remained where it was, it could keep him covered.

The Taliban closed in. Two carried AK-47s, while the third had an RPG-7 launcher over his shoulder.

A germ of a thought was born, and Bolan slid back into the deep cover of the boulder.

"Reef, get out here."

Mahoud joined him. "You want me to do something?"

"Keep your head down and watch that chopper. Let me know if it moves in closer."

"Where will you be?"

"Using your little hidey-hole."

Mahoud frowned, not quite understanding.

Bolan crawled into the gap where Mahoud had been waiting, moving until he could see through the far side. In position the soldier pushed the AK-47's selector switch to single shot, sighting down the weapon until he had the approaching rebels in range. He held the muzzle on his first selected target. The Kalashnikov was an unknown weapon as far as accurate single shooting was concerned. In reality, to use it as a sniping weapon he would have checked the rifle, calibrating it and making sure he knew its eccentricities before going for a hard kill. Right now all he had was his own skill and his past experience as a marksman.

Bolan had picked his man. He shifted the muzzle a little, deciding on a full body shot. He needed a bulky target, not the relatively smaller head. He eased back on the trigger, again not knowing its pull. When the rifle fired, Bolan kept his eye on the target and saw the man react as the 7.62 mm slug hit him an inch above the Executioner's intended spot. Bolan quickly adjusted his aim, allowing for the windage, and his second shot struck directly over the guy's heart. As the Taliban fighter went down, the rocket launcher slipping from his fingers, Bolan turned the AK-47 on the other two, who were much closer now. He snap aimed, his sure hand guiding the muzzle on the targets.

The first rebel, the helicopter spotter, went down hard, a slug having blown through his left hip, tearing out muscle and shattering the bone. He slammed facedown on the ground, kicking and yelling. He still made an attempt to use his rifle, dragging it around to point at Bolan. A final slug impacting against his skull stopped him. The survivor opened up on Bolan's position. His slugs pounded the earth and whined off the face of the boulder, snapping viciously. He began to run forward, weaving as he sprang across the open ground. The Executioner let him get close, ignoring the sharp stone chips that caught the side of his face. He jacked out three single shots that caught the Taliban gunner and kicked him off his feet.

"Helicopter is coming in, Matt," Mahoud called.

Damn right it was, Bolan thought. Just as he had expected.

"Take the rifle," he said. "Keep him interested."

Bolan shoved the rifle behind him, pushing it toward Mahoud with his foot, then wriggled his way out of the narrow space and pushed to his feet.

He could hear the beat of the chopper as it swung in toward the boulder and the single crack of shots as Mahoud started firing.

Bolan ran.

He put everything into the effort, dismissing the threat of the helicopter. His boots pounded the hard ground, muscles straining, lungs pumping.

He got at least ten seconds into his run before the chopper's machine gun opened up. The gunner's shots whacked the earth behind Bolan, the 7.62 mm shells tearing up splinters of rock, throwing gouts of earth into the air. Trying to correct his lagging shots the gunner swung the muzzle and laid down another burst. He over-compensated and the slugs ripped up the ground ahead of Bolan, who veered to one side. He felt the spatter of hard debris against his legs, ignored the threat and powered forward.

He could see the crumpled, bloody shape of the dead rebel ahead of him. The long tube of the RPG-7 lay alongside the body, the loaded rocket head protruding from the barrel.

One chance was all he'd get, Bolan told himself as he covered the final few feet in a headlong dive, ignoring the machine-gun fire. He felt the jar of his impact with the ground, kept moving and snatched at the rocket launcher, fingers closing over the pistol grip, hauling the weapon to him as he rolled away from the dead rebel. He spit out acrid dust that had entered his mouth, forced himself to ignore the looming bulk of the chopper as the pilot attempted to line up for the gunner.

Bolan dragged himself to his knees, the RPG over his shoulder.

The numbers were falling fast.

He could see the open hatch, the hunched figure of the gunner swinging around the M-60.

CHAPTER ELEVEN

Bolan felt the launcher recoil as he eased back on the trigger. The missile burst from the muzzle, trailing smoke as it streaked up at the helicopter. It struck just ahead of the open hatch, penetrating the thin body, and detonated a microsecond later. The front of the chopper vanished in the blast. The stricken aircraft went belly up, the gunner's finger pressing back on the M-60, sending a short burst into the open sky. The wrecked carcass dropped, rotors still turning, and hit the ground. A secondary explosion tore it apart, hurling debris in all directions. Smoke trailed into the air.

Dropping the launcher, Bolan climbed to his feet, backing away from the fierce heat of the burning helicopter. He chose a large rock and leaned against it, feeling the effects of his recent exertions wash over him. Something wet ran down his face and when he inspected it he found it was blood from a gash above his eye.

A sound caught his attention. It was Mahoud joining him.

"I'm glad you are on my side," he said.

Bolan didn't have the energy to reply.

He watched as Mahoud returned to the two dead rebels and relieved them of whatever weaponry he could find, helping himself to an AK-47 and extra magazines. One of the Taliban rebels had been wearing a leather satchel. Mahoud used it to carry the additional ammunition. He also found automatic pistols on the men. When he handed over the weapons, Bolan caught a concerned look on his face.

"What is it?"

Mahoud pointed to one of the dead men. "That one I recognized. Muhadjar Khan. A devout follower of Wazir Homani. He was known as one of Homani's chief enforcers."

"Not anymore. But I understand what his presence means. Homani knows we're here. The helicopter was sent in to back up the ground force. Homani is determined to get to you before we leave the area."

"If he has found out about me, what about the rest of my family? Matt, you understood my stipulations about all of us coming out together. I will not back away from that. I must have my family safe before I attend the peace talks."

"I wouldn't expect you to do anything less." Bolan glanced up from checking his weapons. "Where is your family?"

"They are waiting in an abandoned Soviet outpost near the Afghan-Pakistan border. My wife and two daughters."

Bolan walked to where the dead Taliban spotter lay and picked up the transceiver the guy had been using. He slid the unit pack free and checked it over. It was a Codan HF SSB 2110M model. The tactical machine was state-of-the art military unit, built to demanding MIL-SPEC design. Within its features were transmit-receive and GPS capability. Bolan worked his way through the frequency readout until he logged on to the setting Lieutenant Pearson had given him. Picking up the handset, Bolan began to transmit his pickup request. He was rewarded minutes later by the slow drawl of a communication technician. Shortly, Pearson himself came on the line and they quickly established a GPS lock on Bolan's position.

"Be a couple hours before we can reach you. You okay with that?"

"We've had hard contact with some Taliban," Bolan advised. "They wanted the package, but we managed to persuade them that wasn't going to happen. I can't say there might not be another attempt, LT."

"Understood. We'll make it happen ASAP, Cooper. Just make sure you keep that GPS lock working. Any change, you call it in. Good luck."

CHAPTER TWELVE

"The attack failed. Shehan killed Mahoud's guide, Azal, but the American killed Shehan, then escaped into the hills."

"Has he been located?"

"No, not yet. Our people lost him."

"They lost a stranger in their own backyard? Where did you find these people?"

"I was assured they were the best."

"Something tells me someone lied to you."

"These things happen."

"Not with the money you've been paid to carry out this operation."

"I have instructed our people to keep searching and find Mahoud and the American."

"Instruct them that if they fail to find them it might be better if they stayed in those hills."

Roger Dane cut the call. He remained where he was, staring out the window across the water. The *Crescent Moon* was anchored in Monaco harbor, surrounded by dozens of other luxury vessels. Smaller craft slid by carrying suntanned visitors to the tiny principality. Global economic slowdown had little effect on the ultrarich who flocked to the principality to flaunt their wealth.

Behind Dane the main cabin door opened. Dane didn't turn. He knew who had entered.

"There's been a slight problem, Daniel," he said. "The team in Afghanistan didn't complete its mission. They killed Rahim Azal, but the American took down Shehan and got away into the hills. I just got off the phone with Bouvier. He has his backup people still searching for the American and Mahoud."

"That's not the news we were expecting. I hope you made it clear we can't accept any kind of failure."

"Oh, he understands."

"What about Marino?"

"They have the boy. It went off without a hitch. They have Rafiq Mahoud safely locked up in the cabin we rented."

"At least we have that to fall back on. Mahoud loves his son, and that gives us an edge."

"Only if he loves the boy more than his ambitions."

"Roger, you have a cynical streak and it's showing."

"I like to see it as being aware of human frailty. Sharif Mahoud may be a dedicated crusader, but he is also a devoted father and we all know the strength of filial devotion."

"Keep track of what's happening, Roger. Don't let anything slide. We can't afford any more mistakes. By the way, I came to tell you that Homani will arrive tomorrow morning. He's coming in from his French retreat."

"He wasn't supposed to be here for a couple of days. What's he up to?"

Hartman laughed. "I can't get you to trust him, can I, Roger?"

"I'll admit it. I don't like the man and I don't trust him.

Daniel, I can't feel comfortable around a man who treats me like I was something that came in on the bottom of his shoe. And he never shakes hands."

"The guy is a mullah, Roger. A religious man."

Dane shook his head. "He's an arrogant bastard. He really does believe we're his inferiors. He's only tolerating us because we can deliver him what he wants. Jesus, Daniel, he's using us. Playing us like fish on a hook."

"Puts us in a difficult position morally then, doesn't it?"

"Meaning?"

"You understand me. We're using *him* to get what *we* want. Roger, you should be ashamed."

Dane grinned as he said, "It's different for us."

"Why the hell so?"

"Because we are doing it for good old American free enterprise."

"I'm glad I have you around to keep me on track, Roger. I keep forgetting our primary mission is to fly the flag and keep dear Uncle Sam clean and pure."

"Not forgetting to line our own pockets, too."

"We wouldn't be money-grasping Imperialists if we didn't."

"I'd better go and make sure we have a cabin ready for our visiting mullah," Dane said. "Last time he was on board he kept complaining the towels weren't white enough."

CHAPTER THIRTEEN

Carl Lyons's rental vehicle was a plain, standard model in a light tan color. He wasn't overly impressed with it, but it suited his current role as a field agent for the Justice Department. Lyons didn't want to draw any unwanted attention when he arrived at Rafiq Mahoud's College. It was midmorning when he arrived, and the grounds were busy with students moving between classes.

The sight of all the young people hurrying around made Lyons feel his age. And dressed for it in his gray pants and sport coat. The last time he'd worn a shirt and tie had been too far back to recall. He locked the car and read the direction board, then cut off along the walkway. The only good thing about the day was the fact he was back in California. Sunshine. Palm trees. And from what he was seeing at the moment it still had the monopoly on gorgeous young women.

Inside the main building Lyons checked in with reception, showed his ID, asked for and was escorted to the office of the Dean of Admissions.

Dean Graham Prescott was an affable, tall man who wore an expensive suit and a perfectly formed bow tie. The moment he became aware of who Lyons was, he ushered him through the outer office to his inner sanctum, firmly closing the door.

"Please sit down, Agent Benning," he said, using Lyons's cover name.

As Prescott resumed his own seat behind a desk busy with paperwork, Lyons took one of the seats facing him.

"Is this about Rafiq Mahoud?"

The question came out of left field, and for a heartbeat even the usually unflappable Carl Lyons was caught off guard.

"Why?" he quickly countered. "Is there a problem?"

Prescott cleared his throat.

"I hope not. It's only that Rafiq didn't attend his classes on Monday, or this morning, and no one appears to have seen him since Friday."

Lyons leaned forward, his interest peaked. "Perhaps he's decided to take a little time out?"

Prescott shook his head as he said, "No, no. Not Rafiq. As a student he is incredibly punctual. It's something he prides himself on. In the whole time he has been here Rafiq has never, ever, missed a class."

"Does he live on campus?" Lyons probed.

"Yes. We already thought of that. His room has been checked. It doesn't appear to have been used since he left on Friday."

"How about any special friends? Anyone he might have told if he was going away? A girl, maybe."

"You would need to speak to some of his classmates to find that out." Prescott paused, then continued. "Agent Benning, was it Rafiq you came to see?"

"Yes."

"If you feel reluctant to tell me more, Agent Benning, I have to inform you that we do know about Rafiq's family background. He has never concealed it himself. We understand his father's situation. His *difficult* situation. Dr. Mahoud is a respected figure in his field. Though we here in America can do little to aid his efforts, the man has to be applauded for what he is trying to do."

Just great, Lyons thought. If the news was out on Rafiq's identity, it could turn into open season.

"I need to speak to anyone who might be able to point me in the right direction."

Prescott sat upright. "Do you think Rafiq might be in danger? Something stemming from his father's work?"

"My priority is to find out where the young man is," Lyons said brusquely.

Prescott picked up his phone, dialed a number and had a conversation. When he finished he put the phone down and caught Lyons's eye.

"I've asked for a couple of students to come here to my office. I recall they are friends of Rafiq's. Perhaps they can help."

THE YOUNG COUPLE WAS impressed with Lyons' Justice Department badge. The woman, who introduced herself as Maddy, smiled nervously while her companion, a redhaired, broad-shouldered linebacker, feigned cool indifference. His name was Brad.

"I needed to speak to Rafiq on a family matter," Lyons said. "Now that he appears to have gone AWOL, it gets serious."

"It isn't like him," Maddy said. "I mean, Rafiq isn't what you'd call a geek. In fact he's great to have around. But he's really serious about his studies, and he's never late for class."

"Rafiq would drag himself to class even if he was sick," Brad said.

"If either of you have any thoughts on where he might be, please let Agent Benning know," Prescott said.

"When was the last time you saw Rafiq?"

"Friday afternoon after our last class. He was driving off campus with this girl he's been seeing for the past few weeks." Maddy gave a knowing smile. "I guess he's pretty taken with her."

"You know her?"

"Only from meeting her when she was with Rafiq. It was easy to see how he felt about her. I mean, yeah, she's pretty and all that, but…"

"But?"

"Out of his class," Brad said. "We all figured she was a bit older. More experienced. Rafiq laughed when we told him."

"She isn't attending the college then?"

"No," Maddy said. "She has a job in a local bookstore. She met Rafiq at a beach party. Come to think about it, she just kind of turned up and attached herself to him. Rafiq was flattered by all the attention, but she seemed like a nice girl. We were all glad for him. I mean, he spends so much time at his studies it was nice to see him having some fun."

Lyons's face remained impassive, but he was already experiencing a slight unease.

"Okay. So the last time you saw him, Rafiq and this girl were driving off campus together?"

Brad nodded. "Yeah. They were in his SUV."

"Write down details of the vehicle," Lyons said. "Make and model. License. This girl. What's her name?"

"Callie Jefferson."

"I'll need the name of the bookstore where she works."

"Agent Benning, do you think something has happened to them?" Maddy said. "I mean, with them not showing up?"

"Right now I'm just covering everything I can. The more information I have, the easier it will be to locate them."

"I hope so."

"Any idea where they might have gone?"

"All Rafiq talked about last week was this trip they were going on. Up country somewhere. He was pretty cagey about it. The more we asked, the less he said. I guess he didn't want to give too much away in case anyone followed and caught them...well, you know."

"I know," Lyons said. He slid a couple of printed cards from his pocket and handed one each to Maddy and Brad. "If you think of anything that might be helpful give me a call."

WHILE MADDY and Brad wrote out the details he needed, Lyons stepped aside and called Stony Man on his cell phone, connecting with Brognola and relating what information he had.

"Just a feeling," he said, "but this vanishing act is a little too convenient. I could be wrong and maybe they decided to stay away for a little extra fun and games, but the way everyone talks about Rafiq, he isn't the kind to skip class."

"This is all we need," Brognola said. "The mission is barely off the ground and we've already lost an asset."

Prescott passed over the written data and Lyons dictated the information to Brognola.

"Aaron can run this through the system," the big Fed said. "I'll be in touch."

"Get him to check out this girl. Something doesn't sit right."

THE GUY BEHIND the bookstore counter was middle-aged but still insisted on dressing in jeans and a long flowered shirt. Multiple layers of beads hung around his neck, and his graying blond hair was worn in an untidy ponytail. When he stepped around the counter Lyons saw he had won his own silent wager. The man *was* wearing open sandals.

"Callie? Yeah, I was wondering why she hadn't turned in today. It's not like her. I know she hasn't been here long, but she's always on time. Good worker, too. Popular with the customers." He grinned. "Not surprising with her looks."

"So the last time you saw her was Friday?"

"She finished early."

"She say anything about where she might have been going? Who she might be seeing?"

"Uh-uh. Just said she'd see me Monday. Hey, you think something's happened?"

"That's what I'm hoping to find out."

CALLIE JEFFERSON'S small, rented apartment offered Lyons nothing. He checked it thoroughly. Apart from the cheap furniture, there was nothing to suggest anyone had even been living there. Callie had not put her stamp on the place. There were no clothes, no jewelry. No personal possessions of any kind.

She's not coming back, Lyons decided.

Making his way downstairs, Lyons met up again with the manager of the apartment building. The man had let Lyons into the apartment earlier.

"Any luck?" the guy asked.

"No. I'm guessing she's skipped town. Nothing there except the furniture."

"She paid up front for three months. Cash."

"Looks like you made on the deal," Lyons told him.

The manager spread his hands. "She was a good tenant."

LYONS SAT IN HIS CAR working on his next move. He would never have admitted to anyone, but at that moment he hadn't a clue how he was going to move forward. He needed somewhere to start. But where?

He spotted the diner across the street. It was directly in line with the apartment building.

What the hell, Lyons figured. It was as good a place as any, and he could do with a coffee. So he started the car and swung it across the street, pulling up outside the diner. He went inside and chose an empty stool at the counter.

"Black coffee," he said when the server approached.

"Saw you come out of the apartment building," the guy said. "You don't strike me as the type to stay there."

Lyons saw the man as a talker, and his cop instincts came into play. He pulled out his badge holder and showed the guy.

"I'm looking for someone who could be a missing person. Maybe you knew her."

"Woman, huh?"

"She had an apartment across the street. Callie Jefferson."

"Callie? Yeah. She comes in here every morning for breakfast. You say she's missing?"

"She went away on Friday for the weekend. Hasn't shown up since."

"Hope nothing's happened. She's a nice girl. Wish I could help. Like I said, she use to come in for breakfast every day. Could set my clock by her. Always at 8:20. She'd order her meal, then go make her daily phone call."

"Call?" Lyons swung around on his stool and stared at the pay phone on the other side of the diner.

"That's it."

"Long or short call?"

"Couple of minutes is all. Then she'd have her breakfast and leave," the server replied.

"Did she ever say who she was calling? I mean, weren't you curious?"

The guy grinned self-consciously. "Yeah. Sure I was. Callie must have noticed, so one day she told me it was her mother. Said she called her every day because her mother liked to know she was okay."

Lyons crossed to the pay phone. He took out a notebook and pen and wrote down the company name and the phone's number. Then he called Stony Man from his cell phone and asked to speak to Aaron Kurtzman, the Farm's resident computer genius.

"If I give you the pay phone number and company, can you trace calls made from it?"

"Be even more helpful if you can give me dates."

"Hold on," Lyons said. He returned to the counter. "How far back do these calls go?"

"Three weeks I'd say. Not much longer."

"Always the same time?" A nod. "Go back two weeks max. Calls made every morning at 8:30."

"Might take a little time, but we'll pin it down for you. Anything else?" Kurtzman queried.

"Check out a Callie Jefferson."

"You got it."

Lyons broke the connection.

"I'll have my coffee now," he said, and picked up his mug.

"That information help?"

"Hope so."

"She was a nice young woman," the guy said, wandering off to top up his coffeepot. "Be a shame if anything happened to her."

AN HOUR LATER Lyons's cell phone rang. He had already left the diner and had parked up away from town, waiting impatiently for his return call, resisting the temptation to contact Kurtzman himself.

"Up until two days before your subject went missing, all her calls were to a landline in Los Angeles," Kurtzman said without preamble. "After that, her calls went to a cell. We had to go chasing the signal because after the first contact the cell was obviously on the move. Turns out the end user had a sat phone. Once we pinned down the band frequency it was easier to track. It appears that the user was on a definite run, headed out of L.A. The user settled in a spot somewhere north of where you are now."

"I need that location. Something odd going down here."

"I'll send you a text. If you plan to go looking for your missing pair, get yourself some big wheels. Rough country up there."

"If anything else comes up…"

"I know the drill."

EARLY NEXT DAY Lyons was on the road in his new rental. He had returned to the agency and traded his car for a late-model SUV capable of handling the roughest terrain. The Ford Expedition's powerful 5.4 liter engine would give Lyons the power he needed, and the 6-speed transmission would enable him to cover any ground conditions once he was off road. The SUV was equipped with a DVD touch-screen satellite navigation system, another bonus for the Able Team leader. He was able to tap in the coordinates Kurtzman had sent in a text to his cell phone, giving him a direct route to follow.

He made good time. Two hours' steady driving and he was turning off the main highway onto a narrow road. Lyons scanned the timbered hills as he pushed up the higher slopes. He spotted the odd isolated lodge, smaller cabins, the gleam of water from small lakes. Even they vanished the farther he drove, noticing that the road had become a vehicle-wide dirt track. The forest closed in around him.

Lyons slowed, then stopped, checking his GPS. The readout told him he was less than two miles from his destination. Before he moved out on foot Lyons dressed accordingly. He stripped off his civilian clothing and pulled on combat trousers and boots. A multipocketed hunter's vest went over a short-sleeved cotton shirt, to house speed loaders for his .357 Magnum Colt Python and clips for his Uzi. The Python was in a high-ride holster on his right hip, and a sheathed Cold Steel Tanto knife was on his left.

Right now Carl Lyons was operating on instinct, something about the setup refusing to sit comfortably. He accepted he had little hard evidence to back his gut feeling, but he couldn't shake his bad feeling.

Fully armed, he exited the Ford, pausing to make a quick call to Stony Man and update them on his progress. He laid out the facts in short sentences, asked if they had anything for him.

Stony Man's mission controller, Barbara Price, relayed the information to Lyons.

"Callie Jefferson *is* a false name. Okay, we came up with a number of women with that name but they all check out. Your Callie doesn't."

"Okay, here are my thoughts. A false identity. Callie shows up near the college and makes friends with young Rafiq so that she can lure him away from college and friends when the time is right. She chooses a weekend so that by the time his disappearance is noticed she has him free and clear." Lyons considered his next move. He also fell back on his former career as a street cop. "Do something for me. Have Hal get in touch with local law enforcement. Have them sweep Callie's rented room for fingerprints. They might fall lucky and get something they can use to pick up on her real identity. If they get a hit, pass me the data."

"Get back to you on that, Carl. Hold on. Aaron has passed me something. He got a name for the subscriber of the landline Callie Jefferson kept calling. The guy's name is Greg Marino. We're running a search on his background."

"Okay. Keep me updated."

"Hey, good luck, Carl."

Lyons smiled briefly. Luck was something he needed right now.

THE EX-LAPD DETECTIVE had fixed the location in his mind and he approached unseen and unheard, finally crouching in the heavy undergrowth with his target in sight—a slope-roofed timber cabin, with a porch running the length of the front wall. The roof overhung the porch. An area around the building had been clear cut at some earlier time, though some grass and weeds had started to grow back. Parked in front of the cabin were two vehicles, a powerful-looking 4x4, black, with dark tinted windows, and beside it was an SUV that was the same model and color as the one belonging to Rafiq Mahoud.

Lyons spent some time observing the cabin and the surrounding area. His instincts warned him not to make any hasty moves. He had to establish opposition strength before he initiated any action. The last thing he needed was for some concealed guard to come barreling out of the woods targeting Lyons's back. That said, he also needed to confirm Rafiq's presence inside the cabin.

Alive *or* dead.

Playing a hunch, Lyons decided the kidnappers were more likely to keep Rafiq alive in case they needed his physical presence to convince his father that the youth was unharmed. If they had wanted him dead, a drive-by shooting would have solved that problem quickly. Rafiq was a bargaining chip that could be instrumental in persuading Sharif Mahoud not to participate in the peace talks.

Before he moved again, Lyons took out his cell phone and switched it off. As he zipped the phone back in his pocket, Lyons scanned the area around the cabin. Apart from the section that had been cleared around the building, the landscape was timber-and-underbrush heavy. He was going to have ample cover. He understood it meant the opposition would have the same advantage.

Soft sound caught his attention, but it was nothing more than a breeze rustling its way through the foliage above his head, disturbing the branches of the clustered trees.

Lyons knew his next moves would draw him closer to the cabin and its occupants once he had established the whereabouts of any perimeter guards. There was no easy way to do it, so the sooner he completed his recon…

The presence materialized without sound or scent. Carl Lyons was no beginner at the game. His combat experience with Able Team had developed his skills to a high degree, but this time even those skills were no match for whoever came up behind him. Something swept down in the periphery of his vision and then he felt the solid slam of a heavy blow across his skull that pushed him into enveloping pain then darkness.

CHAPTER FOURTEEN

The rescue chopper arrived a few minutes over the two hours Pearson had predicted. The sight of the cumbersome transport chopper dropping from the sky was a welcome one for Bolan and Mahoud. They scrambled on board and the pilot lifted off.

Bolan dropped to the deck, putting his rifle aside and watched as Mahoud did the same. The ride wasn't exactly comfortable but neither of them cared. Both gave in to the sudden surge of exhaustion sweeping over them and offered no resistance.

The Executioner didn't sleep. His mind was still active and he found it hard to let go. So much had happened since his initial departure from the military base. His chief thought revolved around the undeniable fact that the mission had been compromised all the way down the line. The opposition had been walking almost in tandem with Bolan and Mahoud. There at every turn. Someone was desperate to have Mahoud silenced.

He glanced across at Mahoud. The man looked to be asleep but his lips were moving gently in a silent prayer, hands clasped together at his raised knees.

As soon as they touched down at the base Bolan went looking for Pearson, to request a communications hookup. Pearson took him to the communications center and Bolan was given the use of a satellite phone. Left alone the soldier punched in the code and number that would eventually link him, via the orbiting bird and several cutouts, to Stony Man Farm.

"Striker," Brognola said abruptly, "where the hell have you been? This mission is all over the place. You vanish. Carl has gone off the grid, as well. Can't get a damn word from him. Just don't tell me you went and lost Mahoud."

"I have him. A little bruised around the edges, but he's alive."

Brognola's response was a disapproving grunt. A moment later Barbara Price came on the line.

"Hey, Striker, good to hear from you. I get the feeling it hasn't been a walk in the park."

"Not exactly. And it isn't over yet. Tell me about Ironman."

"He went looking for Rafiq Mahoud. When he got to the college, the kid had already been missing a couple of days. He was supposed to have gone off for the weekend with his girlfriend. Only neither of them came back. Carl did some good old-fashioned police work and found out the girlfriend wasn't as sweet as she made out to be. She'd been making phone calls to a guy who turns out to be involved with certain suspect characters, and the name she gave Rafiq was a fake. Aaron managed to track phone calls and pin down a location. The last we heard from Carl was that he had found the location. After that his cell phone went dead and we haven't heard anything from him since."

"I won't pass that to Mahoud for the moment. The last thing he needs to know is that his son may be missing."

"You have his wife and daughters to bring out?"

"That's next. He gave me the location. Mahoud will stay here under military protection until I bring the family back. Do something for me."

"Go ahead."

Bolan gave Price a quick rundown on the problems he had encountered, emphasizing his suspicions security could have been compromised regarding Mahoud.

"Get Bear to run some deep checks on anyone and everyone. The President and Mahoud are supposed to be the only ones privy to certain details about the extract, but I'm not so sure. The opposition picked up on us too easily. I'm getting vibes telling me there are more interested parties being fielded than we figured earlier. Check it out. Here's something else for Aaron to look at. A piece of equipment." Bolan recited the make and model of the Codan transceiver he had brought back with him. He read off the serial number. "I took this off one of the Taliban gunners hunting for Mahoud. Someone is supplying these guys with brand-new equipment. It might give us something if we could pin down where it came from."

"Understood."

"Aaron just came up with a tie-in for Kate Murchison," Brognola interjected, "the real name of Rafiq Mahoud's girlfriend. She's in the system. Been arrested a few times for assault and fraud. Her photo shows her as young and attractive, but she's known to be a hardass and has a violent temper. Not a nice lady. Word is she's been involved with a guy named Greg Marino for the past couple of years. Marino is ex-military, and was kicked out of the Army for suspected theft of military weapons. Military CID couldn't get enough evidence to convict after their main witness was found dead. All they could do was recommend Marino be discharged. Word is Marino runs a tight little crew ready to hire out to anyone who comes up with the cash. The sad end of my story is Kate Murchison's logged phone calls were to Greg Marino."

"What we need to know now is who Marino is contracted out to," Bolan said.

"We're on it."

"Signing off now."

"Watch yourself out there, Striker."

"Always do," Bolan said.

IT HAD BEEN HARD persuading Mahoud to stay behind. The man wanted to see his family and was prepared to join Bolan. It took the soldier some time to make the man see it wasn't a wise move. He reminded Mahoud of the problems they had encountered getting to safety. Bolan had no intention of exposing Mahoud to further threats. He would have been the first to admit he had little idea who was behind the attempts on Mahoud's life while they had been trekking through the hills. The repeated attempts told Bolan there was a concentrated effort being waged against Mahoud. He had detailed this to Lieutenant Pearson and stressed that Mahoud needed around-the-clock protection.

"The people opposing him are determined, LT. Taliban, rebels, paid killers—call them what you like. Mahoud is their target and they don't give up. His peace initiative has upset a lot of people. Bottom line is, they want the guy out of the picture."

"Look around, Cooper. This is a pretty well-armed camp. I think we can keep Dr. Mahoud secure. If those hostiles try to pull him out of here, they're going to face some heavy resistance."

Bolan nodded. "That's good. I'm going to get some chow, then hit the sack for a couple of hours."

"The medics look after you okay?"

"They did."

Pearson grinned, checking out Bolan's fresh combat fatigues.

"You look a lot better than when you arrived. When you're ready, the chopper will fly you to your drop-off point. They can take you in pretty close. Hostiles are used to our air patrols so a helicopter isn't going to bother them too much. You sure you don't want any backup on this?"

"Grateful for the offer, LT, but I need to work this solo. No offence meant."

"None taken. You got all the equipment you need?"

"I'm fine."

AFTER THREE HOURS of uninterrupted sleep Bolan geared up. He downed a mug of black coffee before he checked with Pearson and told him he was ready to move out. On the way to the helicopter Bolan stopped to speak to Mahoud. The man had accepted he was going to stay behind, but he was fixated on the safety of his family.

"You will bring them to me here alive. You promise?"

They both knew he was placing a heavy burden on Bolan's broad shoulders. They also both knew Bolan couldn't give a hundred percent assurance. Mahoud understood but refused to accept the downside of the mission.

"I'll give it everything I have, Reef."

"Good enough, my friend. Go with God and my blessing."

The waiting chopper, with pilot and navigator, was powered up and ready.

"Good luck," Pearson said.

He stood beside his Hummer and watched Bolan walk across to the aircraft and climb in. The chopper rose smoothly, banking sharply once it reached height and the pilot settled it on course.

CHAPTER FIFTEEN

The outpost clung to the side of a rocky hill, its stone construction crumbling and weathered. At the end of a winding trail stood the village. Dusty and isolated, little had changed for decades. It was all but deserted. The border was less than a half mile from the village. At first glance there didn't appear to be much in the way of movement in the area.

Mack Bolan knew different.

He had been watching both the village and the outpost for a couple of hours, using powerful binoculars supplied by the military along with the rest of his equipment. He wore combat fatigues, carried an M-16 A carbine, with an M-9 Beretta holstered on his right hip. Bolan also carried a 7-inch combat knife, with a black epoxy-coated carbon steel blade. He wore it strapped against his left thigh in a black leather sheath. The M-16 was slung across his back and over his fatigues he wore a combat rig holding extra magazines. In one pouch nestled a sound- and flash-suppressor for the Beretta. Bolan also carried a handheld transceiver, hooked to his waist belt, so he could call for pickup.

His recon had supplied Bolan with relevant information about the situation around the outpost.

The village appeared to have a trio of armed men positioned at the head of the street where they could see anyone approaching the outpost. A light-colored 4x4 was parked between a couple of buildings. He had also spotted two more men watching the outpost from a position two hundred yards down the road.

It looked as if the opposition's intel had located Mahoud's wife and daughters. They were on site, hopefully waiting for Mahoud to show up so they could grab him—or shoot him on sight.

Bolan slid back into cover and checked his watch. A half hour remained until dark. He was forced to wait until nightfall. There was no way he could reach the outpost during daylight hours. There was too much open ground with little cover.

BOLAN DIDN'T MOVE until a good half hour after full dark.

He circled the checkpoint, working his way to the rear, using empty huts as cover. He finally eased between close-spaced huts and crouched just short of the 4x4. He could hear the three Afghanis conversing in Pashto. To one side was a small fire with a metal pot that held steaming tea. Bolan could smell the strong brew from where he crouched.

A keen wind was spiraling across the valley. It tugged at the clothing of the three men, lifting coarse dust that drifted across the area.

Bolan slung the M-16 and unleathered the Beretta. He slid its suppressor from the pouch on his rig and threaded it onto the barrel.

The Executioner clicked off the safety, picked his first target and didn't delay.

The head shot dropped the guy to the ground without a sound.

While the two Afghans spent seconds attempting to source the shot, Bolan racked back the Beretta's slide.

He targeted his second man and caught the guy as the Afghan half turned, starting to lift his own rifle. The 9 mm slug cored in between the eyes, the velocity taking it through the skull and into the brain, pushing out a wedge of bone before it stopped short of exiting fully.

The surviving Afghan gave a yell, his AK-47 rising.

Bolan knew he had to stop the man before he opened fire and alerted the other watchers along the monastery road.

The numbers fell with startling speed.

The Afghan's finger slid into the trigger guard, his eyes searching for a target.

Bolan worked the Beretta's slide, his hand directing the muzzle, lining up on target. The pistol chugged once, brass flipping from the ejection port.

The guy fell back across the fire, Bolan's slug tunneling into his chest and perforating his heart, knocking the steaming tea can aside. His rifle clattered unfired to the hard ground.

The Executioner stepped around the 4x4, checking to see if the vehicle was ready to move. He found the key in the ignition and took it, dropping it in a pocket. The vehicle would be a backup means of transport if anticipated help failed to arrive.

Before he set off along the road he racked the Beretta's slide again. It took him twenty minutes to close in on the two men standing watch outside the old outpost. They were squatting in the dust, blankets draped around their shoulders against the windchill.

Bolan dispatched the pair with a couple of shots from

the suppressed Beretta. He slipped around to the west side of the building, flattening himself against the crumbling stone wall. His instincts warned him to check out the interior before making any deliberate entry. As the mission had advanced, revealing obvious breaks in Mahoud's security, Bolan was now working on the assumption nothing could be taken at face value.

The man's family was supposed to be established here in safety, but hostile forces had been waiting. The thought occurred that when he did get inside he might find Mahoud's family already removed—or worse.

Bolan stayed low, moving along the side of the building until he reached the rear. Thick weeds had grown along the base of the wall, the ground underfoot littered with scattered refuse. Midway there was a small window, next to it a narrow, rotting wooden door. As Bolan closed in on the window, he saw a faint gleam of lamplight showing in the square. Crouching beneath it Bolan picked up faint sound. He pushed upright, keeping his head below the window. The sound was still there, faint but audible.

Someone was talking in a low monotone, then he realized it was someone in prayer. The voice was young, reciting the verses with confidence.

Stepping to one side of the window, Bolan peered inside the room. It was bare of furniture. An oil lamp hung from a hook on one wall, throwing a soft circle of orange light that reached out to show the kneeling figure of a slender girl. She was dressed in jeans and a sweater, with a pair of sturdy boots on her feet. A soft scarf covered her head. When she lifted her head, Bolan got a clear view of her face and recognized her from the photographs in the file Brognola had supplied at the start of the mission.

Amina Mahoud, the younger daughter, was twelve years old, large-eyed and pretty.

It confirmed without a doubt that Mahoud's family was still here.

Bolan moved to the door. Light from the oil lamp gleamed dully through the weathered timber. He checked it. The door was secured by a simple wooden latch, which he raised and eased open the door. It moved easily on heavy iron hinges and made no sound. He opened the door far enough so he was able to look inside the room.

The girl had lowered her head as she continued her devotions, the sound of her young voice as gentle as a warm summer breeze.

Bolan eased inside the room, pulled the door shut behind him and stood silently, his Beretta in his right hand. Out of respect for Amina he waited until the girl completed her prayers.

When she finished Bolan was ready to move. Amina abruptly raised her head and stared directly at him. Her beautiful brown eyes regarded his shadowy figure, flicking briefly to the pistol in his hand. Bolan immediately lowered the weapon, pressing it against his thigh in a nonthreatening gesture. He stretched out his left arm, palm of his hand held toward the girl.

"Don't be frightened, Amina. I'm not here to harm you. Your father sent me to take you away from here. Back to where he's waiting for you all."

She regarded him silently, those innocent eyes full of questions, assessing him with the uncomplicated candor of the very young.

"Is Daddy safe now?"

"Yes. He's at an American military base being guarded by soldiers."

"Has he been arrested?"

Bolan smiled. "No. He's with friends. Safe from the men who want to harm him."

Amina stood, the scarf slipping from her head to rest around her slender shoulders. Her hair was thick and black, shining in the lamplight.

"I'm telling you the truth, Amina."

The girl took a step toward him, her face solemn as she said, "Yes. I know you are. What's your name?"

"Call me Matt."

"Can we go to Daddy now?"

"First we have to tell your mother and your sister, Raika. Are you all alone here?" Bolan asked.

She nodded.

"There are men outside watching us. They're bad men."

"You don't have to worry about them any longer. Let's go and talk to your mother."

She reached to take Bolan's hand, a natural, trusting gesture. They walked out of the room into a bleak passage. At the end of the passage an open doorway led into a larger room that faced the approach road. There was no furniture. Just sleeping bags and blankets on the bare floor. A couple of oil lamps were the only illumination. There was a small butane cooking stove, utensils and cans of food. Water came from a large plastic container.

Two women were in the room, equal in height and build. They were dressed like Amina in plain, serviceable clothing and boots, all-weather jackets.

One of the women turned as Bolan and the girl stepped into the room. Bolan knew this was Mahoud's wife, Leila. She was in her early forties and despite the situation a beautiful woman. She was tall and slim. Her fine, well-drawn features were framed by hair as black as Amina's, and worn in a short style that was both practical and enhancing. She regarded Bolan silently, her eyes keen and not missing the way her younger daughter gripped his big hand with her own. Bolan kept the Beretta as much out of sight as he could, but Leila didn't miss its presence.

"This is Matt," Amina announced brightly. "Daddy has sent him to take us to him."

Leila Mahoud absorbed her daughter's statement in silence, assessing him with her intelligent eyes.

"How do we know? How do we know he has not been sent by Homani?"

Bolan glanced at the speaker. Raika Mahoud was a younger version of her mother. She was nineteen years old, with the same features, but leaner. Her beauty was edged aside by a hardness in her expression. The brown eyes held a fiery defiance that held Bolan's gaze. He noticed that her hands, down at her sides, were pulled into taut, knuckle-white fists. There was a lot of anger in the young woman's stance.

"Yes," Leila said, "how *do* we know you are not from Homani, or any of those people who follow him?"

"Because he said he was from Daddy," Amina said, "and I believe him."

"Oh, come on," Raika snapped. "You're a child."

Bolan felt Amina's fingers grip even harder as she returned her older sister's aggressiveness.

"You are so a bully," she said.

Raika leaned forward, one hand lifting. She was held back when her mother reached out and gently held her back.

"My name is Matt Cooper, Mrs. Mahoud. I was sent to escort your husband to a safe haven and bring you to him. This was a request coming from the U.S. President on behalf of Dr. Mahoud. Your son, Rafiq, is being looked after by a colleague."

"Is my husband injured?"

Bolan managed a slight smile as he said, "The trip out

was a little hectic. We made it with a few cuts and bruises. If Reef is as good a talker as he is a fighter, those meetings are going to be well served."

Bolan noticed the proud rise of Leila's chin when he mentioned her husband's courage.

"Yes, Mr. Cooper, I can tell you he is. And I can see you have gone through a rough journey. You know, there are not many people who call my husband Reef. It is not something he reveals to many people these days."

"You see," Amina insisted. "I told you he knew Daddy."

"You expect us to trust you because you know that?" Raika said. "That is just the sort of thing an assassin would learn to use."

"If I was here to kill you, would I be wasting my time in conversation?"

"Whoever you are, you will be aware of not only my father's skill as a negotiator, but also the fact he has important information hidden away. Perhaps you want to use us to obtain that information."

"If that's the case why have you been left alone here? Why didn't those men outside ask you the same thing while they waited for your father? They would want you alive so that if they capture him he could be threatened with your lives."

"This is all very interesting," Leila said. "Mr. Cooper, we are in your hands. These hills are full of rebels devoutly opposed to my husband. How do you intend to spirit us away? On a magic carpet?"

"The closest I can manage is a military helicopter." Bolan took out the transceiver. "One call and they can home in on the in-built tracker. It should take them an hour or so to reach us."

Leila turned to her daughters. "Make sure you are both properly dressed for the journey. We leave everything else behind."

Amina moved immediately to do as her mother had instructed. It took Raika a little longer. She stared across at Bolan, making no attempt to conceal her hostility.

"Excuse Raika," Leila said. "She is young. Full of conflicting emotions. The past few weeks have been hard on us all. These are difficult times."

Bolan nodded. Yet something was telling him to keep a close eye on Raika Mahoud.

He felt Leila's hand on his arm. She edged him to the far side of the room before she spoke.

"Tell me the truth. How did you get by those men outside?" She brushed the barrel of the Beretta. "I see the silencer on your weapon. Are they dead?"

She was looking directly at him as she spoke. Bolan returned her stare without flinching.

"Yes. The two outside and others near the village."

Leila drew breath, her hand at her throat. "Does this not bother you?"

"It bothers me. But in war these things are inevitable."

"Are we in a war, Mr. Cooper?"

"You understand the answer to that, Mrs. Mahoud," Bolan stated. "Your husband, too. If he had been unable to grasp what it means, he wouldn't have been able to fight alongside me when his enemies surrounded us."

"He is a true believer in peace."

"And sometimes even the peacemaker needs to defend his beliefs. If he remains passive against a direct threat, the spoken word won't always save him."

"Thank you for that. One more thing. My son. Is Rafiq really safe?"

"As far as I understand. I have to be honest with you. Communication with the man looking out for him has been broken. It appears an attempt to kidnap Rafiq took place in California. We are assuming your husband's enemies would want to use Rafiq as a bargaining chip against him as well as you and your daughters."

"To prevent him attending the peace talks."

"And also to persuade him to hand over the incriminating information he has locked away."

"Mullah Homani would do anything to silence Sharif. Anything."

"My colleague went looking for Rafiq. We believe he located where he had been taken. Then communication was lost."

Leila's eyes held a shadow of panic for a few seconds, then she recovered her composure, nodding very slightly.

"We must not tell the girls anything about this for the moment. Will you agree?"

Bolan nodded his reply.

"Thank you for that, Mr. Cooper. Now, I believe you have a message to send."

Bolan made his way to the front entrance and dragged open the door. He stepped into the moon-bright night. Holstering the Beretta, Bolan took out the transceiver and activated it. He keyed the transmit button. A second button switched on the homing signal. He made contact after a couple of attempts. The call was brief, confirming his homing signal had just been received.

Help, he was told, was on its way.

"I've brought you some tea." Bolan turned and saw Amina holding a steaming tin mug out to him. "It's the last. There isn't any milk or sugar, but it is hot and very strong."

Bolan took the mug. She was right. The hot liquid was as she had said.

"It's good," he said.

That drew a girlish giggle from her.

"No, it's really awful," she said.

"The helicopter is on its way, so you'll see your father soon," Bolan told her.

"Mother will be happy. She has missed him so much."

"And Raika, too."

"I suppose. It's hard to tell what she thinks lately," Amina stated.

"Oh?"

"The past couple of months she's changed. She used to be fun to have around. But now...well, she's changed. She never laughs. She shuts herself away. Whenever she thinks she's alone she spends ages on her cell phone. But if she sees me, she ends the call and shouts at me for spying on her." There was a long pause and Bolan detected a gleam of tears in the girl's eyes. "We used to be such friends. But since she was away things have changed. I hate it when she's angry with me."

"Where did she go?"

"It was while we were back in France. We lived in Paris." For a moment her face brightened. "I like Paris. I can speak French." The mood broke and the serious little girl returned. "Raika kept going away. And when she came back everything was different. Daddy said she probably had a boyfriend." Amina made a face. "Why would she want a boyfriend? I don't like boys. Well, except for Rafiq. I know he's my brother, but I still like him."

"You'll be able to tell him that soon."

Amina gave him a condescending look. "I could never tell him that. I'd be so embarrassed. And Rafiq would tell me to run away and play like a good little girl." She gave a deep, heartfelt sigh. "Boys. They just don't understand."

The moment was a breath of fresh air for Bolan. He spent so much of his waking time hip deep in conflicts of one kind and another it was easy to forget the reverse side of life. Where the simple words of a child brought pleasure, dulling the edge of pain and suffering. He looked at Amina Mahoud and in her bright-eyed stare he saw there had to be a better way to exist. Maybe not for himself though. As much as he might have wanted it, Mack Bolan understood and accepted his personal role in man's destiny. Until men like Sharif Mahoud could bring about some kind of peace, no matter how small and fragile, Bolan would need to stand his ground. Honorable intentions still needed someone to offer support against those who sought to destroy them.

"I hope my daughter has not been distracting you, Mr. Cooper."

Leila stood in the open door.

"Right now her kind of distraction is welcome. Thank you for the tea, Amina." Bolan turned. "We should go back inside."

"Of course." As they stepped through the door Leila said, "I feel I should apologize for my distrust earlier."

"No need. You were right to be cautious. And the name is Matt."

"May I call him Matt?" a small voice asked.

"You may call him *Mr.* Cooper."

Amina let her shoulders slump in defeat, but she was smiling when she looked at Bolan. They stepped back through the door.

"Raika?" Leila called.

"I'm here," the young woman said as she returned to the main room. "I went to secure the door at the back. We wouldn't want anyone coming in through there and surprising us, would we?"

"I suppose not," Leila said, accepting the explanation and forgetting it almost in the same breath.

Raika's gaze swept the room, pausing on Bolan for a

fraction, her expression fiercely defiant. She looked through him as though he didn't even exist.

Bolan moved to stand by the front window, unsettled by the young woman's attitude.

He tried to understand his feelings. Almost from his first meeting with Mahoud's family, Raika's presence, her cold disdain whenever they made eye contact generated unease. Bolan wasn't the kind of man to make snap judgments without cause.

In Raika's case that judgment implanted itself.

Bolan had to ask himself why.

Raika Mahoud, what the hell are you up to? he wondered.

CHAPTER SIXTEEN

The pale dawn was barely edging over the horizon when the Army helicopter clattered into view and homed in on Bolan's signal. As soon as it touched down, armed soldiers dropped from the door and fanned out. Bolan led his small group from the outpost, shielding their eyes against the gritty clouds of dust raised by the spinning rotors. They all climbed on board. The pilot increased power and the chopper rose, swinging away from the outpost, the village dwindling quickly.

One of the crew passed around canteens of water. Only Raika refused, huddling alone in a corner of the cabin. After she had drunk, Amina moved closer to Bolan.

"How long before we get there?"

"Couple of hours," the soldier replied.

"And Daddy will be waiting?"

"He'll be there. Now why don't you try to get some sleep?"

She did, leaning her slim body against Bolan, her arms holding on to him. When the soldier looked across the cabin Leila Mahoud was watching, a gentle smile on her tired face. It wasn't long before she slept herself.

Only Raika remained awake, staring moodily out through one of the side windows.

The crew sergeant sat on the deck alongside Bolan. He was a tall, rangy man with a weather-beaten, tanned face and a shock of sandy hair. He draped his big hands across his knees.

"Command warned us we might be getting a visit from the Taliban. Intel says they've been gathering a few klicks west of the base. Operations sent out a couple of teams to confirm. They reported movement. Lieutenant Pearson is going to do his best to get you people out before any attack."

"Thanks for that, Sarge."

"You look like you've been through a piece of war yourself, Mr. Cooper."

"Nobody can say Afghanistan ever lets you off easy."

"No shit. I've pounded dust in some places. This place beats the hell out of 'em all."

"They never tell you about this side of the Army at the recruiting office," Bolan told him.

The sergeant grinned.

"You got that right. Hey, what was your specialty?"

"Sniper."

"Well, I can shoot," the sergeant said, "but you need more to do that sniping stuff. Best I could do was to reach squad sergeant. Name's Harry Munro. That's the Oklahoma Munros."

"Couldn't be any other," Bolan said, grinning.

For the next hour he and Munro talked Army, Bolan falling into the easy camaraderie of fighting men. Not with a little surprise he found himself completely at ease with the soldier. It was as if the years had fallen away and he was back in the service himself. Despite his rough-hewn appearance, Munro was a man with a great deal of sense filling his head. His conversation was relaxed, informative. He learned a lot about the ongoing situation in the country as Munro talked.

"The Afghans I've met—not counting the ones who're shooting at me—are good people. Jesus, Cooper, they've been going through rough times longer than I've been alive. Seems like every damn country in the world has tried to beat them down one time or another. Like nobody will just leave them alone to do their own thing. Poor bastards have a hard time without being shot and bombed every which way. This isn't exactly what I'd call God's country, if you know what I mean. Rock and dust. Don't rain all that much. Hot as hell in the day. Ball-freezing cold at night. Being a farmer here is crap. The land doesn't yield much if they do get it planted. If they're lucky enough to feed their families. And that's what most of them really want. Food and a roof over their heads. But then they get the Russians blowing the hell out of everything. Near enough flatten the place to the ground. Now it's the damn Taliban who want to run the country like somebody switched off the feel-good switch. Ban this. Destroy that. Don't laugh. Don't read books. Kick the women back into the Dark Ages. Then there's the drugs. And the drugs. And the mullahs. If those mullahs could figure out how, they'd turn off the sun and make everybody slope around in the dark, and hell, I'm talking too much. Cooper. Why don't you tell me to shut up?"

"You're doing fine, Sarge. You in for the duration?"

Munro shook his head. "No. This is my last tour. Another three months and I go home for good. It's time I started to look after my own family. Hell, I worked out my time. I'll take my pension and go back to farming. Got two grown-up sons. We'll take over my daddy's spread. Keep it in the family."

"Hope it works out."

"How about you, Cooper? There a family back in the States?"

Bolan shook his head. "No family…" He let the words trail off.

WHEN THEY LANDED Lieutenant Pearson was there to meet them with his Hummer. Bolan made sure the Mahoud family was settled in the vehicle before he turned back to thank the helicopter crew. He shook hands with Munro.

"Hope it goes well for you, Sarge," he said.

"You ever get down to Oklahoma you drop by, you hear? Won't be hard to find us. Ev'ybody knows the Munros."

"I'll remember that, Sarge."

As Pearson gunned the Hummer toward the base he asked, "You get the intel about the possible attack?"

"I heard. How sound is it?"

"It's sound. We're going to get you out ASAP." He paused, then added, "I hope we have enough time to do that."

THEY PLACED A HUT at Mahoud's disposal. While the family spent time together Bolan wandered across to the mess hall and ate. He was on his third mug of coffee when Pearson showed up. He helped himself to a drink and brought it across to Bolan's table.

"You don't look too happy, LT," Bolan said.

"Chopper coming in to pick you up has been held back because of the Taliban. Until we know for sure about this attack, command won't risk an evac."

"I see their point. Slow-moving transport chopper would be an easy target for an RPG. Look at it this way, LT, it means we get to enjoy your hospitality a little longer."

Pearson grinned.

"I'd better go tell the family."

Bolan returned to the hut and explained the situation.

"I was looking forward to another ride in a helicopter," Amina said.

"It'll happen," Bolan said.

In the quiet moment as they considered the current situation the Executioner caught the shadow of concern on Sharif Mahoud's face.

"You worried about something?"

Mahoud spread his hands. "Look what I have brought on my family. I should not have allowed them to come to Afghanistan. This is my fault. In my arrogance I imagined this would convince the people of my sincerity. By bringing my family to mix with them. To talk to them. My foolish pride. My naiveté."

"Sharif Mahoud, you stop that talk right now."

Leila's voice cut through with its fierce tone. There was a strong rebuke in every word.

Bolan glanced at her as she pushed to her feet and crossed to where Mahoud sat.

"How long have we been married?"

"Twenty-five years…"

"And every day of those years I have watched you devote yourself to helping others. Even when you lived in one of those villages you were thinking of others. You built your career. Raised your family. Took us from obscurity to Europe. America. Studied tirelessly to reach where you are now."

"Perhaps I spent too much time on those things. I should have given more to you and the children."

"No. You have given us everything we could ever have wished for. A wonderful life. But most of all you allowed us to share your vision. Listened to us and asked our advice. Now this—your great dream, to bring together the people who have the ability to share that vision, to make a real attempt to broker peace. You bring the voice of sanity into all this madness and hatred. Do you really think we could let you come here alone? We came willingly because your dream is our dream, too."

Mahoud reached out to touch her hand.

"But I did not intend that you should all step into danger. To have to hide away in fear."

"In those villages we visited I talked with people who thanked us because they have been left to suffer and there was no one to speak for them. The simple fact we spoke face-to-face with them meant a great deal. And they were surprised that I had come with you. A woman walking into the danger zone. With her daughters by her side. I think that helped so much to get them to open up to me. They told me of the things they have seen. Death. Destruction. Starvation. They told me of their fears at losing husbands and sons to the fighting. All they want is for someone to listen to their stories. Such a simple thing, Sharif, but because of you they have a little faith now. They held my hands and they said for me to ask you to be their voice. To speak for them. They have no one. Only you. When we were separated and your friends guided us to the outpost, we knew you would ensure our safety as you always have. And Mr. Cooper came and brought us back to you."

Amina embraced her father.

"The children said they were afraid when the fighting came. They asked if you would stop it. Just so they could be happy again."

Sharif Mahoud looked down at the smiling face. When he found his voice again he said, "Am I not a man blessed many times over, Matt?"

"No doubt of that."

Beyond the tight group, Raika Mahoud lay on one of the Army cots, her back to them all. She was feigning sleep. Bolan saw her shoulders tense as she listened to the conversation. She was awake yet made no effort to join her parents.

AMINA HAD FINALLY succumbed to fatigue and slept. Her sister remained on her own cot, still pretending. Bolan guessed she was listening to every word being uttered.

Leila was the one who finally broached the subject they had been ignoring while they settled in.

"The arrangement between Sharif and the President. Wasn't it to be a close secret?"

"Yes." Bolan understood where she was going. "Security has been breached. Somehow Sharif's movements have been transmitted to people who want him stopped."

"Stopped, or killed?" Leila asked.

"Both," Bolan replied.

"Explain to me."

"Opposing groups," Mahoud said. "Working from different agendas. Right, Matt?"

"We have two separate factions at work here," Bolan said. "One has no other intention than to kill you. They see the solution to their goal in your elimination. Plain and simple. If Sharif Mahoud dies, the talks will fall apart and the status quo remains."

"If I had to put a name forward for that, it would be Homani."

"It's no secret Homani has called for Sharif's death on numerous occasions," Leila said. "He declares it openly. Calls on his followers to denounce him as blasphemer. Homani incites the act."

"Will he be attending the talks?" Bolan asked.

Mahoud smiled. "Oh, yes, he will be there. His arrogance will not allow him to stay away. He wants his day. To speak his piece."

"And the other group?" Leila asked.

"A little more complicated," Bolan said. "Sharif dead would only satisfy part of their agenda. They also need to get their hands on the data he has. There's a deeper motivation here—reputations, covert alliances, men in high positions who do not want their identities brought into the open. Important individuals here in the region. I'm also certain there are others in the U.S., maybe even Europe, who see the Middle East as a chance to offer them means of control. The region has mineral wealth and of course oil. They want their hands on the reins."

"This is why they kidnapped Rafiq?" Mahoud said.

Leila had quietly, calmly told him about Rafiq once they had been settled in the hut.

"Coercion. A demand for your data in exchange for the life of your son."

"I would respect them more if they faced me openly. Like men. Not hiding behind my son."

"We're dealing with people who work in the shadows. They arrange their deals behind closed doors. Away from the light because what they do is unlawful. For *their* benefit, not for the good of others."

"And they buy and sell lives in order to maintain their anonymity," Leila said. "Whatever suits their purpose, no matter how much harm it brings."

"Yes. Believe it. These people will sacrifice anyone to remain where they are. Leila, there is a great deal at stake here. Power to control not just wealth, but political aims." Bolan turned to Mahoud. "Without seeing your data I'm guessing there are some surprising names in there."

"Yes. Extremely important and influential figures who are not going to be happy if I expose them."

"Then you must do it," Leila said. "If you expose these people to the world they will lose their credibility. Out in the open where is their threat then?"

"Nice in theory," Bolan said. "But these people aren't the kind to walk away and admit defeat. They would fight back."

"Surely showing what they really are would strip them of their influence. If they were not afraid of exposure, then why the desperate need to silence Sharif and destroy his information? A victory, no matter how small, is still a victory."

Bolan had to smile at her logic.

"Sharif, Leila should do the talking at the conference. There's no way to beat her down."

"I am beginning to see your viewpoint," Mahoud said with a tired smile.

Seconds after Mahoud spoke, the first mortar landed outside the hut.

The explosion rocked the building, dust sifting from the roof. The dull sound of the blast was accompanied by a burst of autofire.

Bolan snatched up the M-16, checked he had extra magazines in the vest and cut across to the door.

"Matt," Mahoud called. "What can I—"

"Stay here. With your family."

The tone in his voice had the desired effect.

Smoke was drifting across the area as Bolan exited the hut. He heard the dull thump of another mortar. It had landed close to a parked Hummer, shredding a tire and rocking the heavy combat vehicle, throwing a dark gout of earth into the air.

Armed figures were moving into view from the north

perimeter of the base, some carrying rifles, others wielding RPG launchers. They moved independent of one another, firing at anything that moved.

The crackle of autofire came from U.S. forces as they picked up the pace of the attack and fought back.

Another incoming mortar landed in the center of a wedge of stacked equipment boxes. Debris was thrown in all directions.

The noise of weapons fire rose to a crescendo. Men were shouting. Bolan saw people falling to the ground as he took his position in front of the building, seeing the raiders coming fully into view through the streaks of smoke.

A Taliban rebel launched himself in Bolan's direction, his AK-47 spitting on full-auto. Bolan shouldered the M-16, caught the man in his sights and hit him in the chest. The rebel spun, then dropped to the ground. Bolan moved forward, tracking a second figure. The guy had an RPG, fumbling with the controls as he attempted a launch. The M-16 cracked sharply, driving 5.56 mm slugs into the side of his skull. The guy's head shattered in a blossom of red as he slumped to the sand.

Around Bolan the compound erupted into a melee of autofire, incoming mortars, the screams and yells of combatants. The crash of exploding RPG rockets. There was little coordination in this maelstrom, simply a clash of opposing fire, each desperate to gain the advantage over the other.

Off to Bolan's right flames erupted from a mortar hit, then came the hiss and explosion from a fired RPG missile as it struck home.

Sound and vision were fragmented.

Actions carried out on automatic pilot.

Each man might have been in his own isolated place,

in the middle of the firefight, yet alone at the same time. There was no time to separate thought from action. Aim and fire, repeat the moves. Select a target and take it down.

Bolan took cover behind the immobilized Hummer, his senses assailed by the smell of scorched rubber and paint as he went down on one knee and tracked a fast-moving Taliban fighter. His well-placed shots dropped the man, catching him midstride. The rebel fell in a loose sprawl, skidding along the ground.

Around Bolan uniformed U.S. combat soldiers had dropped into defensive mode, gathering under the command of their officers. Men like Lieutenant Pearson who deployed his soldiers with a cool professionalism that used them to their best advantage.

In addition to the force attacking the base head-on, there was a reserve number of enemy launching the mortars. The missiles were starting to range in now; their targets, the main storage areas.

From the far side of the base an AH-64A Apache attack helicopter rose from its pad and swept into the area, veering in a wide circle away from the firefight where it gained height. Bolan caught a glimpse of the chopper as it swept in from altitude, behind the attacking Taliban. He saw it was heading for the distant mortars.

The Apache made a recon circuit, turned, then lined up on the targets it had spotted. The white trails bursting from the missile pods preceded the hard slam of the AGM-114 missiles as they exploded. The chopper overflew the target area, dispersing the coiling smoke, rose and came around and opened up with sustained bursts of 30 mm cannon fire, raking the mortar emplacements.

All this took place away from the main area of fighting. Its success was marked by the abrupt cessation of mortar fire.

Regardless of the demise of the mortar attacks, the combatants within the base were still engaging. A pair of Hummers, equipped with mounted machine guns, rolled to the front line and opened fire, scattering the rebels.

Bolan had paused briefly to reload his carbine. As he locked in the fresh magazine, he caught sight of three Taliban rebels converging on the Mahouds' hut. Their maneuver had the deliberation of men who knew exactly where they were going. Nothing like simply making a spur-of-the-moment diversion.

He had no doubt the rebels were targeting the hut because they knew who was inside.

Bolan shut out the noise of battle as he focused on the three rebels and their mission.

The killing or kidnapping of Sharif Mahoud and his family.

Bolan pushed to his feet. Moving around the Hummer, he headed for the hut.

Ahead of him the lead pair had almost reached the door of the hut. The third guy hung back to cover them, his AK-47 ready.

Bolan angled in his direction, raising the M-16. He put two fast shots into the guy, seeing his slugs punch in through the ribs on his right side. The Taliban rebel stumbled, twisting to seek his attacker as Bolan fired again. His double shot struck the man in the head, snapping it back. The 5.56 mm slugs channeled into his skull, exiting in a burst of pressured blood. As the rebel dropped Bolan raced by him, hard on the heels of the advance pair as they stepped through the door and vanished inside.

He heard the tail end of a startled yell as he closed on the hut and barreled through without a pause, his weapon rising, and as he cleared the frame he saw the two invaders.

The closer man began to turn as he heard Bolan's entry. The Executioner triggered the M-16 and fired off a short burst that ripped into the guy's body, turning him so that Bolan's follow-up shots hit their target full-on, chest and throat. The guy stumbled, crashing to the floor.

Still moving, Bolan targeted the second gunner who had maintained his forward run, swinging his AK-47 at Mahoud, who was shielding Leila and Amina.

The crackle of shots filled the interior as Bolan and the Taliban rebel fired together. Out of the corner of his eye Bolan saw Mahoud jerk as a 7.62 mm slug struck his left arm, high up. Then Bolan's own weapon was firing, the hard burst coring in through the back of his adversary's skull, exiting through his face. A bloody spray fountained across the room as the rebel went down. As Bolan moved past the first man he had taken down he triggered a final burst into him and kicked the dead guy's weapon aside. There was no need for more with the other attacker. Bolan's head shots had killed him outright.

Leila had turned Amina away from the dead Taliban, hiding her face as the girl burst into tears. Raika had roused herself from her bed and was standing near her mother.

"Raika, look after your sister," Leila said.

"You all stay here," Bolan ordered, then turned back to the door.

A burst of fire sent 7.62 mm slugs that tore chunks of wood from the doorframe. Bolan dropped to one knee, his M-16 tracking the source of the shots, and picked up on the lone Taliban rebel coming at him at a dead run, firing as he came, his AK-47 on full-auto. The burning spray of shots flew wide. The Executioner shouldered his carbine and hit the guy with a burst to the torso. In the same instant the hard boom of a combat shotgun added its noise as a uniformed soldier ran into view. He hit the rebel with a trio of shots, the destructive impact of the 12-gauge doing maximum damage. The rebel's left arm was severed at shoulder level and his body torn open, pulped flesh blowing out in bloody geysers before he slithered loosely to the dusty ground, nerves shuddering in response.

Bolan checked the area and saw no more attackers, but armed soldiers were racing past.

"Soldier, we need a medic in here. Fast," he told a shotgunner.

"Yes, sir," the man said, and turned away.

Bolan went back inside the hut.

Leila had covered the dead men with blankets and was tending to her husband, binding his arm with a towel, the cloth already red with blood.

Raika stood watching, little emotion showing on her face. Amina stood a few feet away, her big eyes still wide with shock, motionless. When she saw Bolan she ran to him.

"Will Daddy be all right?"

"We'll make sure he is."

Bolan turned as Lieutenant Pearson stepped inside the hut. Dust-streaked, carrying an M-16, he surveyed the scene.

"You need help?"

"Already sent for a medic," Bolan said.

"I'll chase it up." Pearson turned to leave. "You chose an unfortunate time to visit us, Dr. Mahoud."

"In these unsettling days when would be a good time, Lieutenant?"

"You have me there, Doctor."

"What's the situation?" Bolan asked.

"Getting that Apache in the air changed the tide. Damn lucky we have it here on base on a short loan for an upcoming operation. Those rebels lost their advantage once the mortars were hit. They're already pulling back."

"Any losses?"

Pearson nodded, his face expressing his feelings. "Two dead. Five wounded. Three we can handle okay, but two need specialist treatment so we'll be sending them out with your ride. The carrier has better medical facilities."

"The Taliban?"

"Six dead, not including the ones you handled. Number of wounded. We'll treat them then try to find out what was behind the attack. Don't expect much. Those bastards close up if we capture them." Pearson shrugged. "I'll let the spooks deal with them."

Bolan joined him at the door as a medic team rushed into the hut.

"Smart move bringing in a team to try for Mahoud in among the main raiding party," Bolan said.

"You believe it was deliberate?" Pearson asked.

Bolan nodded. "They went directly for the hut. This was no coincidence. Those men had information. Mahoud was their target. Two straight in. The third outside to block interference."

"You think the information came from inside the base?" Bolan's lack of a reply implied as much as a vocal affirmation. "Son of a bitch," Pearson said. He brought his anger under control swiftly. "I'll post guard around the hut until you leave. And *I* was the one who said Dr. Mahoud was safe in our hands. On a U.S. base."

"Don't knock yourself out over this, LT. This mission has compromise written all over it. Been screwed from day one. The sooner we have Dr. Mahoud out of Afghanistan, the better."

"You think that will be an end to his troubles?"

"No way, LT. But I might have a better chance to control the situation away from here."

Pearson cleared his throat. "You really sure about that?"

"Right now, LT, I'm not clear on a lot of things. But I intend to change that as soon as I can."

Even as Bolan spoke the words his mind was spinning over what he had to qualify his intentions. He had very little, and the greater part was hunch, gut feeling, and his suspicious nature.

Not a great deal to work with.

Mack Bolan had lived on the edge before and walked away. It was clear he needed to pull off a similar miracle again.

THE MILITARY CHOPPER flew them across Afghanistan into Pakistan and eventually out over the Arabian Sea where they had a rendezvous with a U.S. Navy aircraft carrier on patrol. The carrier was in international waters and moved farther out to sea once the helicopter touched down. The wounded men from the Afghan base were taken off to the carrier's hospital. Mahoud spent time there having his wound checked out. The Army medics at the base had done a good job, but it was decided to follow up.

Bolan, Leila and the girls were also run through the medical system. They cleaned up and got into fresh clothing. After eating they were assigned to cabins so they could rest.

Bolan had things to do before he relaxed. His status had been relayed to the carrier's captain, and the Executioner was given access to a secure line and made contact with Stony Man.

"Glad to hear your voice, Striker," Brognola said. "Can't give you an update on Ironman. We still can't make contact."

"Let me know when you do."

"You have the family safe as promised. What's your next move?"

"Mahoud needs to get back to France. His data is secured in Paris. I need you to arrange to get us there. The clock is ticking on this. The conference is due soon, so we need to move on this."

"Mahoud wants to return to his Paris home?"

"No. We discussed this on the flight. I advised a safe-house. Don't we have somewhere outside Paris?"

"Château Fontaine. SOG has it on long-term lease. It's self-contained in its own grounds with its own power supply. How do you want to work this?"

"Security can be provided by our blacksuits. They can fly over along with the items on my shopping list."

"I was waiting for that. I'll pass you over to Barbara. Tell her what you need. Meantime I'll requisition flights for you and the Mahoud family. By the time you arrive we should have the house up and running."

"I'm still concerned about the repeated security breaches in Afghanistan. There's something odd about the way the opposition got a line on our moves. Keep Aaron and his team running checks on everyone involved. I need to be ahead of this, or at least running in tandem with the opposition."

"Striker, you sound tired. Go get some rest. It'll be a while until we sort your travel arrangements. Stand down until then."

"Let me speak to the lady, then I promise sack time."

After listing his needs Bolan went to his cabin. His mind was full of unanswered questions and concerns about what lay ahead. He was also thinking about Carl Lyons. Bolan had full confidence in Ironman, as he was fondly known by the Stony Man team, but that didn't prevent him worrying about his friend.

Bolan stretched out on the bunk, staring at the ceiling, convinced he had too much going on to rest. He was wrong. He was asleep within minutes of lying down. His mind might have been active but his body needed to recharge.

CHAPTER SEVENTEEN

On board the Crescent Moon

Ali Asadi waited until he was alone, making his way along the deck and climbing to the upper section. From inside his robes he took a powerful satellite phone and tapped in a programmed number. He waited as the connection was made, heard the soft purr as it rang out.

The man who answered spoke in French, and Asadi replied in the same language.

"We failed," Asadi's contact said.

"Explain?"

"The man the U.S. President sent succeeded in his mission. Every attempt to stop Mahoud was fought off. A number of our people are dead. Even the helicopter I sent was brought down."

"What about the men we inserted into the strike against the U.S. base?" Asadi queried.

"All killed."

"All?"

"Yes. And Mahoud and his family were airlifted out to a U.S. carrier in the Arabian Sea," the contact stated.

The silence that followed was unnerving for Asadi's contact. He wished Asadi would rant and rave at him. He could at least understand that. It would have been better than the empty silence.

"These fools here, even Homani, are still agreeing Mahoud should be captured alive," Asadi said. "They insist this information he claims to have secreted away is too important to be allowed exposure. While I am with them I have to go along with this foolishness. At least while I do that I can use their assets to help me. If I learn of anything that will be useful I will pass it along."

"But you wish *us* to keep after Mahoud?" the contact asked.

"Of course. This damned man is nothing but a curse. His words, blasphemous as they are, will sway many of the weaker members of the peace talks. These men are already in the pockets of the infidels. We cannot let that happen. Mahoud is no fool. He understands the thoughts that drive these men. His words will turn them aside and along the path he and his fellow traitors wish them to walk. Homani has allowed himself to be persuaded by Hartman that there is too much to be lost if Mahoud exposes his information," Asadi said.

"I thought Homani was a true believer."

"Each man has his own personal vision of true belief. Homani is taking the easy option. Hartman promises him everything he wants to maintain his struggles. Weapons. Money. He makes many promises. Homani sees this as an easy option, but fails to realize Hartman's duplicity."

"You do not trust him? This American?" the contact asked.

"He is an American. What is there to trust? They cut your throat while they look into your eyes and smile.

Homani is blind to this. He is an old fool who no longer understands the modern world."

"What do we do?"

"If Mahoud is out of Afghanistan we need to find where he and his family have been moved to. Mahoud will want to regain possession of his data. The man is nothing if not determined. If I had to make an educated guess, I would say he will go back to Paris. That was his base, where his friend Jamal Mehet remained when Mahoud left France. We know he was keeping watch in the city. That was where we got our hands on him. I suspect Mehet was looking out for more than just our people. When we had him, our priority was getting him to tell us where Mahoud was hiding. In retrospect I can see we should have been asking him where this information had been hidden," Asadi said.

"I understood you were not concerned about that."

"Not for the reasons Hartman and Homani have. They want it so they can claim it. That is where I understand Hartman. He sees the power in such data. If he gains control of it, I suspect he will use it himself to buy loyalties and force people to do what *he* wants. And that could include us."

"We would be well rid of him then."

"When the time is right. For now we can allow Hartman to play his game. One of the virtues of our faith is patience. Let these others run around and make their moves. Our prime aim is the death of Mahoud and his family. If we achieve that, the myth will be destroyed as his soul descends into hell. The conference will founder. Alive, Mahoud binds the meeting together. Without him there will be nothing," Asadi stated.

"Until we know where Mahoud is, we can't do very much."

"I will have that location for you very soon. Be assured."

The location was telephoned to Asadi a couple of hours later. The call was brief. Simply the name of the house and location where Sharif Mahoud and his family were. Château Fontaine.

The moment his caller had gone off the line Asadi made his own, passing on the information.

MOHAN BOUVIER TAPPED his fingers against the telephone casing as he considered his next move. There would be no problems getting the men he needed. As many as he wanted. On reflection he decided to go for a small number. There would be less attention paid to a compact group. First, though, he needed to confirm numbers.

He called one of his recon experts, relayed the details about Château Fontaine.

"Is this urgent?"

"Yes. I need the intel quickly."

"I will get back to you."

BOUVIER HAD his update by noon of the following morning.

"Guests number five. Security is provided by a four-man team. All armed. They have two men patrolling the grounds around the château. They swap every four hours. Two vehicles. Is that enough?"

"Perfect. The usual fee will be paid into your account by this evening."

Bouvier finalized his teams.

Four to make the assault on the château. There would also be two other teams, each consisting of driver and shooter. These would be in vehicles waiting to follow anyone leaving the château. Every team member had photo identification of Sharif Mahoud and his family.

"We know this. Mahoud is in France. There are only days left before the conference," Bouvier told his people. "He needs to move soon if he is going to collect his evidence. That means he will leave the château. A good time to deal with him if he does. If that happens, the second team will move in and eliminate his family. This is not negotiable. They must all die. Is this understood?"

CHAPTER EIGHTEEN

Château Fontaine, France

The house was over three hundred years old. Gray stone with leaded windows that reached ceiling height. It was a relic of past glories, now reduced to having only a few of its many rooms utilized. Even the grounds on which it stood were untended, the gardens overgrown, an ornamental fountain long without water. The house had running water but no installed electricity. Power came from a diesel generator standing behind the main building inside a stone enclosure.

Bolan, Mahoud and Leila were in one of the spacious drawing rooms. The two girls were in a nearby room under the protective eye of a Stony Man blacksuit.

"There are likely to be other safehouses," Bolan explained, "but they have connections to main agencies. This place has only ever been used by the group I operate through. We have no affiliation with recognized U.S. security organizations, so I'm not expecting leaks from that source."

"You can be sure of that?" Leila asked. "One hundred percent sure?"

"Leila," Mahoud admonished his wife for her forthright manner.

"She's right to question that statement," Bolan said. "In her place I'd ask the same. Let's face it, too much has happened over the past days to make even me wary."

Mahoud slumped back in the armchair, favoring his injured arm.

"Yes, you're right."

Bolan crossed the high-ceilinged room and helped himself to more coffee from the thermos jug.

"Absolute security? The four men you've met are from my group. We operate covertly. As far out of the agency community as possible. It's as good as it gets, Leila."

The four blacksuits from Stony Man, flown into France on Brognola's orders and the President's approval, were known to Bolan. Château Fontaine had been used on a couple of previous occasions to provide secure bolt holes on Sensitive Operations Group missions. Security had never been breached during the earlier excursions.

"Then I suppose we must hope that is enough," Leila said, smiling at Bolan. "I did not mean to be rude, Matt, but after Afghanistan, and what has happened with Rafiq…"

"I understand," Bolan said.

"How do you think we should proceed?" Mahoud asked. "We only have days before the conference starts. But I need to recover my information first."

"Is it close?" Bolan asked.

"We will need a day."

Bolan knew about Mahoud's data, but lacked detail. The subject hadn't come up apart from references during the Afghanistan episode, and Bolan had let the matter stay in the background until Mahoud was ready to discuss it himself.

"Do you want to tell me about it, Reef?"

Mahoud glanced across at his wife. Her head moved in a gentle, approving nod.

"Tell him," she said.

"When I began to gather my information, it was in the form of notes, all cataloged with names, dates, times and places. My suspicions had grown for some time that outside influences were directing events in trouble spots. The more I looked into it, the stronger my convictions became. I realized there were so many people working in the background I needed to bring it all together in a coherent form. It took me many months to compile my data. I used everyone and everything I could to gather details. I called in favors. Persuaded individuals to pass me any small snippets of information. It was not easy. Like-minded people who were also seeing these inter- woven happenings brought me material. I even had photographic evidence. Some recording of clandestine meetings."

"The amount of incriminating material became a flood," Leila said. "By the time Sharif realized he had enough to accuse the guilty, the mass of data was enor- mous. We had to compress it and commit it to a computer, along with the images and sound bites."

"It was about this time I received word that knowledge of the data had been leaked. Two of my trusted friends, who had helped pass me information, were found dead. Both had been tortured. The trail would eventually lead back to me, so I placed the data onto flash drives. I made a number of copies. I placed these in secure locations without telling Leila. Only I know where the data is located."

"Matt," Leila said, "this information *must* be shown at the conference as part of Sharif's presentation. It will reveal to those with moderate views how they have been tricked themselves. How they are manipulated. Their views distorted and misrepresented. When they see the guilty faces and hear the recorded betrayals, they will realize how much of the distrust has been created by the real traitors."

"I can understand why there's so much resistance to Mahoud attending the conference," Bolan said. "If this data is as explosive as it sounds, you could blow the meeting apart."

"Modesty prevents me from agreeing," Mahoud said.

"Throw modesty out the window," Bolan said. "If you're ready to collect this data, we'll do it tomorrow. Leila, you and the girls stay here. Agreed?"

"Yes. Of course."

"Maybe we can get through this and give Reef his day," Bolan stated.

"We should go and sit with the girls," Mahoud said. "I'm sure Matt has things he needs to be doing."

Bolan waited until he was alone before he activated his sat phone and contacted Stony Man.

Barbara Price spoke to him first. She was having a hard time concealing the concern she was feeling at Carl Lyons's missing status.

"At least you climbed back on the grid," she said. "We can't get any kind of fix on Carl and Rafiq Mahoud."

"He's a resourceful guy," Bolan said. "This isn't the first time Carl has been on his own. He'll show up."

"You know that for a fact?" Price queried.

"I know enough not to give up on the man."

"I guess."

"Has Hal decided to bring in local help?" Bolan asked.

"Enough time has elapsed, so he's contacted the police

and they're going to check things out. As soon as we get any feedback, I'll update you."

"Anything on the kidnappers?"

"Oh, yes. We've pinned down Marino's associates. He seems to work with the same people. Todd Grover. Jake Harper. They were both in the military with him. A third guy called Cujo. Only name we have for him. He's full-blooded Chiricahua Apache and has been in trouble most of his life. And you know Kate Murchison. The guys came up with a further link in the chain. Came from Marino's phone records. Roger Dane. He's second in command to one Daniel Hartman. Hartman is a powerful man who heads a large conglomerate. He has connections within government, military, and makes his billions through contracting weapons and ordnance. Oil. Minerals. Check out anything that smells of power and influence and Hartman's name will be somewhere on the list. Where Middle East politics are concerned you'll also find Hartman involved," Price stated.

"Hartman's name show up anywhere else?"

"Oh yes. The transceiver you picked up gave us a solid lead. Aaron traced it through the serial number. One of a batch sold to a contractor supposedly handling ordnance for a Middle East regime. Turns out the consignment went missing en route. This deal has more twists than a corkscrew. When the cyberteam went right inside the background they turned up a connection with Hartman. One of the companies handling equipment sales is under Hartman's umbrella. It's a small outfit and easy to overlook. Seems Hartman is in business with Mahoud's enemies deeper than we thought."

"Connections to Homani?"

"Not easily apparent until Aaron's team went excavating. On the surface Hartman is just a businessman but pull some of his acquaintances out of the shadows and the pattern starts to show. Aaron's sneaky peek at agency databases have Hartman and Homani linked. For reasons known to themselves, the agency data has been held back."

"Not the first time that's happened," Bolan observed.

"And Hartman isn't a happy camper where Mahoud is concerned. Scuttlebutt has it Hartman wouldn't be sending flowers to Mahoud's funeral."

"Connections and consequences," Bolan said. "Thanks for all that. Just keep me in the frame about Carl."

"Will do. Hey, you need anything else over there?"

"You filled my order to the letter."

"We aim to please," Price said.

IN HIS ROOM Bolan went through a checklist of the equipment Stony Man had supplied at his request. Civilian clothing for himself and the Mahouds. Credentials and cash. Driver's license, passports—the passports stamped with an entry visa that even the keenest-eyed French official would not have been able to fault. The credentials were there as backup if there came a need for them. Stony Man had provided identical backup for Mahoud and his family. It had all been delivered by the blacksuit team and carried with them on their flight from the U.S. aboard a United States Air Force flight to a NATO airfield in France. The four-man team had loaded their baggage into a plain SUV, with French registration, and had left the base for the drive to the safehouse.

As well as the personal luggage, there was a locked aluminum case for Bolan's attention. He had opened the case in his room and checked over the ordnance inside: a Beretta 93-R, complete with a shoulder rig and a 9 mm Uzi. Extra ammunition for both weapons. A knife to replace the one he'd lost in Afghanistan. Bolan had no idea

what or who he might find himself up against in France.
He did acknowledge there would be little goodwill
involved.

Bolan extracted a pair of high-spec cell phones with full
triband and satellite facilities. The cell's batteries had been
charged, giving them long usage. Bolan took out the
charging units and connected them to the room's power
sockets to ensure full power. He was in no mood to have
the cells run down once he and Mahoud left the château.

Sitting at the bedroom's writing bureau Bolan spread
out a small towel from the bathroom and field-stripped the
Beretta and Uzi, checking each weapon thoroughly, then
reassembled them. He knew that John "Cowboy" Kissinger, the Stony Man armorer, would have checked the
weapons before sending them off, and his own examina-
tion wasn't because he doubted Kissinger's skills. Bolan's
life might depend on the ordnance working perfectly at any
given moment. If the weapons failed to perform, the responsibility rested on Bolan and no one else. He wouldn't
have wanted it any other way. He had learned the simple,
but important, lesson drilled into every combat soldier
from day one: his weapons were his lifeline, the difference
between life or death; if he failed to maintain his weapons
and they let him down through neglect, there was no one
to blame except himself. The mantra was repeated continu-
ously throughout the training period and it became as
natural as breathing; there were those who followed it and
others who let it slide: Bolan still remained faithful to the
creed.

With his weapons loaded and placed back inside the
aluminum case the Executioner crossed to gaze out the
bedroom window. Despite the remoteness of the house, he
still possessed a sense of unease about security. He
realized it was most likely an echo of his time in Afghan-

istan, where every move seemed to have been monitored. Where he began to imagine there was an enemy under every rock, behind every bush. Mack Bolan wasn't paranoid. He wasn't the type to believe he was being spied on at every turn, though from the Afghan episode he couldn't have been criticized to have taken such thoughts on board.

Hal Brognola had told Bolan the agreement between the U.S. President and Sharif Mahoud was strictly need to know. He had accepted the statement with his usual reservations. Thinking back to his earlier conversation with Mahoud and Leila, Bolan smiled at Leila's quiet observation on the concept of total security.

"You can be sure of that?" Leila asked. "One hundred percent sure?"

After Brognola's assurance that only the President and Mahoud were aware of what was happening, Bolan had kept his feelings close. The concept of total security was a comforting premise, but never one Bolan felt entirely comfortable with. He understood the world and its complexities, and the belief in secrets kept was, as far as he was concerned, an unplayable rule. It had to do with the fallibility of people to keep those secrets. And the reasons they often failed.

Coercion.

Bribery.

Individual loyalties.

The faith in one person's beliefs held against others. There were too many variables. The weakness of faith, the belief that something worked against policy was justified.

So, Mack Bolan had accepted the mission, aware he was placing his own faith in the words, no matter how genuine in their exposition, of good men. The problem came when those good men expected those around them to keep secrets. It was never going to happen. Secrets had a habit of becoming known to others. Maybe as a whisper, but one able to be picked up by hostile ears. The whisper became a catalyst and the reaction offered the opposition something on which they could act.

Bolan understood the complex scenario attached to Sharif Mahoud's problems. The man had multiple enemies, and those enemies had their sources. Not simply the means provided by those whose sympathies were confined to religious-political opposition to Mahoud's intentions. His data gathering made Mahoud a target.

The soldier watched as one of the Stony Man blacksuits walked the château grounds. The team maintained a steady rota of security patrols. Good practice, Bolan understood, but a dedicated strike force wouldn't be deterred by such a show of force.

Bolan turned from the window as he picked up a sound coming from the hall outside his room. He crossed to the door and opened it, saw the retreating figure of Raika Mahoud as she moved down the corridor. He watched her until she vanished from sight around the corner.

He remained at the door, aware that her room was at the far side of the house. To reach the stairs leading to the ground floor all she had to do was walk from the other side of the landing. Bolan's room wouldn't have been anywhere near her line of travel. To walk to his room would have been a deliberate act.

Had she been listening at his door?

If so, what had she been expecting to hear?

The young woman was a puzzle Bolan wasn't sure he wanted to solve. Her actions aroused his curiosity. Her attitude toward him was also an oddity. Since he had first met her in the outpost in Afghanistan, Raika seemed hostile to him. Bolan failed to understand why. He didn't dwell on it for too long. All he could do was keep her under observation until such times as her agenda revealed itself.

CHAPTER NINETEEN

The following morning Bolan and Mahoud took one of the
SUVs and left the château, Paris their destination.

A few minutes into the journey Bolan said, "Tell me
about Jamal Mehet."

"Jamal? Why would you ask me about Jamal?"

"I need to know all I can about people you have been
involved with."

Mahoud stared out through the windshield. His reflection in the glass showed as a transparent, misty image, and
in his mind he was reflecting on his past association with
the man he had called friend.

"We were friends for over nine years. Jamal was as passionate as I was when it came to our beliefs. We walked
the mountain passes together. Shared our food over camp-
fires. Fought resistance and prejudice. On more than one
occasion we saved each other from death. It was a friendship born out of our times of hardship. When I took up my
doctorate and moved to higher positions Jamal was always
with me. Adviser. Protector. The only one I could turn to
for practical advice when matters became too involved. He

had a natural aptitude for seizing the simple solution within a complex problem."

"How far did this friendship go in terms of telling him things you wouldn't reveal to anyone else?"

Mahoud smiled, glancing across at Bolan. He said, "You are referring to the data?"

"Yes."

"Jamal was the only one, apart from me, who was privy to the entire database. He helped me compile the evidence. When it was complete and copied, the original draft was removed from my laptop. In fact to ensure there would be no chance of anyone recovering it, I removed the hard drive and destroyed it."

"And then?"

"I took the copies personally and placed them in safe-deposit boxes. On my own. Three different banks. I visited each bank, in different parts of Paris, kept nothing on paper about locations or passwords. Those copies are as safe as I could make them. Jamal did not know the location of the banks. This was the only information I did not share with him."

"When you moved on, did Jamal stay here in France?"

"He remained to maintain a watch on certain parties opposed to me. Jamal understood the situation I was in and kept a keen eyes on the Paris situation. The family apartment was broken into and searched. I imagine it was an attempt to locate the data, but whoever did it found nothing of course. They were extremely professional. Nothing was destroyed but when Jamal made one of his frequent visits to check the apartment he discovered the break-in."

"Did he report it to the police?"

"No," Mahoud said with a resigned shake of his head. "It would not have revealed anything. And Jamal, like myself, had little trust in the authorities."

"He told you about the break-in?"

"He called me on my cell and advised me to be even more careful. Jamal seemed to feel this was a determined effort to get control of the data."

"This was just before you were separated from your family?" Bolan queried.

"A few days actually."

Mahoud related a time frame for the incidents.

"Jamal called you. He was found dead four days later, and you had gone into hiding by then."

"Saying it like that suggests…"

"That your opposition is working hard at trying to stop you making the conference. The fact you still have your data locked away must be forcing their hand."

Mahoud fell silent, digesting the cold facts.

Bolan left him to his thoughts, concentrating on driving. They were still a distance from Paris, staying on narrow back roads. Bolan had their route logged into the SUV's GPS unit.

"Call Leila. Tell her to stay alert."

Mahoud stared at Bolan.

"What?"

"I think we might have trouble. Just call her. Now."

Bolan checked the rearview mirror again, confirming his earlier suspicion. The BMW on their tail had suddenly accelerated, closing in fast, coming up hard on their rear.

Beside him Mahoud was speaking into his cell phone, warning his wife to be vigilant and to let him know if anything untoward happened. As he completed his call he saw Bolan reach under his jacket to check his handgun.

The chase car powered to within inches of the SUV's rear bumper, close enough so that Bolan could see the faces of the driver and his front seat passenger. With a further show of raw power the BMW swung out and drew level with the SUV. It held its position before flashing ahead and pulling in front of the SUV.

"I see guns. They have guns," Mahoud said as the BMW slid by.

"Yeah?" Bolan said. "Well, so have I."

The BMW held the center of the narrow road, preventing Bolan from passing.

"Matt?"

Bolan didn't reply. His attention was on a second vehicle that had taken up the rear position. Damn. They had him boxed in. Their next maneuver would be to slow him down, stop, so they could move in and take Mahoud.

He fixed his attention on the road ahead, looking beyond the lead BMW. Fields ran alongside the road. Straggly hedges bordered the fields, with occasional openings for access.

Not the best option, but it was the only option.

Bolan spotted one ahead of the BMW.

"Reef, hang on tight," he said.

The BMW sped past the gap, leaving Bolan with seconds to make his play.

He touched the brake, causing the tail car to drop back and swerve. The gap came up and Bolan swung the wheel, sending the SUV into a sliding turn. The wheels struck soft earth. The heavy vehicle swayed violently, then righted itself as it sped through the gap and into the open field beyond. It threw up sprays of dirt and grass clumps from its rear wheels. Bolan hung on to the wheel, gunning the SUV across the field for a good thirty feet before he slammed on the brakes, bringing it to a sideways stop.

Mahoud opened his mouth to speak and found Bolan already halfway out of the SUV.

"Out," Bolan called over his shoulder. "Under the vehicle."

He reached the rear door and yanked it open, reaching inside to pull his Uzi from the canvas satchel on the floor.

Mahoud dropped to the ground and wriggled awkwardly beneath the SUV.

The rear chase car nosed in through the gap, the driver flooring the gas pedal, sending the BMW powering over the field. Someone leaned out of the passenger front window and triggered a burst in Bolan's direction. The guy's aim wasn't helped by the car's bumpy progress across the field.

Bolan ignored the bullet hits that fell short. He stood his ground, handling the Uzi with the confidence of familiarity. He triggered a long burst that cored in through the windshield and took out the driver. The BMW swerved off course, starting to slow, and Bolan saw the passenger door swing open. The shooter cleared the vehicle, landing on his knees, and made a last-ditch attempt to bring his weapon into play. Bolan altered his aim, stitching the shooter with half a dozen Parabellum rounds. The target went down in a bleeding heap.

The roar of the second BMW alerted Bolan. He half turned and spotted the speeding vehicle coming directly at him. He lowered the Uzi's muzzle and blew out the front tire. The wheel dropped onto its steel rim, the weight of the vehicle sinking it into the ground. The driver attempted to keep control, but the steering had become leaden. The BMW slowed, clearing Bolan's position by yards. As the car passed him, Bolan dropped to one knee, tracked in with the SMG and emptied the Uzi's magazine into the rear of the BMW, keeping it low so the slugs penetrated the body panels and punctured the fuel tank. In reality Bolan knew blowing open a fuel tank didn't guarantee a flame-out. Not unless the gasoline fumes ignited. In this instance luck was on his side. One of the 9 mm slugs caused a spark when it hit metal. Flame showed beneath the BMW. With terrifying speed the fire expanded, reaching back into the tank, and as pressure was created the mass of fuel only had one way out. The tank blew, turning the rear half of the BMW into a ball of flame. The still moving vehicle rolled on a way, the wheels lifting under the force of the blast.

Bolan tossed the empty Uzi onto the SUV's rear seat as he moved past, easing out the Beretta, working the fire selector to single shot.

A front door was kicked open and a figure threw itself out of the BMW. The guy's coat was in flames and he was struggling to discard it. Bolan hit him with a single head shot that dumped him facedown. On the opposite side of the car the passenger door swung open and Bolan caught a glimpse of an auto weapon as its owner thrust it across the roof panel. The 93-R spit out two fast shots. The slugs collapsed the guy's face and blew out the back of his shattered skull. He went down without a sound.

Bolan turned away and returned to the SUV.

"Let's go, Reef," he said.

Mahoud eased himself out from beneath the vehicle, using his good hand to brush grass from his clothing. He surveyed the scene of destruction and death, his lips moving in a silent comment. He climbed in beside Bolan. The SUV swung around and Bolan drove back to the road. He turned back the way they had come. When Mahoud realized where they were going, his face was pale with shock.

"You don't think they will have gone to the château?"

"They knew enough to track us," Bolan said. "They know where the house is."

He pulled out his cell phone and speed dialed the number that would connect him with the blacksuit crew chief.

"Heads up, Morgan," he said, "we just had hard contact with the opposition. On our way back. You might be having visitors."

"Will we get there on time?" Mahoud asked.

"I hope so," Bolan said.

BOLAN SWUNG the SUV in through the stone pillars marking the entrance to the château grounds.

Beside him Mahoud was desperately tapping in the number of Leila's cell phone and getting no response.

"Why will she not answer? What has happened?"

Bolan didn't answer. His mind was on the total situation. He turned the SUV off the driveway and into the closest stand of trees and undergrowth, burying the vehicle in deep. He stepped out, reaching into the rear for the Uzi, reloading it from the bag on the floor. He pushed a couple of extra mags into the deep pocket of his leather jacket. He reloaded the Beretta, head snapping up as he heard one of the SUV doors open.

"No," he said as Mahoud appeared at his side.

"I want to go with you."

"Reef, think straight. You have one arm working. Right now you'd be a liability. I've got enough to think about. Leila, Raika and Amina."

Bolan turned away, breaking into a hard run in the direction of the house. It was fortunate that the original designer had planted trees along each side of the curving drive and they hadn't been chopped down. They provided ample cover.

As the château came into sight, Bolan saw a dark panel truck parked on the circular drive in front of the building. He also saw a figure sprawled on the ground and recognized one of the blacksuits.

Movement ahead of Bolan offered him a brief glimpse

of an armed man wearing some kind of dark blue uniform complete with peaked cap. The Executioner stepped behind a tree and flattened against the trunk. He slung the Uzi and unleathered the Beretta, closing on the sentry.

Bolan moved until he was in range, two-fisted the 93-R and put a pair of 9 mm slugs into the back of the sentry's skull. The guy pitched forward, facedown on the drive.

One man down.

How many inside the house?

Only one way to find out.

Bolan went for the gaping front doors.

As he went up the three stone steps, he heard a woman's voice raised in protest.

He shouldered the doors wide and ran into the wide hall, saw an armed figure halfway up the main staircase. The crashing of the main doors caused him to pause, turning, mouth open. He got no chance to speak. Bolan thrust out the Beretta and triggered it twice. The slugs punched into the guy's chest. He looked down at his body, flattening a hand over the holes, shock etched across his features. Bolan was still moving forward, the Beretta on line, and he fired again. The single shot snapped the target's head back as the Parabellum round drilled in above his left eye and into his skull. He fell back across the stairs, then slid down as his body weight took over.

Bolan stepped by him, holstering the Beretta and bringing the Uzi into play. The shots had attracted attention. A third guy appeared from the corridor adjacent to the head of the stairs, brandishing an autopistol. Bolan raked the exposed body with a burst from the Uzi that spun the guy, his body writhing from the impact.

The Executioner continued to the top of the stairs, peering around the angle of the wall. Again he heard a woman protesting. This time he recognized Leila's strong tones. A man replied. Bolan heard the sound of a slap, then he heard the shriller tones coming from Amina.

"Get away from her."

It was the defiant tone of the young girl's voice that drew Bolan into action. He moved quickly along the corridor, in the direction of Leila's room. Movement at the far end of the corridor caught Bolan's eye. He recognized two of the blacksuit crew. He signaled in the direction of Leila's room and they nodded in acknowledgment.

The door was half open.

A man's voice reached him. He was speaking in a language Bolan didn't understand, but the threat was implicit in his tone.

The room's door was pulled open and Leila appeared in the frame, her eyes wide with fright. Amina clung to her mother's side.

An armed figure was hunched close to Leila. The pistol he carried was pressed against the side of her neck.

Bolan flattened against the wall to reduce his profile. He lowered the Uzi in his left hand and drew the Beretta again.

Along the corridor the pair of blacksuits realized his move and one of them called to the gunmen. The guy's head turned in that direction, ordering them back in stilted English.

The muzzle of his pistol drifted away from Leila's neck for a few seconds as the guy concentrated on his inadequate language skills.

It was the moment Bolan had been waiting for.

The Beretta was lined up, muzzle steady. He stroked the trigger and the 93-R loosed a slug within a heartbeat. It struck just above the right ear, coring in through tissue and bone and tore through the brain, exiting out the far side in a spurt of bloody gore. The gunman was wrenched sideways by the impact, his face slamming against the door frame as he dropped to the floor in an uncoordinated slump.

Bolan raced forward, pushing Leila and Amina aside as he went into the room, his Beretta sweeping back and forth. The room was empty except for a staring Raika sitting on the edge of the bed. Her gaze settled on Bolan's face and once again she returned his look with cold indifference.

The two security men had moved Leila and Amina from the door.

"Clear in here," Bolan said. "One of your guys is down in the drive outside. One still unaccounted for. Go ahead, I'll manage up here."

They moved off immediately.

Bolan dragged the dead man away from the door, then ushered Leila and Amina back inside.

"What is going on?" Leila asked, hugging Amina close to her. "I was so sure we would be safe here. How did they find us so quickly, Matt?"

"Right now I don't know."

"Why did you come back?"

"We'd only gone a few miles and we were hit by trailing vehicles."

"Sharif? Is he..?"

"He's fine. Waiting in the car down the drive."

"It happened so fast. One minute everything was quiet, then we heard shouting and your men told us to go to our room and stay there," Leila said.

"It was scary," Amina added.

"So much for your safehouse," Raika said. "And your wonderful American security men."

Bolan faced her. "I saw one of those men on the ground when I came in. If he's dead, it's because he was defending you. It will be interesting to see where the bullets are. In his chest, or in his back."

"Raika, if you don't have anything useful to say, stay silent," Leila snapped. In a lower tone she said, "I apologize for my daughter."

"Leila, no need. We're all under pressure right now."

One of the security crew opened the door. Mahoud was with him. He rushed to Leila's side and embraced her.

"We found Lewis outside with a couple of bullet wounds in his back. He didn't make it. Jake is out back. Someone took a knife to his left side. He's lost blood but he should be okay. I've called it in to home base. They'll organize medical help." He stood back. "No sign of any other hostiles." He cleared his throat. "I guess we fouled up."

He turned to Leila. "No excuses, Mrs. Mahoud. Happened on my watch, so I'm responsible."

"All of you people have been wonderful to us. As you say, one of your team has died, another is hurt. These attackers are determined to try to hurt us. My family is still alive. There is no blame here. The ones who are to blame are the ones who refuse to leave us alone."

Bolan laid a hand on the man's shoulder. "Go take care of your guys, Morgan. I'll call home and we'll figure out what we need to do now."

BROGNOLA WAS HAVING a hard time disguising his anger.

"Where do these guys keep getting their information? Every move we make they seem right up there with us. Damn it, Striker, it's like we're in a leaky sieve with intel bursting out the sides."

"Is the President up to speed with everything?" Bolan asked.

"He's insisting I update him on all decisions."

"Maybe he should look at security at his end, Hal."

"You realize what you're saying?"

"Wouldn't be the first time the White House has been breached," Bolan reminded the big Fed.

Brognola sighed, admitting Bolan was right.

"I'll get Aaron to run a sneak peek on their security."

"We may move, Hal. I figure if this place has been exposed, they might try again. I don't want to risk any more lives. As soon as I decide and we relocate bring your people back home."

"How will we know where you are?" Brognola asked.

"You won't until I decide to tell you."

"You're running the show, Striker."

"Yeah? Then why does it feel like I'm doing it with someone looking over my shoulder every time I make a move?"

BOUVIER KNEW EXACTLY why he had received no word from the team. No contact meant the strike hadn't gone well. Hamir, the team leader, would have called if the attack had succeeded. Bouvier didn't call himself. If the team had been compromised, any cell phone chatter could be picked up by listeners.

He sat back and debated his next move. There had to be a next move. Something had to be done about Mahoud. The man was Bouvier's prime target. With the conference only days away, operations were going to need to be arranged quickly and with little time for solid backup. Bouvier didn't like to work this way. Hastily mounted operations were more likely to go wrong. There were bound to be unforeseen obstacles.

Bouvier crossed to the bar and poured himself a generous brandy. He stood at the room's high window, savoring the rich bouquet of the mellow liquid as he tried to review the situation from the point of view of the man orchestrating Mahoud's security. The liquor, though an unacceptable drink from a religious standpoint, was one of the vices Bouvier allowed himself, always blaming the vice on his French father; it was, he would say wryly, in the genes.

This American, Cooper, was proving to be a worthy enemy. He operated on his own for the most part—his performance in Afghanistan proved that—and seemed to have a propensity for survival. Worthy or not, the man had to be removed along with Mahoud and his family. Thinking as Cooper, Bouvier decided that the man would be forced to remove the Mahoud family from the château. It was a logical next step. The safehouse was no longer safe. Its security had been compromised, and Cooper would see the possibility as untenable. He would remove the Mahouds and take them somewhere he alone would know the location. He wouldn't even tell his own control. Bouvier saw that as sound logic. The fewer people who knew, the safer Mahoud's family would be.

To his advantage Bouvier could rely on his immediate contacts, plus the added benefit of Homani's asset. He would find Cooper and the Mahoud family. Their mission would be completed and the upcoming conference would be canceled.

Bouvier stared out across Paris, the skyline as familiar to him as the lines in his face. The French-Algerian had lived in France for a number of years, brought there by his parents, French father, Algerian mother. The young Bouvier had a rebellious streak that had brought him into contact with radical Muslims in the city. He had started to hang out in the Marais/Oberkamph quarters. Here, in the 11th Arrondissement, there were many brasseries, cafés and restaurants where he could get both Algerian

cuisine and company. It was here where he had fallen in
with Muslims who, like himself, were disillusioned with
the Western way of life and were seeking active partici-
pation in some kind of resistance. He developed a strong
political attitude, allying himself with discontented
factions. Bouvier's activities and his devotion to the cause
resulted in him being cultivated by the power elite. His
profession in finance and commodities gave him a solid
background when it came to arranging protests and active
missions. After a few years Bouvier came into Ali Asadi's
circle and the man realized his potential, promoting him
as assistant to the master facilitator Masood. Bouvier was
quick to learn and he learned everything his instructor
told him, and more. He quietly took on board more than
even Masood realized, though Asadi wasn't slow to understand the way the younger man worked. When Masood
was unexpectedly killed during a mission in Pakistan, the
group was left without a facilitator. Bouvier stepped in and
proved his worth by assuming Masood's position without
once losing his grip. He knew every contact in a dozen
countries and had financial matters under control. Within
six months it was as if Masood had never existed. And
Bouvier became the new master. In truth he became even
more skilled than the late Masood. His done deals had
resulted in many successful operations, causing death and
destruction to a significant number of the enemy.

As he had in the past, Bouvier looked on setbacks as
no more than new challenges. He thrived on problems. So
he set about putting this one back on track, understanding how important it was to Ali Asadi. The death of Sharif
Mahoud would be a high moral victory. Removal of the
traitor would ensure the continuing state of unrest, leaving
the way open for more recruitment to the cause. Mahoud's
betrayal had been having an effect on many of the mod-

erates, allowing them to claw back many young idealists wavering about joining the ranks of the faithful. His death would show there was no profit to be had in walking away from the ideals of Islam. The moderates—the weak ones—would have much of their power taken away with the death of Mahoud. Without his powerful words and irrefutable appeal to many, there would be a vacuum into which men like Asadi could step.

Although the efforts already expended had failed to remove Mahoud, the sacrifices of the faithful would not be in vain. Mahoud *would* die.

Soon.

CHAPTER TWENTY

He came to with a pounding ache in his skull. He could feel the semi-dried stickiness of blood that had slipped down from his hair and across the left side of his face. Lyons remained in his slumped position, head down, watching the outline of his booted feet slowly come back into focus. He was sitting on a plain wooden kitchen chair, his hands tied with cord behind him. He heard the sounds of nearby movement, picked up the smell of coffee and heard the crackle of wood burning in a fireplace or stove. Streaks of sunlight crisscrossed the floor.

As his hearing sharpened Lyons focused in on voices. More than one. Conversation filtered in and out as he struggled to pick up clear words through the fuzziness that hampered his ability to concentrate. He fought the desire to shake his head. Listened closely.

"Jake, go tell…Cujo…extend his patrol…area."

"You…worried…compromised?"

"Being cautious…all…just go do it."

Lyons heard the thump of heavy boots across the floor. A door opened and closed. He caught a draft of cool air as the door opened, the scent of pine. As the door slammed shut, Lyons felt his ears pop and the rush of clear sound almost made him start.

"Greg, we should clear out of here ASAP."

This time the voice was female.

Callie Jefferson?

"Babe, cool down. No need for us to panic."

"Easy to say. Greg, this jerk-off had a Justice Department badge in his pocket."

"And he's on his own. No radio for communication. Just a cell phone. I never heard of a Fed coming in without backup. If he'd been part of a team, the woods would be crawling with a task force by now. Whoever he is, this joker is running solo."

"But he still found us. Doesn't that tell you something?"

"Tells me he's an idiot. No law dog runs around like the Lone Ranger. They're taught to be team players. Hell, they don't even take a leak without backup these days."

"So who is this guy? Hell, Greg, look at the way he was kitted out. The guy had plenty of firepower. Call him an idiot if you want, but he came ready."

"Okay, I haven't figured him out yet. But I'm damn sure he was on his own. We'll see what Cujo says when he gets back. If there are any more out there, he'll spot them."

"Shouldn't he be awake by now? Cujo wouldn't have hit him that hard."

"Go check."

"Maybe I should slap him awake."

"Kate, you have to curb that violent streak."

"You think?"

A third voice joined the conversation. Another male.

"Your problem, Kate, is too much pent-up aggression. Try some liquid therapy."

"Say what?"

"Take a drink. Works for me."

"Yeah? Well, I'd still rather slap him."

Lyons saw booted feet move into his line of vision. He could see the woman's legs as far as just above her knees. Strong, shapely legs. Tanned and firm. The woman stood with feet apart, muscles working beneath the skin as she braced herself. Lyons knew what was coming. Even so he was slow to react. Fingers caught in his hair and yanked his head back. A hard hand struck him across the left side of his face. It was a solid blow, tearing the corner of his mouth, and it rocked Lyons's head to the side.

"Damn it, I told you he was awake."

Lyons simply let his emotions get the better of him. Ignoring the stinging pain from the blow he swept his booted feet, catching the woman's closer ankle, and continued through. The force caught the woman off guard. Lyons heard her startled yell as his leg-sweep took her feet from under her. He caught a blurred picture as she fell, slamming to the floor on her behind.

"Hey," someone yelled.

Two men rushed into Lyons's vision, each wielding a handgun.

"Son of a bitch."

One of the men thrust the muzzle of a pistol into Lyons's neck.

"I suggest you think very carefully before you try anything like that again."

The woman had rolled to her feet and she came at Lyons in a wild rush, her fists swinging. She managed a full-on blow that clipped Lyons's cheek before the second man grabbed her and hauled her away.

"Let me go, Todd. I owe that fuck."

Todd held on to her. Lyons could see him now. He was

a big guy, with powerful upper body strength. The arms encircling the young woman were massively developed.

"I warned you, Kate," he said. "Too much aggression."

"I am going to cripple him."

Lyons stared at her. Attractive. Blond and blue-eyed; right now those eyes were blazing with uncontrolled fury. Her lips were pulled back from even white teeth. Although she was struggling, Todd's superior strength held her captive.

Lyons felt the gun muzzle draw back, saw movement as the guy holding it stepped away. He was of average height, with dark hair cut short and angular features that kept him the wrong side of being handsome. The guy had a small but deep scar on his left cheek, over the bone. He wore tan chinos and a dark wool shirt.

"Kate, enough," he said simply. "Enough."

The young woman stared at him briefly, then ceased struggling.

"Okay, Todd, you can put me down now."

Todd released her and stepped back, arms spread away from his body. She turned to look at him, unconsciously brushing her blond hair back in place.

"You let your guard down," Todd said. "I told you a hundred times. Don't step in too close. He was waiting for you to do just that."

Kate returned her gaze to Lyons. He watched her, unfazed by the threat in her eyes. He had already stored away what he knew about her. She wasn't disciplined. She let her emotions control her actions. That led to risk taking. He would remember.

"I don't trust him," she said.

Todd grinned. "I'm sure he fucking loves you, too."

The guy holding the gun was studying Lyons closely.

"Agent Benning," he said. "This is not one of your better days."

"It's been that kind of a week."

"So what are you doing all the way up here in the woods?"

"Maybe he's looking for Smoky the Bear," Todd suggested. "He sure needs some tracking advice."

"Oh, Jesus, we all know why he's here," Kate snapped, irritation sharpening her tone.

"I'd like Agent Benning to tell us."

"Greg, for Christ's sake."

More information, Lyons thought.

Greg. Greg Marino, the guy *Callie Jefferson* had been calling.

"I do believe Agent Benning is looking for Rafiq Mahoud. Give him credit, Kate, the guy *has* tracked us all the way here. Nice job, Agent Benning. Pity it won't go any farther. You might have found Mahoud, but it isn't going to get you a pat on the back and advance you up the pay grade ladder."

"The only bonus is going to be a bullet in his skull," Kate said, relishing every word.

"You know, you really have upset her," Todd said.

"In that case my day just brightened," Lyons said.

His cheek was throbbing where the woman had hit him, and he could still taste blood from his cut lip.

"Go fetch the kid," Marino said. "Let him take a look at his savior."

Grover chuckled. He moved across the cabin behind Lyons. A door was unlocked and opened.

"Get out here, kid. You've got a visitor."

Grover reappeared, pushing a reluctant figure in front of Lyons.

"Say hi to each other."

It was Rafiq Mahoud. Lyons recognized him from the photograph in the file Brognola had e-mailed to him. He was a tall, lean young man with dark eyes and a shock of thick black hair. Right now he looked scared as he was pushed across the room to stand in front of Lyons.

"This is Agent Benning, Rafiq," Marino said, grinning. "You should thank him. He's your personal hero. Came all the way here to rescue you from our evil clutches."

"Though he isn't doing too well," Grover said.

"Is it true?" Rafiq asked. "Did my father send you?"

Lyons nodded.

"What I want to see is how he's going to achieve this rescue," Grover said. "Him being trussed up like a Thanksgiving turkey and all. Hey, that would be fun to watch."

Lyons ignored the taunts. He held Rafiq's gaze, hoping the look in his own eyes would at least give the young man some kind of hope. Right now Lyons had nothing else going for him.

"Go and put the kid back in his seat," Marino said abruptly, tiring of the game.

In the microsecond before Rafiq was pushed aside Lyons silently mouthed *be ready*. He didn't know what else to do, so he was surprised when Rafiq gave a brief nod.

A COUPLE OF HOURS later Marino called his crew together.

"Listen up, people," he said. "Change of plan. We move. As of now."

"Why the change?"

"I figured Benning was a loner, up here on his own playing the Lone Ranger. You guys talked, I listened. Tossed it around and it started to come up wrong. The more I thought about it, the more it sucked. Can't figure it all yet, but the last thing we need is a posse of Feds storming in. So we'll ship to another location. We can take the northern back trail out of here."

"What about him?" Kate asked, nodding in Lyons's direction.

"Bring him along in case we need a bargaining chip. You never know. It always pays to have a little extra insurance."

"Keep him tied up, he won't be any trouble," Grover said.

"Let's get the gear into the 4x4," Marino said. "Everybody, let's go."

Kate and Harper collected the backpacks and hauled them outside. Marino followed, dialing a number into his cell.

Grover brought Rafiq and stood him a few yards away from Cujo, who was standing in the open door, keeping an eye on Rafiq and Lyons. Grover moved behind Lyons to free him from the chair.

"You behave, Mr. Agent Man," he said.

Lyons acted in accordance with what Grover told him. He had no choice as long as his hands were still tied to the struts of the kitchen chair. He was going to be freed for him to be taken outside, and during that thin window of opportunity he would have to make his move. Lyons glanced across to where Rafiq stood. The young man was watching Lyons intently and when the big ex-cop made eye contact, Rafiq's brief, nodding response told him the young man was ready.

"Jesus, Cujo, why did you have to tie him to the fucking chair?" Grover said, checking the cord.

"I didn't want him jumping off it and running away."

"Yeah, so now I have to untie his hands to get him off it. Apache logic sucks."

Cujo chuckled. "Go figure, white eyes."

Still grumbling, Grover fumbled with the ties that bound Lyons's wrists. He tucked the UMP under one arm and used his right hand to pull a butterfly knife from a sheath on his belt. Lyons caught sunlight gleam on the steel handles and heard the metallic sound as Grover flipped the knife, exposing the blade, then slit the cord binding his wrists.

Lyons used the split second that left Grover with the knife still in his hand, reversing his action to close the weapon. He rose from the chair, kicked back hard to drive it into Grover's thighs, then turned and snatched the H&K submachine gun from the man. Lyons' fingers curved around the hand grip and he swung the muzzle in Cujo's direction as the man registered what had just happened. Lyons didn't hesitate. He pulled back on the trigger. The triple burst of .45 ACP fire hammered into the wooden door frame inches from Cujo's face, blowing out keen slivers of wood that tore at his flesh. He howled in pain, stumbling away from the door as Lyons fired a second burst, one of the big slugs shredding Cujo's shirt on the curve of his shoulder and clipping flesh.

Cujo flung himself clear of the door. As the man vanished, Lyons turned back into the room, aware he still had Grover at his back. The merc had lashed out to kick the chair aside. Lyons saw the butterfly knife flash open again, the gleaming blade slashing at his throat and the only thing he could do was raise the UMP to protect himself. The blade chinked against the SMG, glancing off, and Lyons swung the weapon in the air, ramming it hard across Grover's skull. The blow was solid, dazing the merc who swayed on his feet. Lyons hit him a second time, across the side of his face. The meaty sound of the blow was followed by a burst of blood from Grover's right cheek. He slumped to his knees and the Able Team leader hit him again, driving him to the floor.

As Lyons stepped over the prone body, he reached

down and scooped up the knife, flipped it to shut away the blade and shoved it in a pocket.

Then he was at Rafiq's side. He slapped the youth's shoulder.

"Hey, let's go. Back door."

Lyons pushed Rafiq into motion. The young man ran ahead of Lyons, directly to the cabin's rear door. He yanked the handle and pushed the door wide, scrambling through. Lyons followed close, heading Rafiq in the direction of the tree line.

"Just keep going," he yelled. "We need the cover."

They hit the trees seconds before the rattle of gunfire erupted. Slugs blew chunks of bark and raw wood from the closest trees. Lyons suspected the shots were meant as more of a warning than anything else. They needed Rafiq alive.

"Which way?" Rafiq asked.

"Straight ahead," Lyons said. "We need to gain distance. Nothing else matters right now."

They ran, pushing through anything standing in their way. Foliage and low branches slapped against their bodies, scratching their exposed flesh. Blood mingled with sweat, stinging, smarting. Dry twigs and fallen leaves snapped under their pounding feet.

Their pursuers were still a good distance behind. They kept coming. They had no choice. If they lost Rafiq, their mission was over. Lyons was another matter. He was expendable, having dealt himself into the kidnap situation. If he was eliminated, it would ease the burden.

Ahead of Lyons the youth stumbled, went down on one knee, but hauled himself upright again and continued on.

The ground sloped away, dropping a couple of hundred feet, the trees thinning out, leaving wide stretches of exposed terrain dotted with brush. Far below Lyons saw the gleam of water.

"Go for it," Lyons said. "We don't have a choice."

Rafiq hit the slope, with Lyons close behind. Their momentum took them at breakneck speed down the slope, feet slamming into the earth as they tried to control their descent. Lyons heard the crackle of autofire. Slugs tore at the ground around them, kicking up dirt and grass. However this came out, Lyons and Rafiq were committed now. They were in a no-man's land, unable to turn back, exposed, with no way of knowing what they might find when they hit bottom. The reckless rate of their descent made it hard for any kind of accurate shooting from the opposition. They didn't want to hit Rafiq, but if a good shot presented itself there would be no hesitation when it came to taking down Lyons.

Rafiq lost his footing and pitched facedown, his momentum dragging along the slope, arms and legs windmilling as he tried to regain control. When he did come to a stop, he made no attempt to climb to his feet. He lay motionless.

Lyons struggled to bring himself to a stop, muscles straining as he fought his downward motion. He dragged himself back to Rafiq, half turned so he could check the upper slope. Three figures, spaced apart, were moving in their direction with measured steps, but still a fair distance away.

"Rafiq? You still with me?" Lyons demanded.

He touched the young man's shoulder.

Rafiq jerked. "Benning, a day out with you is no fun at all." He pushed himself up on his arms, groaning.

"Anything broken?" Lyons said.

"I'll tell you when everything stops aching."

When Rafiq raised his head, Lyons saw blood streaming from his nose. The left side of his face had been scraped raw from hitting the ground. The Able Team leader hooked his left arm under the youth's and helped him to his feet.

"I know," Rafiq said. "Keep going."

He turned and resumed his downward run, limping on his left leg. Lyons swung the H&K into play, laying the muzzle on the distant figures and jacking out a couple of bursts that fell short, but at least warned the oncoming group that the game was far from over. The only consolation as far as Lyons was concerned centered around the fact he had seen only identical SMGs in the cabin. So if his weapon was out of range so were theirs.

The slope began to flatten out. The gleam of water Lyons has seen earlier lay in front of them. A river. Fast-flowing, the water foaming where it swirled around half-submerged rocks. He had no idea where it went, but as far as he was concerned it might prove a way of getting clear of their pursuers.

"Can you swim?"

Rafiq stared at him. "Sure," he said, the realization dawned. "Are you kidding?"

"That river will take us downstream pretty fast," Lyons said, looping the webbing strap of the H&K over his head to sling the weapon across his back.

"And drown us just as fast," Rafiq said.

They were yards from the overhanging bank now.

"We don't have much choice."

He grabbed Rafiq's arm, yanking the youth with him, and, still holding him, launched them both off the bank. They dropped six feet into the water, which closed over their heads, the chill shocking them. The current was stronger than even Lyons had imagined and swept them along as their heads broke the surface. Rafiq was feet ahead of Lyons, his black hair plastered flat against his skull, gasping for air, but using his arms to keep himself afloat. Lyons followed suit, spitting out water that splashed its way into his mouth.

"What now?" Rafiq said, shouting against the noise of the turbulence.

"We let it take us."

"Where—the Pacific?"

Lyons saw white water ahead where the river dropped a level over shallow rapids. He felt the current increase and Rafiq was pulled way ahead of him. There was no fighting the current. It simply swept them along, twisting and turning them at its whim. Lyons felt the bump and scrape of smooth rocks as the rapids held them in its grip, bouncing and tumbling them. More than once Lyons felt himself being pulled beneath the surface by conflicting currents, then thrust into air again. The noise was deafening. The spray created a fine mist that obstructed his vision. In the end he stopped resisting and let the flow carry him.

Eventually the rapids ended and Lyons shook his head to clear the water from his face. He checked out his surroundings, treading water as he did. The water here was calmer, the river almost tranquil. On either side high rock walls rose, topped with greenery. The river banks had given way to rocky stretches.

Lyons looked around for Rafiq. The young man was nowhere in sight. Lyons cast around, wondering if Rafiq had made it.

Any doubts were removed when he spotted the teenager, on the far bank, slowly wading out of the water. Lyons swam in that direction, his body starting to ache from the battering it had received coming through the rapids. As he felt the stones beneath his boots he pushed for the bank. Rafiq was sitting on a large flat stone, watching, a grin plastered across his face.

"That was better than any Disneyland ride," he said.

"You want to go back and try it again?"

"No. It wasn't that good."

Lyons noticed Rafiq was favoring his left arm around his shoulder.

"You okay?"

"Kind of banged my arm on a rock."

Lyons made him take off his shirt. Rafiq's upper arm was starting to show a heavy bruise, the flesh reddened and puffy. The big ex-cop gently probed the flesh.

"Is it broken?"

Lyons shook his head. "No. I think you've sprained the muscles. It's going to be sore though."

Rafiq watched as Lyons squeezed water out of his shirt before he handed it back.

"Were you in the military?"

"No. I was a cop before I moved to Justice."

"But you know this survival stuff?"

"Some," Lyons said. "We get some extreme missions."

"Not baby-sitting stupid teenagers who fall for long legs and blue eyes," Rafiq said.

"I already told you, Rafiq, that wasn't your fault. Callie—*Kate*—is a professional. She's probably done this kind of thing before."

"Well, she had me fooled."

They moved away from the river, hiding themselves in the tumbled mass of boulders and shrubbery that edged the water.

"Right now," Lyons said, "all we need to concern ourselves with is getting away from Marino and his team. Moving to this side of the river gives us some advantage. It's going to take them time to pick up where we came out of the water. We have to use that time to move on. Try to find someplace where we can call for help."

"I guess." Rafiq's expression exposed his anger. "Why

can't they leave my father alone? He's a good man trying to do right things. Why do they want to kill him?"

"Rafiq, you understand as well as I do," Lyons said. "You're not stupid. Nothing's as simple as it looks. If your father makes his peace accord work, a lot of individuals will lose face, political and religious power. That's enough on its own to make Sharif Mahoud a target. The problem is made worse because there's more. Multinational companies stand to lose money and influence, and a lot of those companies are in bed with the hard-liners."

"Armament dealers? Oil companies? That kind of thing?"

"And more. Military connections. Alliances between power brokers."

"It's a rotten world we live in."

"The sad thing is, it's the only one we've got," Lyons said. "Your father is doing his bit to try to make some of it better. His enemies are gunning for him because they are scared he might make that difference."

"You said the man looking out for my father is good. How good?"

Lyons smiled. "He's the best."

"As smart as you?"

"A whole lot smarter," Lyons said without hesitation.

He checked the SMG, pulling the magazine and shaking water from it.

"Will it still work?" Rafiq asked, watching.

"Yes."

"Are you just saying that to make me feel better?"

"Yes," Lyons said. "Does it?"

Rafiq smiled. "What about that Native American, Cujo? He'll be able to find us."

"Let's not make it easy for him."

Lyons finished with the H&K. He slid the magazine

into place and pushed to his feet. They moved off, angling away from the course of the river. They were going to have to climb to reach the higher ground, where at least they would have the timbered slopes to conceal their passage.

Their initial priority was to locate a telephone or some other means of communication. Lyons knew that wilderness areas were likely to have isolated watch towers, lookouts for fire spotting and also for lost trekkers. The towers were usually equipped with radios, enabling communication with ranger stations. If they were lucky they'd come across a ranger station, but the odds weren't good. Lyons needed to find a regular trail, even a fire road. If they found one of those and stuck to it, they would eventually reach some kind of refuge.

He glanced at Rafiq. The younger man was proving to be resilient and capable. At least he wasn't whining about his situation. If he could maintain that attitude, it would go a long way to keeping him alive.

It took them almost an hour to climb up from the river to solid terrain. On relatively level ground, on a ridge, they were presented with a seemingly endless panorama of forested wilderness. It spread in all directions, impenetrable timbered slopes that rolled into the distance, slopes and valleys vanishing into the hazy distance.

"That's a lot of trees," Rafiq said. "So which way do we go?"

"West," Lyons said. "That way."

"Why west?"

"Sooner or later we'll reach the ocean," Lyons said wryly.

Rafiq shook his head. "And that's your best shot?"

"Right now, that's my best shot. That direction takes us away from Marino and his bunch."

"When my father sent me here, he told me it would be

the best way to learn about America, to see the country. He's really getting his money's worth at the moment." Rafiq hesitated. "I shouldn't be joking about Dad. Whatever problems I've got, they can't be anything like the ones he's having to face."

Lyons had been checking behind them, across the wide gorge where the river flowed.

"I shouldn't be too sure about that," he said.

Rafiq glanced to where Lyons was pointing.

On the far side of the gorge figures could be seen working their way to the perimeter.

"I see what you mean."

"Let's move," Lyons said. "It's going to be a while before they reach this side and climb up from the river. We need to make some more distance."

CHAPTER TWENTY-ONE

The apartment was clean and functional. It overlooked the Seine, though the occupant rarely took advantage of the fact. He wasn't in Paris for pleasure, his purpose far from that of a sightseer, even though he was looking for someone.

The man he was seeking was Mohan Bouvier.

The French-Algerian was a facilitator for one of the Muslim cells active in the Middle East. Bouvier's reputation was well known. The man was responsible for coordinating terror attacks in India, across the Middle East, France and as far as London, and importantly for the searcher—Israel.

Ben Sharon, Mossad agent, had been tracking Mohan Bouvier for almost three months, following him across Europe and North Africa, and had eventually located him in Paris. Sharon was closing in. His mission was simple: find and eliminate Bouvier.

Sharon had no problem with that. The activist was responsible for a considerable number of deaths. He had supplied men, weapons and bombs that had been directed and placed so they could carry out indiscriminate slaughter. Bouvier had pulled the triggers and set off the bombs by proxy. Mossad had targeted him for removal.

With infinite patience Sharon had worked his way along the shadowy trail left by the facilitator, until the present day where he had located the man's Paris hideout.

Now all that was left was the final act.

Sharon had been monitoring Bouvier's communications. The man was no electronics expert. He used cell phones and sometime landlines to make his contacts, and it was by monitoring the lines that Sharon had chanced upon some chatter that made him sit up and take notice.

It was one of those lucky happenstances where surveillance for a particular purpose revealed information on an entirely unrelated matter.

When Sharon picked up isolated words and phrases he almost bypassed them. Until they registered in his mind, pushing aside the information he had been looking for.

Cooper.

Sharif Mahoud.

The Israeli sat back and replayed the items on his recorder. Bouvier was talking about an American named Cooper and Dr. Sharif Mahoud, and both names were known to Sharon.

He let the recording run on, grasping the gist of the isolated conversation. From what Bouvier was saying, Cooper was already in Paris though his whereabouts weren't known at the moment.

Sharon's current assignment had occupied his attention over the past few weeks, tending to isolate him from other world events. But he knew about Sharif Mahoud and his attempts to broker a peace accord. The conference included Israel, and despite his skepticism over the outcome, Ben Sharon applauded Mahoud's attempts.

Anything that might generate peace, no matter how

slight, was to be supported. Sharon, a realist, understood
the intense resistance to any form of initiative throughout
the regions. There were those who would fight peace
because it went against their deeply felt religious and political aims. For many, it was personal. For others, it might
mean an interruption of their business dealings in weapons
and other commodities. Those things, no matter how they
might be viewed, were impossible to ignore. Power and
wealth were great catalysts. They brought out the worst
in many, and curtailing such activities wouldn't happen if
certain parties had their way. Maintaining bloody conflict
was their way of continuing a merciless trade.

If Cooper was involved, it meant resistance to
Mahoud's conference had continued beyond what Sharon
had been aware of. The man was courageous and determined. The passion of his enemies would be strong
enough to generate strong opposition against the conference, strong enough for attempts to be made to stop him.

If Bouvier was in the picture, it meant operations were
being mounted against Mahoud. That was what the facilitator did. He brought groups together, arranged times and
places, put weapons and vehicles into the hands of the
ones carrying out the missions.

Cooper placed himself in harm's way to prevent those
things happening. If he was siding Mahoud, the man had
the best there was.

But did Cooper have any information about Bouvier?

Sharon didn't know the answer to that, but he was
going to make sure Cooper was armed with whatever the
Mossad agent could provide.

The Israeli checked his contact file and made a sat
phone call. The number he had been given months ago
would, through a complicated array of electronic routes,
put him in touch with the group Cooper worked through,

on a line the Israeli understood to be secure. He recognized the voice he had touched base with before.

"This is Ben Sharon. Mossad."

"Haven't heard from you in a while," Hal Brognola said. "I guess this isn't a social call?"

"No. I am on assignment in Paris at present, monitoring phone calls involving my target. Two names have come up. Sharif Mahoud and Matt Cooper. My target is a facilitator for terrorist groups. His job is to organize teams who carry out hostile attacks. If he is talking about Cooper and Mahoud, I would guess a strike is being organized. I will try to get more information and pass it on."

"Much appreciated," Brognola said. "I'm sure you know what Mahoud is working on currently?"

"The upcoming peace accord? Yes. We are hoping something good comes out of the meetings."

"Cooper is running interference for Mahoud and his family, trying to keep him safe until the conference. It's a complicated issue."

"If I give you my number, Cooper can make contact himself. It might save time if I can deal directly with him."

Sharon recited his number and also a meeting place if Bolan wanted physical contact.

"I'll pass it along," Brognola said. "Thanks again, Ben. Good luck with your mission."

"*Shalom.*"

HAL BROGNOLA MIGHT NOT have had any idea where Bolan was at the moment, but it didn't stop him making contact to pass along Ben Sharon's message and offer to help. Bolan called his Mossad friend within the hour.

"Thanks for the intel," Bolan said. "I'm interested in what you had to say."

"Is the location satisfactory?"

"Yeah. In an hour?" Bolan asked.

"Yes."

The call ended. There was no need for either of them to say more.

IT WAS RAINING when Bolan showed up at the small restaurant on the Left Bank. It was on a side street off the main drag. Cars were parked in ragged array along the street, some partway on the sidewalk. Rain sluiced down off the gutters, splashing across the cobbled street. Stepping out of the taxi, Bolan handed the driver the fare, turning up the collar of his coat as he made his way to the entrance. A bell tinkled above the door as Bolan stepped inside. The smell of aromatic coffee was welcome. The restaurant was quiet at this time of day. It took only seconds for Bolan to spot Sharon sitting in a corner, facing the door. Shaking rain off his coat, Bolan made his way over and sat.

"Ben."

Sharon smiled and reached out to take Bolan's hand. Then he caught the proprietor's eye.

"Two black coffees, please," Sharon said in French. He then noted the bruises on Bolan's face. "Still attracting the wrong kind of people?"

"It's something I do."

"I remember."

"As I recall, you're not above a little of it yourself."

They halted their conversation as the coffee arrived.

"*Merci,*" Bolan said.

"Can you talk about your involvement with Sharif Mahoud?"

Bolan related the events that had occurred since his arrival in Afghanistan, bringing Sharon up to date with the attack at the château.

"It's no secret Mahoud has attracted plenty of opposition. His intention to head the peace accord has sent resistance sky-high. He's placed himself and his family on the firing line. I can't fault their courage. I only hope it doesn't end badly."

"In the time I've spent with them it isn't hard to see they're united in backing him. The only one who doesn't seem one hundred percent is the elder daughter, Raika. I can't put my finger on it yet, but she seems to stand back from it all."

"I guess it must be hard on them. Having to put their lives on hold because of Mahoud's cause."

"One of our people is on the son's case. Rafiq Mahoud attends a college in California. He went to pick him up and found out Rafiq had been snatched. It was a setup. He was lured away by a young woman, then grabbed. The last we heard was that our guy had tracked them down. After that, nothing."

"The boy's been taken to be used as leverage?"

"Seems most likely."

"Did Mahoud give you any names who could be behind these attacks?" Sharon queried.

"The main suspect is Wazir Homani."

Sharon nodded. "One of Mahoud's main opponents, a real hardass who's radical down to the tips of his shoes. Mossad has a file on him. His favorite rants include Israel, the U.S. and Western society in general. The man loves the sound of his own voice. He encourages his followers to give their lives in the name of God, and tells them all to take up the struggle while he stays in comparative safety behind his personal bodyguards. Never moves without them. They travel around in a bombproof Mercedes."

"Mahoud understands the resistance and won't allow it to put him off. He regrets the way his family has been sucked right into the danger zone. It places him in a dilemma. I feel for him, Ben. He wants to do the right thing but is aware it could cost him dearly."

"You seem to be handling things fine, Matt."

"Facing off against the opposition isn't the problem. Figuring out what's in the background, in the shadows, isn't."

"We seem to be running along close lines here," Sharon said. "I'm chasing down Mohan Bouvier. One of his operations looks to be centered around Mahoud."

"Suggests a home visit might be helpful," Bolan said.

"Just what I was about to recommend."

"BOUVIER LIVES on the third floor, the apartment on the corner that you can see from here."

"Does he live alone?" Bolan asked.

"He has a young woman he dates when he's in Paris. He never brings her to the apartment, however. He goes to her. She lives across the city."

"She's not involved in what he does?"

"No. I ran checks on her. Very solid French upbringing, though not a very active political animal."

"You make that sound unusual."

Sharon grinned. "You should understand the French are normally well into politics. Why do you think lunch takes hours to get through?"

"I'll take your word for it, Ben." Bolan eased the Beretta from its holster and checked it. "Does Bouvier keep protection close?"

"Sometimes a couple of heavies. It looks as if at least one of them could be on duty today. The dark blue Citroën parked at the entrance is his."

"I don't have time to wait for him to leave, Ben. We need to do this now."

"No problem," Sharon said. "Third floor. Apartment twenty-three. I'll go around the back in case there's a second one there. If you go in, leave the door off the latch."

The rain persisted, splashing off the street and making a fine mist at ground level. Bolan saw Sharon slip into the alley next to the apartment building. He stayed on course and pushed his way through the entrance door, which took him into the lobby. As he crossed the lobby Bolan saw the small ground-floor apartment usually occupied by the building's concierge was closed and shuttered. The age-old tradition provided by the usually formidable female guardians was dying out. In this instance the absence of the concierge made Bolan's entry easy.

He took the stairs, his soft-soled boots making no sound. Bolan took out the Beretta and held it against his thigh, muzzle down. He didn't want to cause any alarm if he encountered one of the building's occupants. He reached the second floor without incident. The only sound he heard was a door closing along the corridor at the far end of the building. Stepping onto the third-floor landing, Bolan edged to the angled turn of the corridor that would lead him to Bouvier's door. The corridor was carpeted, and softly lit from sconces. A window at the extreme end would look out over the alley Sharon had chosen. Bolan guessed there would be a fire escape leading up the rear outside wall.

Bolan spotted the door to number twenty-three, and approached it cautiously. Before he had taken more than a couple of steps he caught movement out of the corner of his eye. A dark-suited figure lunged around the angle of the corridor, coming straight for him. The guy was as tall as the American, and broad across the shoulders. Bolan's attention went to the knife that appeared from beneath the man's jacket. He held it confidently, closing on Bolan with deceptive speed despite his bulk.

The way the attacker held the knife told Bolan he was going for a crippling gut sweep. The Beretta in Bolan's hand arced up, but as fast as he was, the other guy reacted with surprising speed. His left arm swatted around and his large fist knocked the Beretta up out of harm's way. The pistol fell from Bolan's fingers as he concentrated on the gleaming blade as it swept in toward his lower torso, clamping his hand around the thick wrist and pushing the blade aside. He swiveled, his back to his attacker, and slammed his right elbow up and back, connecting with the guy's face.

The blow was hard, snapping the guy's head back, blood streaming from a torn lip. The guy grunted, reached out and curled his free arm around Bolan's neck. The soldier snapped his chin down against his chest, preventing a throat hold. For a moment they were poised motionless, until Bolan hooked the guy's right foot with his own, yanked hard and took it off the floor. Left on one leg, the guy lost his balance as the Executioner thrust back. They toppled, Bolan on top, and slammed to the carpeted floor.

The attacker grunted on impact, the arm around his neck slackening. Bolan drove his elbow into the guy's face, once, then again as bone cracked. The man cried out, drawing air into his lungs. Bolan struck again. For a few seconds the guy went limp. Rolling, Bolan twisted the knife arm, gripping it with his free hand, and pulled it across his hip, adding hard pressure until bone cracked. The knife slipped from nerveless fingers. Bolan snatched it up, pushing to his feet. As he stepped away from his attacker, the guy used his good arm to push himself into a sitting position, gathering his legs beneath him as he began to rise. The Executioner steadied himself, then swung his right foot in a brutal kick that thudded against the guy's exposed jaw. Blood erupted from his mouth as his head was whipsawed back. The force of the blow spun him across the floor and he slammed into the base of the wall.

Bolan retrieved the Beretta. He turned to the apartment door again, his thoughts concentrated on getting inside. He needed to learn just how detailed Bouvier's knowledge of Mahoud was, who the man's contacts were.

He raised his right foot and slammed it against the door, level with the handle. Wood cracked and the door flew wide. Bolan went in fast, viewing the large, high-ceilinged room. Little furniture, tall windows, a desk holding computer and telephones.

And four men.

Two were standing, while a third leaned over the desk. The pair on its feet already turned in his direction, their hands reaching for the pistols under their jackets.

The fourth man was seated at the desk, his eyes staring across the room at Bolan. He seemed transfixed, unable to grasp what was happening.

Ben Sharon came into the room behind Bolan, a Desert Eagle filling his hand as he kicked the door shut behind him.

The moment broke.

Sharon triggered his handgun, the .44 thundering as it sent a slug into the closest of the hardmen. Blood spurted from between his shoulders as the heavy slug burst free.

As the guy went down Bolan turned the Beretta on his partner, a 3-round burst hitting his target chest-high, toppling him facedown onto the hardwood floor.

The guy at the side of the desk went for the SIG-Sauer in front of him. Bolan and Sharon fired in the same instant, their combined shots spinning the guy off his feet. He crashed to the floor in a welter of bloody debris.

Bolan focused the 93-R on the man behind the desk,

whose right hand was moving toward the keyboard of his laptop.

"If you want to lose those fingers," Bolan said, "just keep moving that hand."

Sharon headed to the desk. He slammed his foot against the swivel chair and shoved away it and its occupant. The chair rolled across the floor and came to a stop against the window frame.

"Meet Mohan Bouvier," Sharon said. "This is the man who arranged the hit on your safehouse. He's also responsible for countless deaths across the Middle East, Europe and Israel. One of your backroom warriors who send others to do his dirty work for him."

"My work is for God," Bouvier said.

"I forgot," Sharon said. "These cowards always hide behind religion to justify their deeds."

"We fight the jihad. In many ways."

"What would you do without your blessed jihad, the excuse to slaughter and maim in the name of God."

"Your blasphemy will not stop us," Bouvier said.

Sharon smiled as he leveled the Desert Eagle. "I can stop *you,* Bouvier."

"Then I will enter Paradise."

Sharon shook his head in weary resignation. "How can you talk to people like these? Rivers of honey and endless virgins."

Bolan was at the desk, switching off the laptop and pocketing the cell phone Bouvier had set beside it.

"If you don't want to end up in paradise, as well, Ben, we should get the hell out of here before the French cops show up. I've got all I need here. He isn't about to tell us anything and we don't have time to interrogate him."

Sharon nodded, turning away to follow as Bolan made for the door with the laptop. As Bolan reached the door something made him turn. He was in time to see Sharon track the Desert Eagle in on Bouvier. The Mossad agent triggered a pair of .44s that practically sheared off the top of Bouvier's skull, spreading bloody matter across the wall and window.

"Now we've both got what we came for," he said, and followed Bolan from the apartment.

"You have any problems getting in?" Bolan asked.

"No. I left the one downstairs unconscious. He'll have a hell of a headache when he comes around."

"And some explaining to do," Bolan said.

They holstered their weapons as they descended the stairs. Surprisingly there was little in way of alarmed responses to the shooting. Perhaps, Bolan figured, the inhabitants of Paris had learned to stay out of harm's way in such matters. Civilians could do very little in the face of armed aggression. The only sure thing was they might get shot themselves. Self-preservation had become the watchword. Bolan couldn't truthfully blame them.

Nor, he found, did he have much criticism for Sharon's actions. The man was carrying out his agency's mandate. Israel's Mossad had always made it clear they would exercise the ultimate penalty against their enemies, had always made the option clear to the world. In their eyes Israel was fighting an out-and-out struggle against those who denounced the nation and its people. It was a war that had been going on for a long time, and Israel showed no weakness when it came to dealing with combatants.

At the street exit Bolan and Sharon stepped outside, crossing to the far side. They walked to their car and climbed in. Sharon fired up the engine and pulled away from the sidewalk. They had driven a couple of blocks before a pair of police cars sped past, sirens wailing and lights flashing.

"Having Bouvier out of the picture is going to wreck

the system for a while," Sharon said. "As a major facilitator, he linked a great number of cells, had access to funds and suppliers."

"Someone else will step in to fill the void," Bolan said. "It's going to take a lot more than the removal of one guy to seriously stop these people."

Sharon shrugged. "Don't I know it. But at least today we rattled their cage a little."

"Downloading the contents of his laptop might offer us a look at what Bouvier was handling recently."

KURTZMAN WAS BEAMING like a kid at Christmas as he looked over the data streaming in from Bouvier's laptop. Barbara Price leaned over his shoulder, understanding Kurtzman's almost ecstatic pleasure.

"Striker, you hit the mother lode here," he said over the audio link.

"Anything to keep you happy."

"Give me a couple of hours to decipher this clutter."

"I need fast results," Bolan said. "I'm running out of time here."

"It's a priority, Striker."

"Heard anything from Ironman yet?"

"No," Price said. "No contact. The local law located the cabin. There were signs it was occupied. Rafiq Mahoud's vehicle was parked outside, along with another 4x4. They're running a trace on it. They found Carl's rental parked up a few miles from the place. Oh, and there was blood found inside the cabin, and a number of recently fired shell casings. One of the forest rangers who was called in did find tracks leading away from the cabin and heading into the forest away from the area."

"Keep me posted."

"Take care, Striker," Price said, and closed the connection.

Bolan handed over the laptop and Sharon set up the computer connection with his Mossad agency and triggered the download.

Bolan helped himself to a second cup of the rich Moroccan coffee Sharon had made.

"What's next for you, Ben?"

"You need to ask?" Sharon glanced at Bolan. "I'm dealing myself in. And don't tell me you couldn't do with an extra pair of hands."

Bolan raised his cup in thanks.

"If Mahoud can work his miracle at the conference, Israel could benefit, as well."

Aboard the Crescent Moon

"Someone put two bullets into Bouvier's head. The team's dead, as well."

Asadi sat back, shock etched across his face.

Bouvier dead? The man had organized so much for the cause. Bouvier had been the man with all the connections, the knowledge of who and what and how. If he was dead, much of Asadi's backup died with him. It would take a long time to regain the leverage Bouvier had kept at his fingertips.

"Whoever made the attack took Bouvier's laptop and cell phone."

Asadi closed his mind to everything else as he sought to make sense of events. The conference was coming up fast and Mahoud still lived. It changed things. Asadi wasn't quite sure how to make his next move.

"Still no reports on where Mahoud is now?"

"No," the informant said. "He was moved very quickly after the attack at the château, before we had a chance to regroup. No one seems to know where the family is now."

"Keep looking," Asadi said. "If you discover where he is, get directly back to me."

After putting away his phone, Asadi left his cabin and made his way to the deck of the *Crescent Moon*. He needed to report to Mullah Homani. The pretence had to be maintained at least for the present.

MULLAH WAZIR HOMANI stood at the rail, seeing the activity in the harbor, though his attention wasn't completely focused on it. His mind was occupied with other matters. Mainly Sharif Mahoud. The man seemed to be leading a charmed life. Over the past few days Mahoud had survived all things directed toward him. He had come through the trek across the Afghan hills to reach safety in the American military base. His family had been brought out, despite the Taliban watch over them, and they had all walked away from the personal attack during the rebel strike at the U.S. base. Since relocating in France, a second attempt to deal with the Mahoud problem had gone disastrously wrong, and the latest report from Paris had informed Homani of the death of Mohan Bouvier.

It wasn't the actual death of Bouvier that concerned Homani, but rather the implications behind that death. Mohan Bouvier held knowledge, his contacts, suppliers, cash deposits held in various locations. He had an ability to arrange and organize. All was gone now that the man was dead. Homani regretted the material loss, away and above the demise of the man himself. Human life was cheap. The loss of one man was insignificant. What had rested within Bouvier's brain was irreplaceable. It was going to take time and effort to rebuild Bouvier's store of knowledge.

Time was something Homani was running out of. He had already set a small team of his trusted people the task of trying to rebuild Bouvier's information bank. It

wouldn't be easy, but they were patient men, faithful ser-
vants of God, and they would devote as much time as
they needed. The fact that Bouvier's killers had walked
away with his computer meant their work would be so
much harder. They would find a way, Homani knew.

In the meantime the problem of Mahoud still remained.
Since the abortive strike at Château Fontaine the man and
his family had disappeared. They had obviously been re-
located, but no one seemed to be able to find out where.
Until they were found, the possibility of another attempt
against Mahoud remained moot.

A soft footfall behind Homani made him turn. He saw
it was Asadi. The expression on the man's face informed
the mullah he had no good news, either.

"I expect you have come to tell me Bouvier is dead?"
Homani inclined his head. "I already know. You are not
the only one with informants."

Asadi looked taken aback, unused to being spoken to
in such a manner.

"So we are still stumbling around in the dark?" Homani
went on.

"This American protecting Mahoud is no fool. Where
he has taken the family is beyond us at the moment, but
we will find them."

"I seem to recall the same promise earlier." Homani
held back from saying anything further. He sensed Asadi's
frustration. Whatever else he might have been, Homani
retained the ability to understand human frailty. Asadi
was angry with himself. A personal attack on the man
would do nothing except raise his defenses and cause him
to doubt his own ability. So he changed tack.

"What are they saying in there? Our dear American
allies?" Homani queried.

The words almost made Homani choke. His need to

remain close to Hartman and his odious second in command, Dane, was placing a great deal of strain on him. Play-acting didn't suit him. He wanted rid of them. But until he could establish himself as the supreme master at the conference, he was going to have to remain their "friend."

"They're like children. All they do is chatter on about regional stabilization. Redistribution of resources. Take from here. Increase financial strength there. I swear that if I have to listen to much more, I will slit their throats myself and bleed them on their expensive carpets.

"They talk about our lands as if they already owned them. And we are nothing but figures they can move around at will. Their smugness appalls me. Like all Americans, they really believe money is the answer. That with it they can buy the world and everyone will fall to their knees in gratitude."

"Ali, have patience. When we have what we need from them, our day will come. They will be shown the way. Made to realize we are more than foreigners who dress in robes and spend our days in prayer. They have no understanding that we are guiding the way. Let them throw their money and weapons at us. We take it all, and when we are ready we will give the orders and watch them crawl on their knees at our bidding."

"I sit at that table and I listen. These fools talk too freely because they believe I am with them. All morning I have been forced to hear about their plans to deal with Mahoud. This information he is supposed to have. They are worried about it. They seem to believe it is of great importance, that it could bring down many people here and in America and Europe. Do you think this is so?"

"Sharif Mahoud is a clever man. If he has been collecting all this material, and I have no reason not to believe it to be so, then there is the chance it could bring many down."

"Good or bad for us?"

Homani smiled. "A good question. If it eliminates the credibility of respected men, then we could use it as a weapon to strengthen our own cause. Belittling a man, especially one who has great pride, can have an effect as damaging as a bullet."

Homani's cell phone rang. Asadi watched his expression change as he received the message.

"Good," was all he said at the end. He lowered the cell. "We have them. A small hotel in Paris."

"I will assemble a team," Asadi said.

Homani raised a hand. "Let us wait before doing anything," he said. "If Mahoud believes he is safe, he will go and collect his data. He has to collect it before leaving for the conference. Once he has it, we can move in and take it."

"And then?"

"Then he can die."

CHAPTER TWENTY-TWO

Cujo checked that his weapon was secure, turned without a word and waded into the water. He pushed against the current, maintaining a direct line as he crossed.

"That Indian is crazy," Grover said.

"No. He's mad because he was shot and Benning got away."

Grover touched the side of his face where Lyons had hit him. The top of his skull was still aching, too.

"Don't remind me," he said.

"Todd, you must have let him get too close," Kate mimicked.

"Hey, look at him go," Jake said.

They watched Cujo wade ashore and start up the side of the gorge, moving in a sure-footed way that took him up the rocky slope fast and easy.

Marino slung his weapon across his back. He took the transceiver clipped to his belt and activated it.

"Move out, people, this isn't a vacation we're on. We lose that kid, we don't get paid. Remember?"

"Who needs money when we're having a fun time?" Kate said. "Jesus, this water's cold."

Grover laughed as he followed her into the river. "You should wear pants."

"Todd, you don't have the legs for shorts like these."

"Will you two quit the small talk," Marino said. "It's like running a kindergarten class."

He raised the transceiver and began to speak into it.

"At least Cujo is getting his kicks," Harper said, spotting Cujo just before he vanished from sight over the lip of the gorge.

"I hope he saves enough for me," Kate muttered sourly. "I owe that son of a bitch Benning."

"You're just grumpy 'cause you wet your shorts," Grover said.

CUJO LOOKED BACK once as he reached the top of the gorge. The rest of his crew was starting to cross the river. He shook his head at their struggles through the current. They were going to be a long way behind. He had no intention of waiting for them.

He cast around and found the tracks left by Benning and Rafiq. The others were going to have to do the same. He figured Marino the most likely to pick up the trail. He was the most experienced of the group after Cujo. Marino had served and knew his battlefield techniques. He'd keep the others on track. The Apache hoped to have the matter sorted by the time they caught up. The boy would present no kind of a problem. Benning was another matter. The guy had proved himself by his break-out from the cabin. The thought made Cujo aware of his shoulder. It still ached from the slug that had creased it, tearing flesh and leaving a tender wound. The side of his face was still tender where he had pulled out the wood splinters. It made him wary of the man. And he hadn't forgotten Benning had a loaded gun.

Cujo swung his own weapon from his shoulders, made sure it was ready for use, then loped forward into an easy, distance-eating run. His eyes scanned the way ahead, keeping the tracks left by Benning and Rafiq Mahoud in plain sight.

His quarry had no vehicle, and were on foot, without food or water. Benning had looked fit, the boy less so. He would slow Benning down. The Justice agent would stick with him. Mahoud was in his charge now and Benning's training would click in. He would do everything he could to keep the boy safe, even if it meant putting his own life at risk. That was the way those agents were indoctrinated. Nothing else mattered except the safety of their charges. It was the kind of dedication Cujo understood.

Loyalty.

Honor.

Sacrifice even.

The problem was these days most people had forgotten those things. Cujo held to those traditions. They had been inbred into the Apache psyche for generations.

When he caught up to Benning he would still kill the guy, because that was what you did to an enemy. It didn't mean you couldn't respect him.

An hour later Cujo felt he was getting close. Benning had tried to reduce his sign, using hard ground whenever he could. Twice Cujo lost the tracks. When that happened he took time to study the ground, searching for where Benning and the boy had been forced to return to softer ground. Cujo had already seen that Benning was moving steadily west, so it proved easy to pick up the tracks again.

Crushed grass. Broken twigs on the brush. Benning was good but he was no Apache. Once Cujo found footprints in wet mud where his runaway pair had crossed a patch of ground softened by a runoff from a spring bubbling from underground. There were knee prints close by, too, where they had paused to drink from the water source. Cujo drank from the chill water himself before moving on.

He abruptly stopped, freezing on the spot as he sensed something out of place.

The prints in the soft mud.

Too obvious. Meant to catch Cujo's attention.

They were made deliberately, because Agent Benning wouldn't be so clumsy as to accidentally leave them.

Cujo saw a flicker of sunlight reflecting from metal off to his right, coming from a patch of brush.

Gun, Cujo thought.

He reacted immediately, throwing himself to the side, but realized his mistake as a shadow fell across him from behind.

Carl Lyons's body slam threw Cujo forward. The Apache stumbled and Lyons dropped to the ground, twisting his body into a powerful leg sweep that took Cujo's feet from under him. He slammed to the ground, the impact winding him briefly. Lyons rolled to his feet, a booted foot slamming the SMG from Cujo's hand. Lyons snatched the weapon from the ground and hurled it aside. Grunting in annoyance Cujo sucked air back into his lungs and powered off the ground. As fast as he was, he walked into a solid right fist that smashed into his jaw, tearing open his lower lip. Lyons followed through with an equally heavy left that cracked hard against his adversary's cheek. It split the flesh, snapping Cujo's head around.

The Native American pulled back to give himself breathing space and a chance to gather himself. His head hurt from the stunning blows. Disregarding the pain, he lunged at Lyons, catching him around the waist. Cujo was no lightweight. He planted his feet apart and lifted the

Able Team leader clear off the ground. He held the position for long seconds, crushing the man in his powerful embrace, until Lyons slammed the point of his elbow down across the base of Cujo's neck. Lyons repeated the blow a few times, feeling his opponent's grip slacken a little. As the man's grip eased, Lyons planted his open palm across Cujo's face and pushed hard, forcing the man's head back.

Lyons could feel blood wet against his hand. He drew his palm back, then slammed the heel of his hand into Cujo's nose. He put every ounce of his strength into the blow. Cujo's nose disintegrated, cartilage collapsing. Blood gushed from the crushed nose. Cujo howled, shaking his head from side to side in pure agony, his long hair fanning out. His concentration broken, Cujo lost his grip and Lyons was able to slip free. He grabbed handfuls of the Apache's hair and yanked his head down without hesitation, swinging his right knee up to connect with the man's face. Lyons followed with an elbow punch to the throat. Cujo toppled backward and fell stiff-legged to the hard ground, the back of his skull slamming down hard.

Bending over the Apache, Lyons checked the man's pockets. Cujo wasn't carrying anything of interest, apart from a heavy bladed knife in a leather sheath, which he took. Lyons crossed to where Cujo's H&K had landed. He ejected the magazine and tucked it behind his belt, then threw the empty weapon into the center of a spread of tangled brush. Turning back, he crossed to the patch of the brush that had caught Cujo's attention. Leaning forward he pulled out the H&K he had wedged into the tangle; it was the SMG, catching sunlight, that had attracted the sharp-eyed Apache.

"Rafiq, you can come out now."

The young man raised himself from a grassed-over depression where he had been lying. As he joined Lyons, he was unable to prevent himself from looking at Cujo's prone form, shaking his head at the bloodied face.

"I've never seen anything like that before," he said. "Is he…?"

"Dead? He could be," Lyons said. He placed a hand on Rafiq's shoulder and turned him away.

"Why didn't you shoot him? I mean, he had a gun. Wouldn't it have been less risky?" Rafiq asked.

"Maybe," Lyons said as they moved away. "Think about it. Shots would have told his partners where we were. Drawn them here faster."

"Oh. Yeah, I see that now."

"Here, take this and try not to cut yourself." Lyons handed over the knife he had taken from Cujo. "It's sharp."

"I'll do my best to remember that," Rafiq said with a grin.

Ahead, the spread of undergrowth and trees began to thicken again. They were still out in the open when Lyons caught an all too familiar sound.

He stood and searched the sky. The sound became sharper. Rafiq had heard the same noise. He thrust an arm to the north.

"There. A helicopter. You see it, Benning?"

"I see it," Lyons said, watching the distant dark spot growing larger. And it appeared to be heading directly for them.

"Hey, look at him come."

Lyons was looking, and he was beginning to wish the helicopter wasn't coming on so fast.

"Could be a rescue party from your agency," Rafiq said.

"It's not," Lyons said. "And it isn't from the Forestry Service."

"So who is it from?"

"You want me to spell it out in simple words?" Lyons asked.

"I guess not."

"So let's hit those trees as fast as we can. At least we'll have cover."

They picked up their pace, breaking into a run as the helicopter swooped down, angling in from the right, and the sharp stutter of autofire reached their ears. Bullet hits kicked up grass and dirt. The chopper roared in over their heads, banking sharply to turn and come in again.

It was, Lyons decided, coming in too fast.

Too soon.

Too damn soon…

CHAPTER TWENTY-THREE

Kerim nudged his partner.

"There they are," he said. "Mahoud and the American."

"I see them," Rashid said.

He leaned forward and turned on the ignition. The Renault's engine caught, ticking over quietly. Kerim took out the transceiver he carried and thumbed the transmit button.

"We have them in sight. Dark blue SUV." He read the license plate. "Follow the plan. We cannot afford to make any more mistakes. It was foolish when they tried to take Mahoud earlier, before he had picked up the data. If Mahoud does get his information, then we can take him. Not before."

Rashid concentrated on the SUV, moving as it did, and merging with the traffic. He stayed at least three vehicles behind the SUV. A quick check in his rearview mirror confirmed that the other two cars had fallen in behind him. While Kerim spoke into the transceiver Rashid watched the SUV, ready to turn if it did.

They drove at a steady pace. Traffic wasn't heavy, which, to Rashid, was both good and bad. It meant it was easy for him to keep the SUV in his sight, but on the negative side it could leave him open to being spotted if he stayed on its tail for a long time. There was nothing Rashid could do. He would have to stay where he was and hope Mahoud and the American failed to realize they were being tailed.

Ten minutes later and Kerim spoke rapidly into his transceiver.

"They are heading for Pont Neuf. Pont Neuf."

Pont Neuf was one of the many bridges spanning the Seine. It was a wide, stone-built bridge that led across the river and would bring them into the 1st Arrondissement or District. Paris was broken up into twenty of these districts, laid out on both sides of the river.

Rashid, who knew the city well, eased into position so he would not miss the bridge approach. As traffic was funneled into position he was staring ahead, making sure he still had the dark blue SUV in sight. He began to nod his head as a realization came to him.

"They will head for the second district," he said. "The 2nd Arrondissement."

"Yes," Kerim agreed. "The financial district."

ONCE THEY HAD CLEARED the bridge Mahoud directed Bolan through the streets until he saw the building that housed the Paris branch of a Swiss bank. Bolan pulled in just beyond it, cut the engine and they climbed out, Mahoud leading the way into the bank. Crossing the floor, Mahoud presented himself to the young woman seated at the reception desk. Bolan stayed well back, his eyes lingering on the entrance. Mahoud filled in a small card and handed it to the woman. She smiled and tapped into her keyboard. Mahoud was requested to press his right thumb on an electronic pad that read his print. The woman acknowledged the positive response and signaled to one of the waiting assistants. The man gestured for Mahoud to follow. Bolan watched them go through a door that would lead them to the safety vaults.

Mahoud returned within a few minutes. He nodded to the young woman and joined Bolan.

"I wish all matters could be resolved so smoothly," he said.

They walked out of the bank and crossed to the SUV. As they climbed in, Bolan checked his door mirror, confirming something that had been nagging at him for a while. His concerns were validated as he pulled away from the curb.

He had spotted a Renault saloon after they had cleared the bridge, and now it fell in a number of cars behind them.

"We have company."

"You are certain?"

"I wasn't sure until we turned into this street. Then the guy parked a few cars back. And I don't think he's alone."

As he drove, Bolan constantly checked his mirrors. The Renault held its place.

"What do we do?"

"They're not going to leave us alone," Bolan said, "so we'll have to lose them."

"That sounds easier than I expect it to be."

"Reef, we outsmarted the Taliban in Afghanistan. Don't say you're going soft on me."

They drove for a while, Bolan working his options. His main concern centered on Mahoud's safety. He hadn't forgotten the man had a wounded arm, which could hamper Mahoud if they got themselves into a compromising situation. The identity of the men following them was also something Bolan was thinking about. Two groups were after Mahoud.

One group simply wanted him dead. The other seemed intent on taking him alive to gain control of the incriminating data the man had on him right now.

In either case Sharif Mahoud's life was threatened. As his family had been threatened.

In the end there would be only one outcome if the opposition, from whichever camp, got close enough to take Mahoud.

It wasn't an outcome Bolan would tolerate. And as he had taken the job of protecting Mahoud, it was up to him to prevent that happening.

Bolan turned off the main drag and took the SUV on a course along side and back streets. They were moving out of the up market areas, Bolan choosing the tight, narrow places, where old buildings hung over the shadowed routes. He realized that as he moved away from the busy boulevards he was also leaving behind the heavier traffic, and before long the Renault was the only vehicle behind him, staying back, but no longer hiding its presence. Farther back Bolan could also see the two other vehicles. The only saving grace was that the narrowness of the streets prevented the other vehicles from overtaking them.

"What if we hit a dead end, Matt?"

Without a word Bolan swerved sharply, running down a crooked street that wound its way past empty properties. Some were in stages of demolition.

"It may be a silly question," Mahoud said, "but do you know where we are?"

"No."

Behind them a large SUV, the last in line of the backup cars, accelerated and bulled its way past the other vehicles. It scraped against brick walls, raising a cloud of dust, then drew level with Bolan's vehicle, the driver swinging in to smash against Bolan's vehicle. The soldier retaliated, feeling the impact. A rear door window on the other SUV shattered. The two vehicles ran in tandem for some yards, slamming into each other as each driver tried to push the other off course.

Up ahead Bolan spotted a chain-link fence edging the sidewalk. He let the ride continue, waiting for his moment and fighting the twist of his steering wheel as the other SUV maintained its body slamming. As his vehicle reached the chain-link fence, Bolan hit the gas pedal and edged his vehicle forward, the nose of the SUV clearing the front end of the other vehicle. He slammed hard on the pedal again and wrenched the wheel around, hitting the other SUV on the extreme leading edge of its front wing. The impact was enough to push the SUV off line. The front end rose as the vehicle bounced over the curb, hit the chain fence and burst through. It was only as his front wheels dropped into empty space that the SUV's driver realized there was a drop on the other side of the fence. The vehicle crashed over the back edge of the sidewalk and hit the rubble below, rocking crazily, finally tilting to one side.

Bolan felt himself thrown forward as the Renault hit the rear of his SUV, Mahoud gasping as his seat belt bit into his ribs. The SUV's rear window blew in as a burst of gunfire erupted. As the SUV came to a jerking halt, Bolan jammed the gearshift into reverse and floored the gas pedal in the same instant he let out the clutch. The SUV, tires screaming and smoking, leaped backward and collapsed the Renault's front, riding up over the fender for a few moments, wheels spinning wildly before it fell back to the street.

"Stay down," Bolan yelled.

The soldier kicked open his door and rolled out onto the street, his Beretta sliding into view from inside his jacket. He moved at a crouch along the length of the SUV, putting a 3-round burst into the Renault's driver as the guy emerged from the car.

BOOTING OPEN his passenger door, Kerim heard the sound of shots and saw Rashid stumble back, a pained expression on his face as he went to his knees. Fear clawed at Kerim's stomach. He had never been under fire before, and despite all the training he had received from his instructors the SIG-Sauer P-226 felt heavy and alien in his hand. He wasn't sure which way to turn, unaware in his agitation how long a time had elapsed since Rashid had been hit.

He caught a fleeting glimpse of a shadow moving on the other side of the Renault and turned, but the shadow had gone. When he looked again he saw the shape of the American leaning in through the driver's side of the car. The man's hand rose. Kerim saw a gun but didn't hear the shots. There was a stunning impact that wrenched his head around. For a moment he experienced the sensation of having been struck by something brutally heavy, and then he was down on the dirty street, his body out of control. He died not even knowing that Bolan's triple burst had removed half his skull and reduced his brain to bloody fragments.

A HAIL OF SHOTS from the tail car behind the Renault slammed into the bodywork, leaving ragged holes in the pressed steel.

Bolan crouched at the rear corner, watching briefly as he assessed his targets. One of the two occupants of the car had leaned out to fire the SMG he was carrying. Flicking the select lever to single shot, Bolan eased the forward hand grip down, enabling him to steady the

Beretta. He was still hidden from sight by the bulk of the
Renault, so the other guy had to move, leading with his
weapon. As he cleared the edge of his open door, Bolan's
finger stroked the 93-R's trigger and put a slug directly
between the gunner's eyes. The guy fell back, his finger
jerking the trigger to send a burst of 9 mm slugs skyward.

Bolan heard the tail car's engine roar as the driver
jammed down his foot. The car shot away, swerving back
and forth as the driver tried to maintain a steady course in
reverse. Leaning against the Renault's trunk Bolan took
steady aim and triggered three shots into the windshield
on the driver's side. The car made a half-circle turn before
its rear slammed into the front wall of one of the derelict
buildings. The door sprang open on impact and the driver
slumped from his seat.

On his feet Bolan made his way around to the passenger side of the SUV to check on Mahoud.

"I am all right," Mahoud said.

Bolan heard a rattle of loose rubble. He turned in time
to see a bloody hand reach up to grip the edge of the
sidewalk. Then a second hand appeared, clutching a pistol.
Bolan crossed and stood waiting. The guy climbing up
from the rubble was too busy concentrating on his effort
to notice Bolan until he pulled himself into view, his head
exposed.

"A wasted effort," the Executioner said evenly as he
launched a full-on kick, the sole of his shoe connecting
with the man's head. A brief cry faded just as quickly as
the guy spun backward, his arms thrown wide as he
slammed down on the piled rubble. Beyond him Bolan
saw the wrecked SUV, a motionless form hanging out of
one door.

Returning to his own vehicle, Bolan fired up the engine
and engaged the four-wheel drive before boosting the

power. The front wheels spun, gripped. Swinging the wheel, Bolan cruised along the street and took the first turn he came to.

"That data of yours had better be dynamite, Reef," he said.

"It is." Mahoud held up the slim flash drive he had collected from the security deposit box. "When we return to the hotel, I will show you what I have."

Bolan took out his cell and called Sharon.

"Ben, we're on our way back. Stay sharp."

When the Mossad agent didn't answer immediately Bolan suspected a problem.

"WHAT HAPPENED, Ben?" Bolan asked.

"The girl has gone. Raika."

"Kidnapped?"

"No, that's the mystery. Everything appeared normal until Leila went to check. Raika wasn't in her room. No signs of a struggle. But there was a note in Raika's own handwriting. Leila translated. It simply said, 'I can't put up with this any longer. I have to leave. Tell Father I ask his forgiveness. Raika.'"

"Does Leila have any idea where she might have gone?"

"No. There was some talk about a possible boyfriend, but Leila had nothing above that."

"Okay, we'll talk later. Ben, we had another attempt on Sharif. We're clear now. It means the hotel has been identified. We need to move. Do it now. Get Leila and Amina out now."

"I'll take them to my apartment." Sharon gave Bolan the address. "Meet us there."

Bolan told Mahoud what had happened. The man slumped back in his seat, shaking his head.

"I have been fearing this," he said. "Too much. I have put them through too much. Is it any wonder Raika has had enough. This is not a life for a young woman. Raika is bright and smart. She should be making her own way in life, not following me around the world on my quest for peace." He gave a brittle laugh. "What a joke it is becoming. Here I want to unite troubled factions and all I am doing is putting my own family into dangerous situations. My son has been kidnapped and my daughter has walked away because she can no longer exist as a fugitive. Sharif Mahoud, peacemaker to the world, and his splintered family."

It took them over thirty minutes to reach Sharon's third-floor apartment. The Mossad agent let them in, locking the door once they were inside.

Amina ran to her father and hugged him.

"Raika is a silly girl," she said. "I know she has gone to see her boyfriend. She should be with us. You need us, Daddy."

Mahoud was almost in tears. He couldn't even speak. Leila went to him and they moved to a corner of the apartment to talk.

"I feel bad about this, Matt," Sharon said. "It was my job to keep them close and a slip of a girl fooled me."

"No one blames you, Ben. I've been concerned over Raika's behavior since Afghanistan. But what can you do apart from shackling them to the bed? Raika's young. The truth could be simply that she *has* reached her limit."

Sharon held out the note he had found. It had been written on a small sheet of hotel stationery. The address of the establishment was printed across the top. Halfway down was Raika's message. Bolan read the words. He glanced across the room at the Mahoud family—young daughter, the adoring mother and father. Raika's family. A close unit from what Bolan had seen and heard.

He looked at the neat writing on the note, penned by a steady, unhurried hand. Not hastily scribbled as a last-minute goodbye.

Deliberate.

Thought out.

So why had Raika only asked for her father's forgiveness?

Not her father *and* mother?

He folded the note and slipped it into his pocket.

CHAPTER TWENTY-FOUR

"We've got them spotted."

Greg Marino picked up the rattle of autofire behind the caller's words.

"Don't hurt the kid," he snapped. "We need him alive. You can take down that fucking agent, but keep Mahoud breathing."

"How close are you?"

"We're on our way. Keep me updated." Marino closed the transmission. "Move out."

"Where's Cujo?" Grover asked. "He must be close by now."

"Benning is no beginner," Kate said. "Could be he took Cujo down."

"If he did, he's got my respect," Harper said.

"Touchy feely crap," Marino said. "This bastard has run off with our paycheck. Hartman will go apeshit if he finds out we didn't get the kid. You understand what's riding on this deal? We get this right and Hartman gets what he wants, we could all be sitting pretty for the rest of our days. Screw up he'll send out a cleanup team to hunt *us* down. That's how big this is."

"Message understood, Greg," Grover said. "Now ease off, buddy, before you explode."

Marino strode ahead, his eyes on the ground, searching for tracks. He had a natural aptitude for following trails, though even he would have stood aside for Cujo. The Apache could track in the dark with a hood over his head. This time around, though, Cujo was being thrown off by his anger at Benning getting off a shot that had creased him. Cujo was on the trail with pride dictating his actions, and that wasn't the way to track. It had to be done with total detachment. Marino just hoped the man's feelings didn't get in the way.

TWENTY MINUTES LATER Marino's worst feelings were justified when they came across Cujo's body. No one said anything initially as they stood around the bloodied corpse. Marino knelt and checked out the man's vital signs. He shook his head as he stood.

"Christ, look at the state of him," Harper said. "Looks like someone ran over him with a locomotive."

"Benning is no desk jockey," Marino said. He pointed at the bruising on Cujo's throat. "Hit him so hard he crushed his throat. Cujo choked on his own blood."

"Why no gun?" Kate asked.

"Benning didn't want to fire shots that might warn us," Grover said. "Smart."

"That means he's got the SMG he took from Grover," Marino said, "plus an extra magazine from Cujo."

"Cujo's knife has gone," Kate said.

"No way he's going to hand over the kid without a fight," Harper said.

Marino activated his transceiver and spoke to the chopper pilot.

"They're a half mile east if you found the Indian. We

spotted him from the air. Benning and the kid took to the trees up ahead. Not going to be easy to flush them out. Plenty of cover for them and it'll be dark in a couple of hours."

"How far is the closest help?"

"Nothing for at least twenty miles. There's a fire road about twelve miles from where they went into the timber, but hell, they won't find anything else," Marino said.

"Stay around as long as you have fuel."

"Will do. Give me the word and I'll drop the gear I brought," the pilot told him.

"Okay. Out."

"DO YOU THINK they can still see us?" Rafiq asked.

They had been moving for at least forty minutes, weaving in and out of the dense timber. The ground underfoot was covered by a thick layer of fallout from the trees. It provided a more than silent carpet to deaden their passing. Now they were motionless, with the silence of the forest around them, Lyons was able to pick up the sounds of the helicopter. Subdued but still around.

"I don't know where that chopper flew in from," Lyons said, "but he has to go back eventually. His fuel isn't going to last forever, and he needs enough to take him back to base."

"Great. So all we have to do is run around in circles until his tank dries up," Rafiq said.

"Something like that. Good thinking, kid."

"I make a joke and he takes me seriously."

Lyons glanced at his watch. "Sunset's in a couple of hours. He isn't going to be able to track us in the dark. Don't they teach you anything useful at that college?"

"Bush craft isn't on the subject list," Rafiq commented.

"Maybe it should be."

Looking up through the canopy of green overhead, Lyons tracked the helicopter by its proximity. The sounds of the rotors drifted in and out of earshot. The chopper was trailing them and most likely reporting back to Cujo's partners. Lyons didn't expect the helicopter to do much more than that. As long as he and Rafiq stayed deep within the timbered terrain, they were reasonably well protected. By the same token their pursuers were going to catch up with them eventually and being at ground level they would have no problem closing in on Lyons and Rafiq.

"You rested enough?" he asked.

Rafiq grinned. "I thought we stopped so *you* could catch your breath."

"You like to run?"

"College long-distance track team."

Lyons secured his SMG, tapped Rafiq on the shoulder and said, "Let's go, then, frat boy."

He headed out, Rafiq falling in easily beside him as they sprinted through the trees. Lyons set a variable course, wanting to make it hard for the helicopter overhead. They covered a long stretch of ground, following the rise and fall of the forested terrain until Lyons spotted a deep ravine that cut through the timber. Brush and timber had grown along the sloping sides, heavy ferns spreading in wide green fronds. Lyons found an easy access to the place where the ravine commenced, and, leading the way, took himself and Rafiq down into the shadowed bottom. At that depth there was no way the spotters in the helicopter could see them through the drop of the ravine and the dense coverage of greenery. He led them into the gloom of the natural crevice. It was cooler down there, too. Lyons saw a gleam of water. It was a spring flowing from a rock shelf some feet above their heads. Cool, clear water ran down the rock to a small pool and a runoff.

"Refreshments, too," Lyons said.

They splashed water on their faces and drank from the spring.

"You managed to keep up," Lyons said.

"Hey, you didn't do too bad for an old...older guy."

Lyons put up a silencing hand, tilting his head to listen to the fading beat of the helicopter.

"It's moving away," he said.

"WE LOST THEM," the pilot called in. "The forest is too dense and we can't see them."

"Okay," Marino said. "Head back and wait for my call."

"You pick up the stuff we dropped?" the pilot asked.

"Yeah."

"Good luck."

"Jesus, he's sitting up there thinking he's had a hard day," Kate said. "All he does is fly around in circles."

Marino fisted one of the supply packs and threw it to her. Kate caught it and slung it from her shoulder.

"Hey, Sheena, Queen of the Jungle," Grover called, "you want to carry mine, too? Help develop those girly arms."

"Come over here, village boy, and I'll show you girly arms."

Harper was crouching, peering along the frosted floor.

"Tracks," he said. "They were here. Prints go that way."

"Let's go, let's go," Marina snapped. "They still got a good lead on us. It'll be dark soon."

As they moved off, Grover said, "We'd better catch them before then. Isn't going to get any easier."

"We can still move," Kate said. "You forgot there are flashlights in the supply packs?"

"How will that help?" Grover asked.

"We'll be able to see our way."

"And they'll be able to see the beams from the flashlights. They can pick us off one by one," Marino said.

"Great suggestion, jungle girl," Grover said, a wide grin plastered across his face.

Kate stayed silent this time, deciding not to make any more novice suggestions.

THE RAVINE RAN northwest for a mile, then started to veer to the west. It provided good cover but underfoot the ground was treacherous, the undergrowth and ferns hiding potholes and rotted timbers.

Lyons called a halt and they flopped to the ground. Though the ravine had seemed cooler when they had entered, their steady march had made them aware of the heat trapped within the ravine and overgrown greenery. Now they were dripping sweat with every move. Their clothes clung to them.

"If I lose any more sweat, I'm coming out of here minus twenty pounds," Rafiq said.

"You got that much to lose?"

Lyons pushed to his feet and they moved off again, working their way along the ravine floor. After a quarter hour Lyons noticed the ravine sides were starting to shallow out. Another half mile and they were out of the ravine and back on what served as level ground. He noticed, too, that the trees were spaced out. The dense forest was behind them. They were emerging onto a wide plateau of open terrain. There was still an abundance of brush and fern, but the timber was petering out.

They reached the edge of the tree line. Sloping ground stretched ahead, undulating green hills and depressions. Lyons checked out the western horizon and saw the rich colors of the setting sun. It was moving with an exaggerated slowness behind the far horizon. Shadows were forming. The sharp profiles of the landscape blurred and merged together as the dusk increased.

"Now we get to sleep under the stars?" Rafiq said. "You know, I was expecting to do that with…I can't even remember her real name now, but you get the idea."

"I do," Lyons said. "Just don't get any ideas, kid. I'm a light sleeper."

"As if, Benning. You're not my type."

"COLD CAMP," Marino said. "No fires."

In the packs the helicopter had dropped they found clothing, sleeping bags and food, bottled water. They distributed the contents of the packs.

"No damn hot coffee?" Kate grumbled. "I'm going to make that son of a bitch, Benning, suffer for this."

"Here," Marino said, tossing her a can of beans. "Just pretend they're heated up."

"You're so not funny, Greg," she snapped back.

"If your young boyfriend hadn't run off," Grover said, "you'd have something to keep you warm tonight."

"Something you'll never get the chance to do."

"Ouch," Grover said.

"We'll run three-hour watches. Jake, then Grover, then Kate. I'll take the last watch. We'll move out soon as it's light."

They ate their cold rations. Harper picked his spot and took up his watch while the others wrapped themselves in the sleeping bags and settled down. There was little talking among them. The day had been long and fruitless. They had lost one of the crew but had failed to catch their quarry.

Of the four it was Greg Marino who lay awake for a long time, running over the day's events. Up until the arrival of Agent Benning things had been working to plan. The cabin had provided a secure place to hold the Mahoud kid. Kate had played her part well, keeping an eye on the kid until they received the get-go. She and Rafiq had driven up-country, taking the side road that led into the wilderness area. The kid hadn't suspected a damn thing. He was still smiling when he'd walked through the cabin door. That smile had faded the moment he was confronted by Marino and the crew. He had seen their expressions, the guns they had been holding, and he knew that plans for a fun weekend had come to an abrupt halt.

CHAPTER TWENTY-FIVE

"This is not working," Rafiq said.

Lyons had called a brief halt. He glanced across at the younger man.

"What?" he asked.

"We could be walking like this for days. For all we know in circles. They call these places wildernesses for a reason. Because there isn't an end to them."

"What's the alternative?" Lyons asked. "Sit here and wait for that crew to find us? They won't be bringing bottled water and a change of clothing, Rafiq. They want you, to make a bargain with your father." Lyons let a hard edge creep into his voice. "If they do get what they want, what do you think happens then? Not a happy ending. They kidnapped you, Rafiq, and the Law comes down hard on kidnappers. So letting you go free isn't an option. Understand?"

Rafiq did understand, though he might not have wanted to accept the truth. He knew Benning was right. The people pursuing them were not about to give him up even if they got what they wanted.

"Okay, you win, Benning. Maybe I'm just not the outdoor type. It's just…"

"Rafiq, you're doing fine. It might not seem like it, but we're getting there. Hell, I think I can smell the salt in the air from the Pacific."

Rafiq actually grinned. "No you can't."

"I can smell something."

"Most likely the bullshit you're feeding me."

Lyons slapped him on the shoulder. "Saw through me, huh?"

"Like a pane of glass."

They moved off, Lyons taking the rear so he could make constant checks of their back trail. He had no doubt that Marino's crew was still on their tail. Now that they had full daylight they would be moving fast, hoping to catch up to Lyons and Rafiq before they hit a regular trail and maybe even company.

The terrain they were now moving through was mainly timber, with occasional breaks in the tree line where they were forced into the open. The undulating landscape, tending to downward slopes, concerned Lyons each time they hit an open stretch. He couldn't do anything about that. As long as they stayed on their westerly course, they would eventually break out of the forested wilderness, but he had no idea how many more miles they needed to travel before that happened.

By midmorning they had covered another wide stretch of open ground. Walking some ten feet ahead, Rafiq turned to speak. Before any words left his mouth, Rafiq froze, his eyes widening in alarm, and Lyons knew their time advantage had come to an end.

The Stony Man commando didn't pause to consider his next move. He simply made it. Powering forward, he covered the distance between himself and Rafiq in long strides, throwing out his left arm, the palm of his hand slamming into Rafiq's chest. As the boy went down, Lyons followed him. They hit the ground, rolling, Lyons aware they were still a distance from solid cover.

"Stay low. Head for the trees and keep going."

Rafiq did as he was told. Gathering his legs under him and bending low, he ran.

Lyons turned on his back, heard the hard thud as a slug hit the ground only inches away, the crack of the shot following. He felt dirt rattle against his side as he twisted to face his attackers, the SMG snapping into position. He triggered a couple of quick shots and saw the group scatter as his slugs struck close by. He swung the H&K, tracking one figure and jacked out a trio of shots. The target paused, stumbled, but kept moving into cover.

Using the brief confusion, Lyons pushed upright and took off after Rafiq. He saw the young man vanish in the trees. At least they had achieved that.

A hail of slugs pounded the earth around Lyons's weaving figure. He ignored them, refusing to let himself be put off his stride. As he felt the welcome protection of the forest close around him, Lyons heard the whack of slugs tearing at the trees, spitting splinters of bark and wood into the air.

He could make out Rafiq ahead of him, moving fast. At least the kid knew how to obey an order. Lyons broke into a sprint behind him, wondering how bad his target had been hit.

"SON OF A BITCH," Grover mouthed.

A slug had ripped through his left hip, narrowly missing bone. It had gouged a raw chunk of flesh free, leaving a bloody wound. Perched on a low rock, Grover continued to curse at what he considered his bad luck.

"I don't mind you swearing," Marino said, "but sit fucking still so I can tie this dressing down."

"You want us to keep after them?" Harper asked.

"Go. Just go."

Harper and Kate moved off.

"I am getting severely pissed off with Benning," Marino said.

"Really? How do you think I feel? The bastard shot me. A few inches to the fucking right and I'd be singing soprano."

"Nah, he was too far off to hit a target that small."

"Funny guy."

Marino finished binding the dressed wound. "You'll need to take it slow. You're still bleeding some."

Grover hitched his pants back up and reached for his weapon.

"I'm not about to miss out on this. You go ahead. I'll catch up."

"Yeah?" Marino queried.

Grover nodded. "Get the hell out of here."

"THIS IS GETTING CLOSE," Rafiq said when Lyons caught up to him.

"You think so?"

The rattle of autofire cut through the forest. They heard slugs hitting the trees. The shooting was more random than accurate. Their pursuers were just letting them know they hadn't quit.

"That way," Lyons said, steering Rafiq off to the north.

The outcroppings thrust up from the forest floor. Large rocks and boulders, bleached by the weather, were covered in part by green moss. As they reached the outer groupings, Lyons guided his charge in through the overlapping stones. He could hear the pursuit getting closer. At least the rock barrier would offer them protection and maybe give Lyons a chance to hit back.

He urged Rafiq on. They pushed deep in among the rocks until the kid held back.

"Take it easy here," he said.

Lyons glanced ahead and saw the grassy area set in the curve of rocks. It was roughly oval in shape, reaching ten feet or so in width, with a sudden drop-off at its extreme edge. Lyons judged the drop to be around forty feet to more rocks and tangled vegetation.

"We should go back," Rafiq said. "No way out there."

Autofire crackled harshly, slugs pinging off stone.

Lyons grabbed Rafiq and shoved him roughly down into a gap between high boulders. He crouched, seeing armed figures moving in their direction.

Okay, Carl, you walked us into this corner, now get us out, he thought.

He crouchwalked a few yards to draw any incoming fire away from Rafiq, then dropped and prepared to wait until the opposition moved again.

Lyons didn't have long to wait.

CHAPTER TWENTY-SIX

Harper broke cover, his face expressing the anger he felt, his patience worn thin by the protracted chase. He moved over the clustered rocks, his gaze fixed on Lyons's last position. The second he locked on to Lyons he opened fire with his H&K. Lyons heard the solid thunk as the .45-caliber slugs gouged the stones behind his head. He leaned forward, bringing his own weapon on line, then dug in his heels and hauled himself to his feet. Harper registered Lyons's move, twisted to meet the Able Team chief head-on and misjudged his step. He stumbled, sliding down on one knee, and Lyons hit him with a pair of hot slugs from his own weapon. They cored in through Harper's chest, breaking a couple of ribs in the process. The mangled slugs still had enough energy to shred their way into Harper's pumping heart, damaging it beyond repair. Harper flew back under the force of the heavy slugs, slamming down on his shoulders, and lay struggling against the pain engulfing his upper body. Blood pumped from the open wounds, spreading across his front until his ravaged heart shut down.

Kate Murchison was closest to Harper. Seeing him go

down, she allowed her anger to dictate her actions and stepped from cover, triggering her subgun recklessly. The weapon jacked out a short burst, then locked on a misfire. Instead of dropping back into cover she raced in Lyons's direction, covering the gap in a few long strides. Out the corner of her eye she saw Harper's bloody body stretched out across the rocks and a yell of sheer rage burst from her.

LYONS HEARD the wild yell, turned and saw the unmistakable figure of Kate Murchison as she erupted out of cover. She was moving fast, swinging the empty SMG at Lyons's head. He ducked under the swing and she reversed, swiping at him again, still yelling. Her rage had kicked aside any restraint as she launched herself at him. Her weapon slammed against Lyons's, spinning it from his hands.

Her booted foot flashed forward, catching his right thigh. The blow was enough to knock Lyons off balance long enough for her to swing the UMG subgun again. It clipped the side of his head, drawing blood as it gouged his flesh. The blow stunned Lyons and gave Kate the opening she needed to body slam him. They fell from the final boulder, sliding down the smooth side and slammed to the grassy ledge below. At any other time and place Lyons might have enjoyed such proximity with a supple female form, but this young woman, showing surprising strength, was out to do him harm.

As they fell to the ground, with Kate on top, she swung a hard right fist that slammed against his jaw, snapping his head around with bruising force. Fingernails scraped bloody furrows along Lyons's jaw. He threw out a blocking arm as she drove another blow at him, caught her wrist and twisted hard, heard her pained gasp. The pain forced her to pause briefly, and Lyons used that pause to backhand her across the side of her face. The blow pushed her back, exposing her to the full force of Lyons's follow-up as he planted a booted foot against her taut stomach and pushed her away from him.

The action lifted her off the ground, sending her sprawling. She rolled, pawing at her bloody mouth. Throwing her useless weapon aside, she came at Lyons again as he pushed to one knee. She slammed into him hard, the force of her contact pushing Lyons backward, and he had to fight to maintain his balance. Kate was throwing everything she had at Lyons, her blows erratic but telling when they landed. Without warning she stepped back, reaching behind her, the hand snapping forward holding the handle of a slim switchblade. The keen-edged sliver of steel caught sunlight as it shot into place. Kate circled, the knife moving as she looked for an opening.

"I'm going to slice you apart," she said. "I owe you."

Lyons stayed silent. He let her do all the talking. He could sense her anger building, pushing her toward an impulsive move. When she went for him Lyons almost missed it. He felt the blade slice across his forearm, drawing blood. Kate's eyes shone with satisfaction. Her confidence made her reckless, almost clumsy, when she thrust again. Lyons had her measure now and he caught her knife wrist, hung on to it and turned sharply. He drew her arm across his shoulder and used her forward motion as a fulcrum to lift and throw her over his shoulder. She arced above him, her body twisting in midflight and Lyons caught a glimpse of her horrified features just before she cleared his body and went over the ledge screaming. She was still screaming when she hit the base of the drop forty feet down.

GROVER HEARD THE RATTLE of autofire and realized his partners had caught up to Benning. Ignoring the savage ache from his bloody hip, he increased his pace, limping badly, but determined not to miss out. He owed Benning for the pain he was suffering.

The mass of rocks confronted him and he scrambled over them, eager to be in on the finale. In his rush he stumbled, scraping his injured hip. He felt the blood starting to weep again, but ignored it. Sweat glistened on his face as he pulled himself to the top of a curving boulder and looked down.

He saw Harper, down and bloody, and caught a final glimpse of Kate as Benning flipped her over his shoulder, spinning her into empty space. Her shrill scream froze him for a moment.

He dragged up his UMG, his hands trembling, and as he drew down on Benning Rafiq Mahoud yelled out a warning. His shot went wild.

Benning cut across the ledge, making a dive for his weapon feet away.

Turning to keep the moving figure in his sights, Grover put weight on his damaged hip and it burned with pain.

He moved the muzzle again, searching briefly for Benning.

And saw the man bringing his own SMG on line.

LYONS SNATCHED the UMG from the ground, rolled on his back and jerked the trigger as he pulled Grover into his sights.

The H&K fired on full-auto, expending the remaining shots in the magazine. He saw the slugs pound Grover's body, turning the merc half around. Grover fell on his back, sliding down the face of the boulder, body limp. He slammed to the ground facedown.

"Benning."

Lyons glanced around. It was Rafiq, gesturing wildly. He was pointing to the far curve of the boulders. As Lyons looked that way, he heard the slam of a shot, felt something tear into his left thigh. The impact knocked him off his feet. Pushing back on the pain, Lyons lunged upright and stumbled in the direction of Rafiq's shelter. More shots crackled, slugs kicking up gouts of dirt. Lyons half fell over the protruding rock and hit the ground hard. For a moment he lay stunned, the pain from his wound triggering nausea.

Then he felt hands grasping his shirt, dragging him forward.

"Come on, Benning, this is no time to be lying down on the job."

Lyons got his good leg under him and pushed himself upright.

"This way," Rafiq urged. "There's cover."

Lyons wiped sweat from his eyes and saw they were moving into some kind of cave. It looked to go a long way back, and Lyons saw light at the far end.

They moved yards into the cave before Lyons heard the scuff of boots behind them. He hauled himself to a stop, leaning against the cave wall.

Greg Marino was there, his weapon aimed at Lyons.

"No more running, Benning. I'm tired of chasing you."

He centered the weapon.

Rafiq stepped around Lyons, shielding him with his own body.

"You'll have to shoot me first."

Marino's laugh had a nasty edge to it. "Maybe I'll do that, sonny."

"And lose your bounty?" Rafiq said.

"The hell with that," Marino said. "It would be worth it to just get rid of you."

Lyons felt something pushed against his hand. It was

Cujo's big hunting knife, the one he had passed to Rafiq. The kid was returning the knife from where he had it tucked behind his belt. Lyons grasped the handle in his right hand, feeling its solid weight. Rafiq was giving him a chance. A slender one. Maybe the only one they might get.

Marino had moved closer, his UMG still centered on Rafiq.

"You kill me, your employer isn't going to be very pleased."

"*He* won't be pleased? How the hell do you think I feel?" Marino snapped. "My crew is dead. My friends."

"You should have chosen better," Lyons said.

The muzzle of Marino's weapon wavered slightly.

"Boy, step aside. I'm going to blow that fucker away."

"Rafiq, move your butt," Lyons growled, and used his left arm to push him to one side.

Lyons's right hand raised the knife to shoulder height, then snapped forward, releasing it in the same moment Marino realized what was happening.

The steel blade spun through the air.

Marino pulled the H&K's trigger as Lyons dropped to his knees. The .45 slugs slammed into the cave wall over Lyons's head.

The heavy knife buried half its length in Marino's right shoulder. He howled in pain as the keen steel penetrated flesh and muscle.

Clenching his teeth as he pushed to his feet, Lyons went for the merc as Marino's weapon sagged in his grasp.

They came together in a savage embrace. Lyons grabbed at the handle of Cujo's knife and worked it back and forth. Marino screamed in agony. The subgun slipped from his fingers. Blood was gushing from the deep wound. Marino slammed a hard knee into Lyons's side, the blow knocking the Stony Man commando off balance. His wounded leg was threatening to give way and when Marino retaliated, pushing Lyons backward, he was unable to resist.

Marino came at him in a rush, catching Lyons full-on and slamming him back against the cave wall. Air was jolted from his lungs. Lyons grunted on impact, sucking breath back into his body. He lost his grip on the knife handle and Marino reached up with his left hand. He grasped the knife and dragged it from his flesh with a wild roar of defiance, turning it back on Lyons.

The big ex-cop saw it coming and swayed away from the keen edge of the bloody blade. He followed with a blinding strike from his right fist that slammed across Marino's jaw. The blow was powerful, delivered with all of Lyons's strength. It pushed the merc off balance and gave Lyons the momentum to follow through. He lunged forward, grabbing Marino's knife wrist and forcing the arm away. Marino recovered quickly, ignoring the pain engulfing his lower face and spitting blood from his mouth. He slammed a bunched fist into Lyons's side, over his ribs, drawing a gasp from his opponent's lips. Lyons countered, delivering a forearm slam into Marino's throat, then braced his good leg against the cave wall and pushed forward, forcing Marino to step back.

The moment Marino shifted his footing, Lyons hooked his right foot between the merc's legs and kicked the left foot off the ground. With Marino disadvantaged, Lyons about-faced, dragging the knife arm across his shoulder, used his hip to boost Marino off the cave floor and threw him over his shoulder. They were still close to the cave wall and Marino slammed into it. He dropped to the ground in a struggling heap, immediately turning his body to come to his feet. Lyons moved in quickly, stamping down hard on the hand holding Cujo's knife. Bone snapped and flesh split. The knife slid from Marino's grasp. Lyons kicked it out of reach.

Blood streaked Marino's face. His front was sodden with blood from the pulsing knife wound. Despite his injuries Marino was far from defeated. He rose to his feet, big hands clawing for a grip on Lyons. The Stony Man commando had no intention of getting into a close-quarter clinch with the man. Marino was a strong man and he was no beginner at close combat. Carl Lyons had a simple credo when it came to such situations. When the other guy was intent on doing harm, there were no gentlemanly rules to apply. It was a simple case of one dying and one living. Lyons had no death wish. With him it was do whatever was necessary to end the conflict.

Do it fast.

Do it hard.

And do it to the other guy.

Marino's stance told Lyons he was about to launch himself into some martial arts attack. If this had been one of those dumb movies Lyons would patiently wait until his opponent delivered his fancy move. Only this wasn't make-believe and Lyons had no thoughts on letting it happen. He took a quick forward step and blocked the merc's arm with his own. Lyons felt the force behind the strike the second he delivered his own punch. A hard fist that impacted against Marino's nose with extreme force, crushing it flat. Blood spurted in all directions, flowing down over Marino's mouth and jaw, spilling across his already blood-soaked shirtfront. The extreme pain stopped Marino in his tracks, and Lyons used the momentary paralysis to his advantage. He closed in on Marino and encircled his neck, gripping his own wrist to complete the move. He increased pressure, crushing down on

Marino's neck until he heard the crunch of the spine. The merc struggled in an attempt to lessen the effect, his hands reaching up to paw at Lyons's arms. The outcome was inevitable. Lyons braced himself, maintained his hold and gave a final, brutal twist. Marino arched briefly, his body shuddering, then became a limp weight in Lyons's arms. The Stony Man commando released his grip. Marino dropped to the cave floor, all resistance gone, in the formless way that only the dead could exhibit.

Leaning back against the cave wall, Lyons glanced across at Rafiq. He was motionless, his gaze flickering back and forth between Lyons and Marino.

Lyons decided he'd had enough and let himself slip to the cave floor, his back to the wall. He felt around in his back pocket and took out the butterfly knife he'd had there since leaving the cabin. He spun the knife, opening it and held it out to Rafiq.

"What?"

"Go cut some strips off his pant leg. Use them to make a pad and tie it over this damn bullet hole. If we can stop the bleeding, I can take a rest for a while."

Rafiq looked unsure but he did what Lyons told him. When he came back his face was pale.

"I could have done without that," he said, holding up the strips of material.

"I'll apologize later. Now cut my pants so we can get at the wound."

"What next? Are you going to ask me to cut out the bullet?"

"Not while your hand is shaking like that," Lyons said.

Rafiq managed a weak smile. He watched as Lyons did what he could to bind the wound.

"One last thing," Lyons said. "Go check those bodies.

See if they have any water bottles on their belts. After that I won't ask for anything else."

Rafiq returned with two water bottles. He passed one to Lyons.

"Sit down, Rafiq," Lyons said, taking the bottle and drinking. "Warm, but at least it's wet."

"Benning, we look a mess," Rafiq said. "Dirty. Bloody. I'm hungry and I don't think I'll ever be clean again."

"You'll feel better later. Believe me."

"I can't say it's been fun, Benning, but thanks for what you've done."

Lyons smiled briefly, leaned his head back and rested for a while. He still felt weak, bruised from head to toe, but decided he could walk.

"I think it's time we got the hell out these woods, kid. You up for that?"

"Best thing I've heard in days," Rafiq replied.

They made their way through the cave and emerged on the far side.

"We still heading west?" Rafiq asked.

"One thing for sure," Lyons said, "I'm not walking all the way back to that damn cabin."

Rafiq handed over one of the UMGs, now fully loaded.

"You think we might need this?"

Lyons took the weapon and checked it.

"Never can tell," he said.

Rafiq had picked up Cujo's knife, as well. When they reached the trees again he hunted around until he found a suitable lower limb. He chopped it from the tree and lopped off the smaller twigs, fashioning a crude crutch for Lyons.

"Hell, Rafiq, we'll make a mountain man out of you yet."

Sometime later they heard the distant sound of a helicopter. Lyons drew them into cover.

"You think it's that same one as yesterday?" Rafiq asked.

"Could be. We'll stay here until we know one way or another."

Lyons watched the chopper descend. It was casting back and forth and after a while he realized it was flying a search pattern. When it got close enough to identify, Lyons realized it was a police search and rescue unit. He pushed to his feet and stepped into the open, waving his arms. Rafiq joined him and they saw the helicopter turn in their direction, starting to fly lower.

"When we get out of here," Rafiq said, "can you ask them to fly us over the ocean? Just for a look. I'm sick of the sight of trees."

"Rafiq, you've got a deal."

CHAPTER TWENTY-SEVEN

"While I was trailing Bouvier, I took photographs of the places he went, the people he met with. I think there are some shots your people might be able to make use of. I haven't had time to sit down and review the shots myself, but you're welcome to check them out."

"Sounds good," Bolan said.

"We could download the images to your people," Sharon said. "Let them have a look and run them through their image databases. They might pick up something I've missed."

Bolan nodded. The images were loaded from Sharon's digital camera into the laptop. Bolan placed them in a folder and sent them in an encrypted form to Kurtzman. His accompanying e-mail asked for a full analysis and ID of anyone in the photographs. He received a reply confirming the arrival of the file and a promise to get back if anything showed up of interest.

"WE IDENTIFIED this guy straight off," Kurtzman said. "Mullah Wazir Homani. Radical guy. Lays into anyone and everything that is not strictly Muslim. There's no half-measures here. According to his way of thinking, we should all be wiped out. Scary guy. Definitely not on our list of friends."

"Isn't he connected to Mahoud?" Price asked.

"Yes, but not in the way you might expect."

Kurtzman swung his wheelchair around, catching Akira Tokaido's eye. Tokaido was Stony Man's ace computer hacker.

"Put them out of their misery," he said.

Tokaido tapped his keyboard, transferring from his monitor to one of the large wall screens. A number of photo images were displayed. Plainly taken through a long-distance lens, the shots were still sharp enough for identification.

"According to the date on the images, these shots were taken a few weeks back. Now the guy in black is Homani. Behind him in white we guess is one of his followers. The two in the badly fitting suits are his bodyguards. Younger guy next to Homani is Sharon's mark, Mohan Bouvier. The one I want you to look at closely is the woman with the group."

Brognola pushed to his feet and moved a little closer to the screen. He examined the image, turning to stare across the room at Barbara Price.

"Am I seeing right?" he asked her.

Price nodded. "I guess you are, Hal."

The young woman was Raika Mahoud.

"That isn't everything," Kurtzman said. "Look at the icing on the cake." He used his keyboard to move across the screen. "Almost missed this first time around."

"What are we looking for?" Brognola asked.

"This," the computer expert said.

He isolated a portion of the screen and began to enlarge it. The high-definition monitor on the wall held their attention as the captured image expanded under Kurtzman's skilled fingers. The section he was enlarging was of the rear door of the car. As the image grew, still hazy, Kurtzman cleaned it up, sharpening the outline and increasing the detail until he had an identifiable face.

"I know that face," Brognola said.

"You should," Kurtzman said. "Just to be sure we ran it through our facial recognition database and came up with a positive match. It's Corey Mandelson."

"And he runs the CIA's Paris section house," Brognola finished. He stepped up closer to the wall monitor. "What the hell is he doing with Homani, Bouvier and Raika Mahoud?"

"Good question," Price said. "I wish we had the answer."

"Aaron, you find out everything you can on all. I don't care whose toes you tread on. I want to know the connection. You know the drill."

"Hal, what about Mack and Carl? If there's something going on here, we need to find out if it's going to affect them."

Brognola glanced at her. "You think? Anyone managed to make contact with Carl yet?"

"No," Tokaido said. "I have a repeat signal going out to his phone, but it's still dead."

"Damn. All this cutting-edge technology and we can't even talk to the guy."

"Nothing we can do."

"So we sit around and twiddle our thumbs?" Brognola said testily.

Price crossed the room and faced him. "Hal, take five. Go have a walk outside. Let us do our jobs. Go call the President and update him."

"Yeah. I'll go call the Man and tell him we have squat. Nada," Brognola stated.

He walked out of the room, leaving a protracted silence in his wake. The tension could almost be felt.

"That went well," Carmen Delahunt, the former FBI agent, said solemnly.

Silence again until Price rounded on her.

"Oh yeah," she said, and then promptly burst out laughing.

Moments later the whole crew joined in.

"I think I'd better go find Hal," Price said as the laughter died down. "Guys, keep digging. We need some answers."

"We're on it," Kurtzman said.

PRICE MADE HER WAY outside and went looking for Brognola. She found him leaning against a fence, chewing ferociously on a cold cigar. She stood beside him and they remained silent for a couple of minutes.

"Hal, they're doing their best, and concerned about Mack and Carl. Every one of them has been at their station 'round the clock since things started happening. If they could pull results out of the air, don't you think they'd do it?"

Brognola took the cigar out of his mouth and stared at the frayed end, rolling it back and forth between his fingers.

"I used to love smoking these things. Every time I feel like firing one up I get a guilty feeling." He cleared his throat. "Just like I'm getting right now." He threw the cigar on the ground and crushed it under his shoe. He ran his fingers through his hair and smoothed his jacket down, turning to face her. "Is my tie straight, Miss Price?"

She adjusted the knot and arranged his shirt collar as she said, "It is now, Mr. Brognola."

They returned to the main building and made their way back toward the cyberunit.

CHAPTER TWENTY-EIGHT

"Sounds serious," Sharon said.

"As it can get," Bolan replied.

The Israeli turned from the open window. He was aware of Bolan's unease.

"I'm listening."

"It concerns Raika Mahoud," Bolan said. "Hear me out, Ben, then give me your opinion, because I could be way off. I hope to God I am, because if not this is going to hurt some good people."

Bolan crossed to the steaming coffeepot and poured himself a refill. He took a long swallow.

"From day one, when I meet Mahoud's family in Afghanistan, Raika has been a step away from everyone, as if she's removed from what's been happening. Nothing I could pin down. Just that she was remote, distant. She made it clear I wasn't included in her circle of friends. I put it down to the situation at first. She had a shell around her, isolating her from everything.

"Then we were deliberately targeted at the U.S. base when the Taliban hit. Again at the château and when Mahoud and I went to pick up his data from the bank."

"With you so far," Sharon said.

"The run of security breakdowns," Bolan said, "got me thinking someone close had been passing locations to interested parties."

Now it was Sharon's turn to show concern as Bolan's unspoken assumptions crystallized. He studied Bolan closely, saw the expression in the man's eyes and full realization slammed home.

"You believe Raika has been passing out locations, betraying her own father?"

Bolan took out the note Raika had left behind. Sharon read it, glanced at Bolan.

"Is it genuine?" he asked.

"Leila conformed the writing is her daughter's."

"You believe Raika left willingly?"

"Yes, Ben, read the message again."

Sharon scanned the note. "So what is it I'm missing?"

"Last line."

"...*tell Father I ask his forgiveness*...so she regrets leaving."

"You notice there's no mention of her mother?"

Sharon acknowledged with a brief nod. "Okay, maybe a little odd."

"I'm stepping way out of the box here, Ben. I think that last line is a plea to Mahoud. Raika is asking forgiveness for something she's planning to do. To her father."

Sharon digested the statement.

"You believe Raika is involved with the opposition planning to assassinate her father? She's been feeding them information?"

"It wouldn't be the first time loyalty has shifted within a family."

Sharon smiled at the truism. "I can't disagree there, but it doesn't have to mean betrayal. What about the boyfriend angle? Maybe Raika has run off to be with him. To get married even. That's happened before, too."

"A possibility. But I rate it pretty thin backed up against the rest of my evidence."

"Something I missed?"

Bolan nodded. "I wanted your input before I showed you this. It came through on my cell earlier. From my people after they ran through the download of your pictures."

He displayed the text message and handed the cell to Sharon. The Israeli read the message through twice before he looked back at Bolan.

"You recall where that shot was taken?"

Sharon nodded. "A private house on the edge of the Oberkamph district. I'd been trailing Bouvier and saw him go in and waited around. He came out with a girl and two men. I recognized Homani, but not the second man. Only just got a shot as he climbed into the car. I had never seen Raika Mahoud before that day, so I didn't know who she was until I met the family. And I didn't pay that much attention to her the day I took the shot. It was Bouvier and Homani who took my attention." Sharon shook his head in frustration. "Damn, I must be getting old. Letting something slip by me like that."

"Up close and personal can sometimes be too close," Bolan said. "Your principal was Bouvier. You recognized Homani because he's a known figure. The others were strangers to you. It would have come when your people processed the shots. Don't sweat it, Ben."

"So what do we do? That house could be a transit point for Homani's cells. Might be worth a look."

"Exactly what I was thinking," Bolan said. "Let's make it a night call."

"And Raika?"

"We keep everything about her between ourselves until it proves out, or doesn't. Agreed?"

"Agreed," Sharon said.

THE HOUSE WAS on the fringe of the Oberkamph. It wasn't run-down, but moving toward it. It stood among other buildings in similar condition, the worn facade of houses long past their best, but still able to offer a reasonable environment.

Bolan and Sharon were in the Israeli's vehicle, parked in shadow at the end of the street. They had been there for almost twenty minutes, watching the target house. During the time they had been waiting, no one had entered or left the building. Traffic was light on the poorly lit street.

"What do you think?" Sharon asked. "Time to move?"

"I think so," Bolan said. He glanced at his watch. "Almost nine."

They were both dressed in a somber black, holstered pistols beneath the zip jackets.

The men exited the car, stepped across to the sidewalk and approached the house. Bolan touched Sharon's arm as a light came on in an upstairs room.

"Someone's home."

The house was set back from the street, behind a low wall with iron railings and a metal gate. The gate was set wide open. Bolan and Sharon slipped through and moved quickly to the front of the house. Little light from the street reached the front of the building, so they were hidden by the shadows.

They moved around to the side and made their way along the concrete path edging the place. There was a high brick wall separating the house from the neighboring property. The house was larger than either man had assumed from the front. It went a long way back. When they reached the rear they saw a generous though over-grown garden.

"Door here," Sharon said.

Checking the window beside the door, Bolan looked in on a deserted kitchen. An open door on the far side showed light in the passage beyond.

Bolan tried the door, which was secured. Sharon examined the lock, then produced a slim leather case that held lock picks. He chose a couple and inserted them in the lock. He juggled the slim metal rods, patiently working them against the lock's interior mechanism until he was rewarded with a soft click. He replaced the probes in the case and put it away. When he opened the door a couple of inches he felt around the frame for any alarm sensors. Found nothing. Even so he opened the door just wide enough for he and Bolan to slip inside. Sharon carried out further checks on the door in case he had missed any other alarm device. He closed the door once he was satisfied, making sure the lock stayed open.

"I take it you've done this before," Bolan said.

"Only a few hundred times."

There was an electric kettle on the work surface nearby. Bolan put a hand on it and found it warm.

"Been used recently," he said.

Sharon had left his Desert Eagle at his apartment and brought along a .40-caliber Glock 23. He slipped a matte-black AAC Evolution suppressor from inside his jacket and screwed it onto the threaded section of the Glock's barrel.

"Let's do it," Bolan said.

They crossed the kitchen, moved into the passage and along to the foot of the stairs.

"I'll check the front room," Bolan said.

Sharon nodded and started up the stairs, his passage silent.

The door to the downstairs main room was standing partway open. Bolan nudged it with his foot, the door swinging wide. He leaned in to check the room. Empty. Not even any furniture.

Bolan retreated, started to turn, then heard the soft creak of a floorboard behind him.

He spun, faster than anyone might anticipate, and faced a pair of hardmen. One had a knife, the other, closer to Bolan, nothing. He lunged forward, hands reaching for the soldier. His move temporarily blocked the knife man. Bolan brought the Beretta up from his side in a powerful sweep. The cold steel slammed across the guy's exposed jaw, laying the flesh open to the bone. Blood began to wash from the ugly wound and the guy stumbled back into his partner, pushing him against the far wall. Following through, Bolan hit his attacker again, not holding back. The 93-R's solid weight delivered brutal blows. Bone crunched above the guy's left ear and he stumbled and dropped to the floor, too stunned to even cry out. Wanting him out of the fight, Bolan slammed a hard boot down across the back of the guy's neck, driving him facedown on the floor. The man didn't move again.

In the seconds from the initial attack, the guy wielding the knife recovered his balance. He launched himself forward, words tumbling in a torrent from his lips, his knife threatening as he closed in on Bolan. The language might have been foreign, but the force and intention behind the words was universal. Bolan stepped back, conscious of the slashing blade in the guy's hand. He felt the slightest touch of it across the front of his jacket and knew the leather had been cut. Before the guy could reverse his action Bolan struck, catching the knife wrist and forcing it down and away from his body. His hand holding the Beretta knuckled in and slammed the barrel hard across the bearded jaw. The man grunted under the stunning impact, but recovered and launched a hard knee of his own that slammed against Bolan's ribs.

Swiveling his body, Bolan twisted the guy's wrist savagely until the choice was for the man to drop the knife or have his bone snapped. He chose the former, the knife thudding to the floor. Bolan slammed the back of his skull into the face behind him and heard a satisfying crunch. Continuing his aggressive stance he about-faced, circled the guy's neck with his gun arm and caught hold of his own wrist, closing the grip. He pulled the man in tight, ignoring the rain of blows to his body. He could hear the rasp of the guy's labored breathing and increased his choke hold. The guy's frantic struggle used up all his remaining energy. Bolan pushed him against the wall, reducing the man's ability to fight back. Frantic jerking became slower as a lack of oxygen impaired the man's resistance. A final tightening of his hold took the guy over the edge. Bolan let the deadweight go.

He turned to climb the stairs and found Sharon bending over a still figure on the landing. Sharon had a bloody knife in his hand. The guy on the floor had an ear-to-ear deep incision in his throat weeping blood.

"Problem down there?" the Israeli asked.

"Not anymore."

Sharon returned his knife to its sheath and pulled out his pistol.

The Israeli indicated the door along the corridor. Both he and Bolan could hear a murmur of voices from the room.

They placed themselves at the door, one on each side, weapons ready.

"Be my guest," Sharon said.

Bolan hit the door with his booted foot, the powerful

blow taking it cleanly off the hinges. The shattered panel flew into the room, followed by Bolan and Sharon.

Of the four men in the room only one reacted fast enough to get off a shot from the handgun he snatched from his belt. The 9 mm slug hit the plaster wall over Sharon's head. The Israeli returned fire, his suppressed Glock sending a pair of slugs into the shooter's chest. The guy stumbled backward over an armchair.

Bolan had moved aside the moment he cleared the doorway, Beretta already tracking in on the startled men clustered around a desk holding a sophisticated computer setup.

One guy snatched up a matte-black SPAS combat shotgun, swinging the heavy weapon in Bolan's direction, mouthing a wild rant. The only word Bolan recognized was *Allah*. There was a wildness in his eyes that told Bolan all he needed to know. He dropped below the level of the weapon a microsecond before it discharged, the solid boom filling the room with sound. The high impact of the blast dug a hole in the plaster wall behind Bolan as he swung the Beretta two-handed, triggering a 3-round burst that hit at an angle, shredding its way into the guy's chest cavity and ravaging heart and lungs. One of the slugs burst from the left shoulder, ragged and bloody debris from the wound misting the air.

Sharon turned his Glock at one of the other two men and exchanged shots. The man went down in a gasping heap, clutching his bloody throat where Sharon's slugs had penetrated.

The surviving man sprang up from his chair at the computer and launched himself at Bolan as the American stood upright. The move caught Bolan off guard. The guy slammed into the Executioner, wrapping his long, muscular arms around him and shoving him across the room.

Bolan heard Sharon's warning yell. He couldn't understand why the Israeli was shouting.

What he hadn't seen were the glass-paned doors behind him leading into a smaller room. His attacker's full-on charge propelled them in the direction of the doors. They struck with their combined weight, shattering glass and splintering the wood frames. Bolan felt the back of his legs catch the lower section of the doors, felt himself falling, with his screaming attacker clinging to him. Glass and wood debris from the shattered doors followed them down. They hit the floor, wrestling against each other to gain the advantage.

Bolan forced back the other guy's head, his free hand wedged under his opponent's jaw. When he realized he was still holding on to the 93-R, Bolan slammed the solid metal of the pistol against the other guy's skull. The guy grunted, blood welling from the deep gash, but he still clawed for Bolan's throat, fingers digging in. Bolan hauled the Beretta around, jamming the muzzle beneath the guy's jaw and triggering a 3-round burst that blew out through the top of the man's skull, taking brain, bone and flesh with it. The guy's lifeless form slumped against him until the soldier rolled it aside.

Bolan groaned as he staggered to his feet.

Sharon appeared in the doorway. "Are you okay?"

"I'll ache in the morning, but at least I'll *have* tomorrow morning," Bolan replied.

"If you want some late-night reading, come take a look what I found." Sharon led Bolan to the desktop computer. "These guys were busy. I think we walked in on their major planning cell."

The Mossad agent pointed to items on screen, indicating recognizable words and phrases in among the script: Hamas, the Gaza Strip, Haifa, Sharif Mahoud.

There were references to a number of Middle East and Afghan locations. Dates. Other political and religious figures from around the regions.

"These are invited members of the conference," Sharon said. "This whole document reads like a timetable of upcoming events. Mossad had picked up background details on suspected attacks, but we had little more than that. Electronic chatter, I believe it's called, coming from various locations. Nothing concrete." Sharon thrust a hand at the screen. "This all starts to make sense of it."

"Ben, make copies. You can send it to your people. I can do the same. There's stuff that needs translation."

Sharon searched through the desk drawers and found a pack holding flash drives. He placed the first one in a USB port and began to download the computer's data.

Bolan spotted a cell phone on the desk. He picked it up and checked the call list, both made calls and received. There were repeat numbers, showing that certain ones had been used a number of times. He dropped the phone into his pocket and turned back to look over the rest of the room. A collection of printed images had been tacked to a section of the wall. Up close Bolan saw there were pictures of Mahoud, others of him with his family, images of Rahim Azal, now dead somewhere in Afghanistan, Jamal Mehet, murdered here in France because he was a friend of Mahoud.

Whatever else Mahoud's enemies were, they had put a great deal of effort into the attempts to kill him. Their intelligence gathering had been thorough.

Sharon came to stand beside Bolan. He studied the images.

"Mahoud has upset a lot of people," he said, and Bolan nodded. "I purged the computer," Sharon added. "Here, this is yours."

He handed Bolan one of the data sticks.

They walked out of the house and returned to their parked vehicle. Sharon turned and drove them back in the direction of his apartment.

CHAPTER TWENTY-NINE

Corey Mandelson emerged from his Paris apartment building, keying the remote for the Volkswagen Touarcg SUV. He opened the driver's door and slid onto the leather seat, pulling the door shut.

The click of the passenger door alerted him but he was too slow to do anything about the man who took the passenger seat beside him.

"Both hands on the wheel," the man said. He had an American accent.

"Who the hell—"

"I talk. You listen."

The man gestured with his right hand, held below window level so that only Mandelson could see the pistol resting across his thighs, the muzzle aimed at the CIA section chief.

"Start the car. Ease into the traffic and drive."

"Where to?"

"Give me a tour of the city. Enjoy it because it could be your last opportunity to view."

Mandelson rolled into the busy flow. Like any cosmo-politan city, Paris suffered from too much traffic, especially at this hour in the morning. It seemed every Parisian was going to work.

The man sitting beside Mandelson was clad in dark, casual clothing. Black pants and sweater. A thin leather jacket. His dark hair framed a strong face that still bore, though fading, the marks of recent violent activity. Mandelson chanced a quick look at the guy. Icy blue eyes stared back at him.

"Do you realize who I am?" Mandelson said.

"I know exactly who you are," Mack Bolan said. "By the way, I like the car. Standard CIA issue? Or does it come with your status as Paris section chief?"

"If you know so much about me, you'll realize the trouble you are in."

"You have that the wrong way 'round, Mandelson. I'm not the one with the problems."

The first flickering of unease stirred in Mandelson's stomach. His fingers gripped the leather-bound steering wheel a little too tightly, making his knuckles gleam white.

Bolan held back a smile. He noticed a fine sheen of sweat forming on Mandelson's forehead.

"You'll have to help here," Bolan said. "Just a couple of details I can't quite fit into the puzzle. What were you doing visiting Wazir Homani and Mohan Bouvier at a terrorist cell safehouse in the Oberkamph district a few weeks back? Bad slip there, Mandelson, because it was photographed."

The man's profile swam in and out of focus for a few moments before Mandelson made him.

Cooper.

The American who had seemingly stormed through Afghanistan and hauled out Sharif Mahoud and his family, and had been doing the same here in Paris.

There had been two hits on sites that came under Ali Asadi's jurisdiction.

First Mohan Bouvier's place, leaving the facilitator dead.

Then the strike against the safehouse Cooper had just mentioned. The local cell had been wiped out and valuable data taken.

Asadi was already climbing the walls over the hits. Mandelson had been catching all kinds of grief over the incidents from the man. He had even had a call from Homani, expressing his dismay at the events and demanding Mandelson look into them.

And now the son of a bitch responsible was sitting in Mandelson's car, pointing a gun at him, and not being coy about what he obviously knew.

"You realize I have a team of CIA operatives I can call in to rain down on you, Cooper. Just one call and I can make you disappear. Damn you, I work for the U.S. government."

"I think I'm right to say you *did* work for the U.S. government," Bolan said. "Until you sold out to potential enemies. You obviously made a pretty sharp deal there, Corey. Those offshore bank accounts. And the Swiss ones. Some hefty deposits there. You got shares, too? Maybe some MidEast oil? I wouldn't go expecting them to pay out next time you log on. They've been kind of frozen. I hope you made a cash withdrawal recently. There won't be any more coming."

"The hell you say. You can't touch my personal accounts. It's not legal."

"Nor is dealing with known terrorists. No need for me to list all your misdemeanors, Corey. You know what you've been doing. Unfortunately for you, so do we."

"We could make a deal. Work this out," Mandelson said. "If you understand my background, you'll know there's big money to be made. Some of it could be yours."

Bolan could almost smell the desperation in Mandelson's voice. He had realized his situation and was playing his only card.

"Anything you want, Cooper. Name your price."

"Okay, I'll make a deal, Mandelson. Give me the information I want, and maybe I won't shoot you right now."

Mandelson didn't know which way to turn. If Cooper was telling the truth and his hideaway funds had been discovered and frozen, then he had nothing to back himself with. The cash incentives deposited in his offshore and Swiss accounts had been his lifeline. His career had stalled and he had known for a long time his advancement wasn't going to happen. He had upset too many people back at Langley, and though nothing he had done gave them the power to push him out completely, the CIA had its own way of dealing with malcontents. So they had sent him to France, where he had been given charge of the Paris station. The people already there knew their jobs. They had resented Mandelson's appointment and he became a token figurehead. Langley waited him out, expecting him to put up with the posting until he'd had enough and put in his own papers. Mandelson understood the power playing, so he kept his head down, did his job while looking around for something he could work to his own advantage.

He found it when he was approached by Roger Dane and drawn into the world headed by Daniel Hartman. Mandelson was aware of Hartman. The man had a reputation and his activities were observed by the agency. Hartman was surrounded by powerful, influential figures from government and military, each with their own reasons for keeping the man protected. In return Hartman saw to it that any friends were well treated. Mandelson let himself be sucked in. It all seemed so easy. The advantages

of being under Hartman's wing began to pay off quickly
and Mandelson's personal circumstances became more
than tolerable. He was discreet nonetheless, understanding that suddenly displaying his new status would immediately arouse suspicions, and Langley would have
pounced on anything they could use to discredit him.

Eighteen months on and Mandelson was well and truly
part of Hartman's organization. He was able to supply
Hartman with useful information regarding political situations in Europe and the Middle East. Swathes of information came through the Paris station, from various sources.
It would be out, analyzed and forwarded to Langley. From
time to time Hartman would request data financial information that involved Europe and the UK, Russia and her
former satellites. He also had an insatiable appetite for
news on strategic flashpoints. Mandelson understood
Hartman's interest here. The man was involved in
armament production. The supply of ordnance. Hartman
realized no boundaries. Weapons were weapons. If there
was a market, he would supply. The same went for
Hartman's interest in natural resources. Oil. Minerals.
Mining rights. The list was endless. The people Hartman
had within his circle were the faceless fat cats who profited
from the misery and suffering of others.

Mandelson quickly allowed himself to become absorbed into that society. The money piling up in his accounts was all the incentive he needed.

When he was asked to assist in the Mahoud matter,
Mandelson agreed readily. He had heard about the man
and his dedication to striving for some kind of peace initiative. Hartman had pointed out that Mahoud was liable to
upset a very profitable apple cart if he pulled off his am-
bitious plan. By this time Mandelson was in deep. He
couldn't simply walk away. He understood enough about

Mandelson to realize it was not the done thing to desert ship. Hartman's influence was wide spread. The old phrase "I know people" meant just that with Hartman. The people he had in his pocket were truly powerful. Betray Hartman and all the man had to do was pick up a phone and Corey Mandelson would vanish from the face of the Earth.

At this moment in time Mandelson was caught between two bad choices.

Turn on Hartman—he was dead.

Refuse to help Cooper—that could have the same result. Mandelson was aware of the hell the man had been raising since he had shown up as Mahoud's protector.

What had started as a pleasant day was rapidly going down the toilet.

"You expect me to go against Daniel Hartman?" Mandelson gave a strangled laugh. "Might as well pull that trigger right now. You realize what a bastard he is? You do not cross Daniel Hartman."

"I want to find Raika Mahoud. And don't turn all coy, Mandelson. You know who I'm talking about."

"How do *I* know where she is?" he said, still trying a last-minute bluff.

"Because you work for Hartman and he's in bed with Homani and Asadi, until they decide you're no longer any use to them. It's time to look out for yourself, Mandelson. Nobody else will. Right now I'm the only one who can give you some kind of protection. Help me, I help you."

"How? If you say you worked out that I've turned, there's no way out for me. Once Hartman knows, he'll have me taken down because I know too much about his operations. Cooper, I'm fucked whichever way I run."

"Let's say I won't take it any farther if you furnish me with information on Homani. Give me that and I'll walk away. You take your chances with Hartman and your CIA buddies. Best I can do. Play straight with me and I promise I'll give you a fair run."

Mandelson considered the offer. It was the best he was about to get. Somewhere along the line someone, somewhere, might catch up with him. He smiled. Might? His days were numbered. But at least Cooper would slip the leash and allow him his last chance.

"Give me time and I'll call you. We fix a meet. I hand over what you want, then you turn your back and I walk. Deal?"

Bolan nodded. "Deal."

CHAPTER THIRTY

Hartman's anger manifested itself in a protracted silence. Only Dane understood. He raised a hand to placate Asadi who was working himself toward another argument. Dane gestured and guided Asadi out of the cabin. He closed the door, a nervous smile edging his lips.

"What is going on in there? Why does he just sit and refuse to speak?" Asadi asked.

"How do you express yourself when angry?"

"What?"

"It's a serious question, Mr. Asadi, sir. How do you show your anger? Frustration?"

"With strong words. I sometimes rage when matters do not reach a satisfactory conclusion. And the way things are progressing right now, you will soon have an example."

"Yes. When Mr. Hartman is in that state he simply retreats into himself. He doesn't raise his voice. He doesn't show signs of rage. He remains outwardly calm. Inside he is working out his anger and attempting to reach a solution."

"And when will he make his decision known to us? Understand me, Dane. I have little patience left. Things are not going well for us. We have lost men and equipment. And still, that damned man, Mahoud, is alive. Hartman and you. Homani and myself. We came together through a common enemy. Each of us wants Sharif Mahoud dead. Removed so that he will not attend the conference and spout his vile words. Yet here we are, only days away from the conference and we are unable to stop Mahoud. It would not amaze me if I saw that rabble-rouser walking on water. Something needs to be done and quickly. Now we learn that Mandelson has turned away. Seen with the man Cooper. He will not answer his phones. Stays out of sight. For all we know he may have given Cooper important information that could place us all in danger. No, this is not acceptable any longer. If Hartman cannot bring matters under control, I will sever our ties and make my own decisions."

Dane could understand Asadi's reluctance to carry on the way things were going. The man controlled a large group of dissidents. His own power and status was substantial. He was a formidable ally, and he would be a devastating enemy. Asadi's record when it came to terror attacks was impressive, and before the recent death of Mohan Bouvier, his intelligence network was the envy of many cells. If they lost Asadi, the effects would be dire as far as Hartman's Middle East operations were concerned. He held great sway across a wide area. Asadi's word meant a great deal to those who saw the continuing fight the only way to achieving their aims.

Asadi was astute enough to know that Sharif Mahoud's words could have such an effect, too, but in an opposite direction. Mahoud talked peace. He talked cooperation between factions. A resolution of old feuds. He was a superb orator, able to command respect when he stood in front of an audience. It was that ability to draw in the crowd and point out to them the futility of endless conflict, the destruction of communities and the misuse of religion and politics. Asadi feared the strength of Mahoud's arguments, the man's ability to persuade his listeners to at least consider an alternative. He was also concerned over the evidence Mahoud had gathered that might expose the transgressions of individuals attending the conference. Any underhand tricks, concealed deals between parties, anything that might suggest secretive alliances between groups or individuals would create a situation Mahoud could grasp and use to his advantage.

And Corey Mandelson's undesirable behavior wasn't helping things.

"Mr. Hartman is endeavoring to ensure the ongoing matters turn in our favor," Dane stated. "We must allow him his time to make his decisions. Do you understand, Asadi?"

"I understand that all the grand talk and gestures have not exactly worked out. We are no further forward than we were when we started. That is what I understand, and that is what concerns."

Asadi turned and gestured to one of his bodyguards. He spoke to the man in his own language, denying Dane any way of knowing what he was saying. The bulky man nodded, then walked away.

"I will be returning to the Cannes," Asadi said. "Contact me if your Mr. Hartman reaches his decision. I will be at my hotel."

"If that is what you wish. You are more than welcome to remain on board. *Crescent Moon* is always at your disposal."

Asadi's smile was icy, words just as bitter. "There is a certain truth in the saying 'keep your friends close and your enemies even closer.' Perhaps a little distance will allow Mr. Hartman an opportunity to reflect on that."

He walked away, descending the companionway to the lower deck. Leaning on the rail, Dane watched as the *Crescent Moon*'s motorboat pulled away and headed for the harbor.

Now what was Asadi up to? And what the hell did he mean about friends and enemies?

Unfortunately the man had been correct in his summation of their combined efforts at containing Mahoud. From Afghanistan to Paris, Sharif Mahoud had evaded them. Even his incarceration in the Taliban camp had come to nothing. The American, Cooper, had broken Mahoud out and they had escaped, taking on the teams sent to deal with them.

Was Asadi pulling out of the deal? Deciding to go on his own?

If he did, Hartman wasn't going to like it. The truth was, they had no real control over Asadi or Homani. They had come together in the face of a common enemy— Mahoud. They all had their reason for eliminating the man. He represented a real threat with his damned peace accord. Plus the added complication of his secret information. That meant different things to them all. Power over the individuals who might be politically and religiously affected by exposure. The ability to force them to toe the line by whoever held that information. There were a number of possibilities.

Hartman, Homani and Asadi all had their eye on the brass ring. Each had his own agenda, and their alliance was now starting to crumble.

Dane made his way to the main cabin. He saw Hartman raise a hand. He went inside and crossed to face his employer.

"I heard the boat leave. Has someone gone ashore?"

"I'm afraid it was Asadi. He decided to return to his

hotel. There were matters that needed his attention. Daniel, he's not happy. He sees the situation as a disaster."

Hartman smiled. "My feeling is Asadi doesn't have the vision to see this through."

"Where does that leave us?"

"Doing what we're good at. Sorting out problems, in our own, or someone else's backyard." Hartman smiled. "Don't look like that, Roger, we're not down and out yet."

"We lost the advantage of having Mahoud's son as a bargaining chip."

"But we still have other aces to play. If Asadi wants to opt out and do it his way, he might succeed and we still get what we want. In the meantime we move on."

"What do we do about Mandelson? If he does have a terminal change of heart, he could cause us problems."

Hartman nodded his agreement. "I think our best option here would be to cut all links with him. Have everything we've ever done where he's linked wiped from databases. Same with the money he's been paid. Have it taken off the books."

"And Mandelson?"

Hartman smiled his empty smile. "I'll look for his obituary in the newspapers. Very soon."

Dane reached for the phone. "Decourt is available."

"Good. Before you call, arrange for us to fly back home. Coming here to cement relations with our Middle Eastern friends hasn't quite achieved the results I was hoping for. And the way responses have been working against us, I don't want to wake up and find we have an unwelcome guest in the form of that man Cooper. Time we returned to our native soil, Roger."

It was the best news Dane had heard all week. He preferred the U.S. to these foreign countries. In these days of electronic business dealing there was no reason they had

to be on the spot. It was entirely possible to fix their deals
and screw the asses off their associates while sitting in
New York or Miami.

The thought of returning home cheered Dane and he
was almost humming as he walked up on deck. Leaning
against the rail, he turned on an unused, disposable cell
phone and tapped in a number.

His call was answered on the third ring.

"Jason, I'm going to arrange for a courier to deliver
something to you. Usual rates and procedures will apply."

"Time scale?"

"Immediate. This is important."

"Understood."

The line clicked dead.

Dane methodically stripped down the cell, snapping the
SIM card and dropping all the items over the rail into the
water. He turned back to the cabin and went to his office
where he put together the information, including photographs, that he was about to courier to Jason Decourt.

"Can't say it's been much of a pleasure, Corey," he
murmured to himself. "What the hell. You're going to die
a rich man."

He found that amusing and was still chuckling over it
hours later.

CHAPTER THIRTY-ONE

Mullah Wazir Homani had remained within his private study for most of the day. He made several telephone calls, none of which gave him the answers he wanted. He deliberated, made his decisions. After his midday prayers he called in his most devoted follower, an intense, lean young man named Yusef Masada.

Masada, as always, wore a white robe and skull cap. His serious demeanor was more than simply his utter devotion to Homani and God. The young man was the only survivor of an attack by American bombers that had mistakenly targeted the family home. Pulled from the rubble after three days, Masada hadn't been expected to live. Severely injured, his body terribly burned, though his face and hands had not been touched, he spent long months in hospital. His recovery had been slow, but his faith and the ministrations of Wazir Homani, a longtime family friend, had helped him pull through. Once recovered Masada had joined Homani, devoting his life to the mullah's cause and was constantly at his side. He never questioned Homani, saw only the positive in everything the mullah said or did.

He stood at Homani's desk, looking down on the man he respected with every fiber of his being. Homani indicated he sit on one of the chairs.

"I should not sit in your presence, sir," the bearded young man said reverently.

"Am I not your master, Yusef?"

"Of course, Mullah Homani."

"And my word is always to be obeyed?"

"Without question," Masada replied.

Homani spread his hands. "Then sit."

Masada did what he was ordered.

"You have been following the events of recent weeks?"

"Yes."

"Then you must be aware that my association with Asadi and the American, Hartman, have not produced the results we expected."

"Any association with Americans is bound by God's grace to fail. They are desecrators of every aspect of life. Corrupt. Without honor, or humility."

Homani allowed the young man his say. He wanted, needed, Masada's revulsion at the mere mention of anything American. His sheer hatred fueled the fire of his loathing.

"That was my first mistake. I am aware of Hartman's influence. His ability to supply material things we need. He also has widespread connections within our communities. I would have been a fool not to have taken advantage. We must allow ourselves to use the capitalist society to give us things we cannot obtain so easily. Once that has been accomplished, the Americans will be cast aside as dirt from beneath our shoes."

This time Masada didn't speak. He might have disapproved of any kind of connection with Americans, but he was wise enough not overstep the mark in front of the mullah.

Homani let the silence drift for a moment.

"I see now that Hartman, for all his wealth and power, was not the man to solve our problem."

"Sharif Mahoud?"

Homani nodded. "Yes. We both understand the need to eliminate Mahoud. The man's views are dangerous, as we know. His appearance at the forthcoming conference would generate unrest. He is a clever man, I cannot diminish that. His rhetoric could easily sway many of the delegates toward his views, and if that occurs, much of my own influence would be weakened. And we are not unaware that Mahoud is in league with the Americans. Even the U.S. President has sanctioned Mahoud's presence at the conference. Even to the extent of sending one of his infamous assassins, this man Cooper, to assist Mahoud."

Masada's head rose sharply and for a moment he seemed ready to rise from his seat. A gentle movement of Homani's hand calmed him.

"I may be getting old, Yusef, but my senses have not been dulled. The power of words is great. Simply observe how they spring from the pages of the Koran and bestow their truths on our faithful. In his own way, Sharif Mahoud holds that strength within his words, though he mouths those words as instructed by the infidels."

"Then he must be stopped," Masada said.

Homani nodded, seeing the interest gleaming in the younger man's eyes. He leaned forward across the desk, eager to keep the momentum of the moment.

"Yes. Mahoud must be silenced permanently. And I believed the honor should go to you, Yusef."

"You consider me worthy of accepting such a task, Master? I am less than nothing. When my family died, I was not considered worthy enough to enter Paradise. God looked on me and turned me from the gates."

"My son, He did such a thing because He had greater plans for you. Your time had yet to come. Now it has, and if you do His bidding, then your entry into Paradise will be of greater significance. Yusef, accept this gift from God."

Masada's gaze lowered with humility. "If this is your wish, Mullah Homani, then I accept and offer my life if it will accomplish my mission."

"Getting close to Mahoud would have been difficult. But I believe I have found a way. We are fortunate to have within our ranks another faithful to the cause who has come back to us. Someone willing to stand next to you in the moment of your triumph."

Homani rose and crossed the room to a door at the opposite end. He opened it and beckoned to someone.

"Yusef, here is your way to Mahoud's side."

Masada raised his eyes and looked on the vision of loveliness he had believed he would never see again. He rose clumsily to his feet, a rare smile crossing his face.

"For this I will go to Paradise fulfilled," he said.

And Raika Mahoud smiled back at him.

CHAPTER THIRTY-TWO

Carmen Delahunt had been scrolling through the images from Ben Sharon's camera, moving forward, then back as she studied the high-definition monitor. She was so intent on her task she didn't notice the time slipping by until Barbara Price came to stand behind her, placing her hands on the high back of the comfortable chair.

"How about a mug of Aaron's coffee?" Price said.

"Yes, that would be nice."

"Now I know you're onto something."

Delahunt leaned back, tearing her eyes from the screen and eased her chair around. She took a moment to stretch.

"Did I just say yes to Aaron's coffee?"

Price nodded. "You did."

"I need to get out more."

"So tell me what's got your attention."

Delahunt took a breath. "Something has been bugging me about these images. I might be imagining it. Take a look yourself and see if you spot what I have."

Price pulled a spare seat alongside Delahunt's and sat.

"So what am I looking for?"

"These four shots. All taken within a minute or so of

each other. Ignore everyone except for Raika Mahoud and the young bearded guy in white. I'll show them in order for you."

Delahunt keyed in the strokes that would display the shots in order, on a loop. When number four was reached, the display returned to number one again. There was enough of a time delay to allow the viewer a reasonable look at each shot.

"Take your time," Delahunt said.

Price let the display run a few times. Then she began to toggle back and forth. Delahunt could see she was studying the images closely, as she herself had been doing. Finally, Price sat back.

"He can't take his eyes off her," she said.

"Just what I thought," Delahunt said.

"Maybe this is the mysterious boyfriend Mack told us about. I'd better get this to Mack."

BOLAN ABSORBED the news in grim silence. "Any other information?"

Price cleared her throat. "Aaron has had the team working overtime on all the names we've come up with. Now we have Mandelson locked in with Hartman, he's trawling every call and e-mail coming from Hartman's sources. Electronic chatter is netting us some interesting snippets. Our friend Hartman's CEO, Roger Dane, keeps popping up. That man is a serious communicator. We can connect him to Ali Asadi, couple of high-flyers from the armament industry and some influential bankers, one of whom has been under investigation for illegal dealing."

"Under investigation suggests nothing has been proved yet?"

"These are slippery guys, Striker. Hartman is a man

with connections. He works suspect deals across the board and doesn't seem to care how many lines he crosses."

"The threat of Mahoud's revelations seems to have unnerved him. He's been doing his best to suppress it and have Mahoud eliminated."

"Nothing like having all your dirty deeds brought into the open to touch a raw nerve."

"Keep the guys digging. Anything they come up with, Hal will know how to use."

"Do you think Raika Mahoud is going to do something crazy? I just don't get this deal of hers with Homani."

"I'm trying to get a handle on it myself," Bolan said. "Are we any closer to who leaked the deal between the President and Mahoud?"

"Uh-uh. Aaron has Hunt on it full-time, but no joy." Price was referring to Huntington Wethers, a former Berkley professor of cybernetics.

"Okay. Keep me updated."

"One last thing. We isolated this young guy's face and ran him through facial recognition programs. His name is Yusef Masada. Aaron found a sheet on him in Agency databases."

"After asking permission?"

"Of course," Price said. "What kind of an outfit do you think we're running here?"

"So what did we learn about Masada?"

"A U.S. raid launched missiles that hit off target. Masada was the only survivor. He was badly burned and spent months in recovery. It appears our friend Mullah Homani was a family friend. Took the young man under his wing and brought him into his group. Masada became faithful to the mullah. He spent some time in a training camp where, according to reports, he became proficient in weapons and explosives. He's wanted on suspicion of

being involved in at least three car bombings in Afghanistan and an assassination in Iraq. He's known to have developed a pathological hatred of anything American. His
profile suggest he's a dangerous individual."

"Can you send me a photo image?"

"It's already on its way through Sharon's e-mail link.
You watch out for this Masada, Striker."

When the image came through Bolan took Sharon
aside, showing him the picture. He briefed the Mossad
agent on Masada and explained the link between the man
and Raika Mahoud.

"Your people are very perceptive," Sharon said.

"They're usually right when it comes to something like
this," Bolan said. "Homani will use this attraction to his
advantage. He'll get Raika to move Masada in close to her
father. Possibly use the pretext Masada *is* her boyfriend
and she's been with him. Now she's had a change of heart
and wants to bring him to meet her family."

"Masada gets close and takes out Mahoud?"

"Our information told us Masada trained in the use of
explosives as well as weapons. What if he shows up
wearing a bomb under his clothes?"

"Homani could persuade him the sacrifice was necessary, a chance for Masada to earn his entry into Paradise."
Sharon glanced across the apartment where Mahoud and
his family were seated. "If Masada succeeded, he could
wipe out the whole family. And if Raika is with him?"

"We discussed this before, Ben. If Raika has joined
Homani, she might well be willing to sacrifice herself to
fulfill his wishes."

Sharon scrubbed a hand through his hair in a gesture
of frustration.

"My God, this gets worse."

"Nature of the beast," Bolan said. "We need to find

where Homani has Raika and this Masada before they decide to do anything."

"I'll get the word out to all my contacts," Sharon said.

"I'm still hoping Mandelson might come through. Thin chance but it might happen."

"The man has few options left."

BOLAN TRIED TO REST. Until they came up with answers, there wasn't much else he could do. He was on a brief stand-down now that the Mahoud family had been moved out of Sharon's apartment and taken to the U.S. Embassy. Through Brognola, Bolan's request had been passed to the President. Agreeing to the decision, the President had called the ambassador and requested Mahoud and his family be escorted there, where they would stay until the time of the conference.

Mahoud had been clearly disappointed that Bolan was stepping aside, but he understood the choice of location. In truth he was grateful that his wife and daughter would be safer at the embassy.

"Will I see you at the conference?"

Bolan smiled. "I expect so. Someone needs to cover your back."

"It has been an interesting time, Matt Cooper. And a privilege. I owe you a great deal. I owe you my life."

"If I recall, you did a great deal of covering my back out there, Reef."

"Thank you for my family."

"Your family can speak for itself," Leila said. She put her arms around Bolan and kissed him on the cheek. "Thank you. Stay safe, Matthew Cooper."

Amina cried unashamedly as she clung to Bolan. He held her in his arms as she touched his cheek.

"Try not to get hurt anymore," she said. "You do seem to fall down a lot and get cuts and bruises."

Bolan couldn't resist a wide grin at that.

"I will try to avoid that, young lady."

"And see if you can find Raika," the girl said. "Tell her she should come back home. And bring her boyfriend, too, if she wants. Even though she is a pain, I do miss her."

"I'll do what I can."

Bolan kept recalling Amina's final request. He understood the feeling behind it, but he was still doubtful any reconciliation was on the books.

He tried to get some sleep, but it was hard to get there. It seemed he had only closed his eyes for a moment when his cell rang. Bolan sat up as he recognized Corey Mandelson's voice.

"One hour." He gave Bolan a location in the city. "Just you. Anyone else and I walk away. No games, Cooper. I might be a loser in this but I know my job. I'll spot any backup. You want Masada and the girl, do what I ask. No games."

CHAPTER THIRTY-THREE

Bolan was at the rendezvous point early. He paid the driver and stepped out of the cab. It swung around and disappeared the way it had come. The sky was heavy with storm clouds and rain started to fall as he made his way along the narrow, deserted sidewalk. Long-established antique and art shops lined the street, though they were not doing much business at the moment. Bolan turned up the collar of his coat.

The crooked line of the street segued into a small church just before it curved off to the right. Bolan spotted the low stone wall that bounded the entrance to the church grounds. It had an arched stone frame formed above the wooden gates. A figure hunched in a tan trench coat stood beneath the arch, water dripping from the stone overhead.

It was Mandelson. He had a cigarette in his mouth, and he was dragging on it heavily.

"I know, they're bad for my health," Mandelson said as Bolan reached him. "Doesn't seem to matter much now."

He thrust his hand into one of the trench coat pockets and took out a slim flash drive. He handed it to Bolan who dropped it in his inside pocket.

"It's all on there. Location of Homani's retreat, as he calls it. The son of a bitch uses the place for recruiting followers. They get the full indoctrination there. Go in wide-eyed and full of hope, come out the other side card-carrying extremists just itching to earn their tickets to Paradise."

"Is that what happened to Raika Mahoud?"

"Did it ever. She came ready to denounce her dear daddy as a spawn of the devil. A puppet of American culture. That girl carried so much hate for what Mahoud's doing. She was already halfway turned on day one. It must have been like Christmas and New Year rolled into one for Homani. Sharif Mahoud's precious daughter. He gave her the full treatment and she lapped it up. Couldn't listen to enough of his propaganda. By the time she went back home Raika was all fired up. She would have done anything Homani wanted."

Mandelson dropped his cigarette butt and fired up a fresh one.

"Raika is the one sending information about Mahoud's locations?" Bolan asked. "Using her cell to set her father up?"

"Smart girl," Mandelson said. "Homani and Asadi worked on her really well. The spying work was her first mission. She picked up on the details about Mahoud's deal with the U.S. President. He told his family what he had arranged, so Raika had the information straight from her own daddy. Even knew your name. When they all went to Afghanistan she was phoning in regularly with everything Mahoud talked about. When you picked the family up in Afghanistan and took them to the Army base, she called in and told Homani just where you all were."

Mandelson paused to drag on his cigarette.

And it was then the first bullet struck him in the chest.

It was a heavy caliber that burned its way through and blew out a hole between Mandelson's shoulders on exit. The sound of the shot filled Bolan's ears as he saw the CIA man twist away from him, his face rigid with shock. Before Mandelson's knees had started to buckle, three more shots hammered at his body, each one capable of inflicting a fatal injury. As Mandelson fell, another shot sent a slug screaming past Bolan as he threw himself away from the bullet-ravaged target. This slug hit the wooden gate, blowing chunks of timber into the air. More shots followed, but Bolan had swung around the side of the archway and dived over the low wall. He struck the rain-sodden lawn on the other side, pulling his body to the base of the wall, his right hand working inside his coat to unlimber the Beretta.

Mandelson was down and there was no point in checking him. The shooter had known what he was doing. His shots had been well placed. Fired for maximum effect, the slugs had ensured Mandelson wouldn't be walking away from the attack.

More shots slammed into the stone wall, confirming that the shooter wanted his second target now.

Mack Bolan.

With the 93-R set for triple bursts, Bolan moved along the wall until he could risk a low-profile look. Recalling Mandelson's position when the first shot struck, Bolan figured the angle. The most likely shooting spot was a narrow alley between two of the shops some way back along the street. The rain made it hard to get a clear view into the shadowed alley.

He waited, wondering if the shooter had moved away now Mandelson was down.

He wiped that thought.

The guy was still out there, biding his time and hoping

Bolan made the first mistake. Mistakes were what often ended this kind of situation. One of the opposing parties got tired of waiting. Or figured it was safe to come out.

Time was running out for both of them. Though the street was empty, due in part to the rain, Bolan felt sure someone inside one of the shops had called the police. It wouldn't be too long before the cops showed up. Bolan didn't want to get involved with the local law. French police tended to be a feisty bunch, prone to lots of shouting and brandishing pistols that came with obligatory itchy trigger-fingers. And the French authorities became very belligerent toward foreigners indulging in unlawful shooting matches on the streets.

Bolan glanced over his shoulder. Beyond the squat gray bulk of the church tall trees filled the area. If he could get himself lost in the timber he might be able to slip away and lose the shooter. Bolan saw no profit staying where he was. He had no hot desire to become involved with the shooter and his heavy artillery.

Between Bolan and the church building were a straggling number of headstones sticking up from the grassed area. They were large enough to provide cover. He could use them to work his way to the church itself, then move along the side and into the trees.

With his mind made up Bolan pushed away from the wall, staying as low as he could. It worked for the first few yards, but it made moving awkward.

The shooter, seeing his target backing off, opened up with a volley of shots that cleared the low wall and burned air over Bolan's head. He reached the first set of headstones, slipping behind as slugs began to smash against the weatherworn stone, blowing sharp chips into the air.

As the shots faded into silence, Bolan chanced a look back and saw the dark figure coming across the street, heading for the church.

Shooting on the move with a big rifle wasn't conducive to accurate results. Bolan decided to use that fact to cover him. He pushed his feet under him, rose and powered away from cover. He had gained a few yards when the thunder of the shooter's weapon reached him. The slug clipped the headstone he was passing. Bolan felt something slice across the back of his left hand, leaving a stinging reminder. He spotted a solid-looking headstone in his path and vaulted over it, turning and dropping into its cover.

Raising his head, Bolan saw the dark-clad figure slide to a halt, raising his rifle. The guy was well inside the Beretta's range now. Bolan braced his wrists on the top of the headstone, tracking in quickly.

The rifle fired. The large-caliber slug passed through Bolan's jacket at shoulder level without touching flesh.

Bolan's finger stroked the 93-R's light trigger and it spit a 3-round burst. The 9 mm Parabellum rounds were on target. The rifle shooter stepped back, his eyes wide in the pale blur of his face. The rifle sagged. Bolan hit him with two more triple bursts and the shooter fell stiff-legged onto his back, the rifle jerking from his slack grip.

Upright, Bolan slid the Beretta back into its holster and closed his coat. Now he could hear the approaching sound of sirens. It was time to leave. He turned and made his way down the side of the church, moving into the trees where the shadows swallowed him.

The Executioner was moving on. The end of his mission was in sight now. Just one more phase to complete.

CHAPTER THIRTY-FOUR

The Loire Valley was a region of natural beauty, vineyards and an almost pastoral tranquility. Mack Bolan had made the trip from Paris to confront one of the many faces of evil. His thoughts were far removed from anything the Loire might offer.

Mandelson's data had described the route and what they would find at the end of the journey.

The retreat, based on an old farm estate, was described as a place of peace and harmony, where the words of Islam could be contemplated in restful surroundings. The first part was correct. The house and outbuildings were original structures, the stone and timbers worn with age. The farm stood in extensive lands, surrounded by green fields, timber and a thin stream winding its way down from low hills. The farm stood isolated, the closest neighbor over three miles away.

"Chose the spot well," Sharon said.

Bolan had parked the SUV off road. He was checking out the farm through a pair of powerful binoculars. There was little movement around the site. No sign of any kind of work going on. Mandelson's information had indicated there was a permanent armed staff of at least six, who made certain Homani had no unwelcome visitors. He did spot a couple of men at the front of the main building where three cars were parked. Neither man appeared to be carrying a weapon but it was possible they had pistols under their coats.

"I have to ask this," Sharon said. "Matt, you haven't told me what you intend if you face off with Raika."

Bolan glanced at him. "Because I'm not sure. Take her back to her family. To somewhere she can be talked out of her condition. It's something I can't give you an answer for, Ben."

"Whatever you do, don't allow feelings to cause you to stall when it happens. You understand that?"

"It's what worries me." Bolan understood Sharon's concern. "I won't let it compromise the situation, Ben." He put the binoculars aside. "Let's get this done."

Bolan eased the SUV deep into the trees and undergrowth edging the narrow approach road.

He and Sharon, clad in combat gear, performed a final check of their weapons and moved out, using the natural terrain and heavy foliage to cover their approach to Homani's retreat.

Corey Mandelson's background on the place had informed them the farm, outwardly innocent, had been internally altered to provide a training ground for Homani's acolytes. His trainees went through religious and combat indoctrination in the cellar area under the main house. Here were soundproofed sections for weapons practice and training in physical combat. The farm had become a breeding ground for Homani's extremist cells. The mullah chose his people, grounded them, then sent them out to do his bidding. Homani selected only a few pupils at any one time, preferring smaller numbers who were solidly trained, rather than too many who might be inefficient.

It took Bolan and Sharon half an hour before they reached the perimeter of the farm property. Concealed in long grass with a simple wood fence the only barrier, the pair took its time looking over the place. They scanned the eaves of the buildings for video cameras, but saw no sign of electronic surveillance.

"Someone's coming this way," Sharon said.

They watched the patrolling sentry strolling along the beaten path that ran parallel to the fence. He was a stocky man, casually dressed. Up close Bolan was able to spot the pistol in a shoulder rig exposed as the guy's light windbreaker flapped open. He also carried a compact transceiver, and as he neared where Bolan and Sharon lay they could hear the intermittent chatter coming through the set.

The sentry passed by, moving on, his solid, measured tread suggesting he had been tramping the perimeter for some time. As dedicated as any sentry might be at the start of his patrol, it became boring after a long shift. Senses dulled and slackness started to creep in.

"No point waiting until his partner shows," Sharon said. "You agree?"

Bolan nodded, swung his Uzi and pushed to his feet. He eased over the fence and cat-footed after the sentry. The guy never saw or heard a thing. Bolan stepped up behind him and encircled the guy's neck, pulling him tight as he applied a choke hold. The transceiver slipped from his hand as Bolan's grip tightened, the effect of the hold rendering the sentry unconscious. Bolan lowered the limp figure to the ground. He picked up the transceiver and switched it off. As Sharon joined him, the Executioner slipped the pistol from the sentry's shoulder holster. It was a 9 mm SIG-Sauer P-226, with a 15-round magazine. There was a second magazine in a belt holder. Bolan slipped it free and pocketed it.

"Let's go," he said, pushing to his feet.

They cut across to the wall of the closest building, flattening against it.

Before either of them could move on, a warning shout alerted them. It came from their right. Following the call, the stutter of autofire broke the comparative silence, slugs peppering the ground just feet short.

"Break off," Bolan said.

Sharon moved to the left, while Bolan dropped to a crouch, bringing up the SIG and sighting in on the bulky figure of the auto shooter. The guy was large, heavy-bodied, and he moved awkwardly because of his size. He also presented a good target. Bolan's pair of 9 mm slugs slammed into his chest. The guy stumbled, looking down at his punctured body, then went down hard.

Bolan, on his feet, sprinted past the downed sentry, rounding the end of the building. The main house lay ahead, across a stretch of open ground. He remained at the corner of the building, using it as cover. From behind he heard the unmistakable thunder of Sharon's Desert Eagle.

A pair of armed figures tumbled out of a rear door of the main building. Both were carrying 5.56 mm SIG auto-rifles. They set off across the open space, moving in a line that would bring them to his position.

Bolan stepped into view, the P-226 already at arm's length. He put two fast shots into the closest guy, punching the 9 mm slugs into his lean frame, then switched to the second man. The autorifle crackled as the guy's finger hit the trigger hastily, the burst of slugs going wild. Two 9 mm bullets put him down in a pained flurry. He was jerking in spasms as Bolan closed in and placed a third shot into his skull. As he moved past, Bolan scooped up one of the autorifles, tucking the P-226 behind his belt.

He reached the rear wall of the house, pressed against it as the door flew open again. A tall, dark, bearded man eased out, hesitating when he saw his two partners on the ground. He raised his autorifle and tracked it back and forth, searching. As he came around to where Bolan was waiting all he saw was a dark blur. The soldier had his own weapon on line, and he hit the guy with a short burst that flipped him off the step and dropped him to the ground in a bloody heap.

Bolan stepped up to the rear door and grasped the handle. He jerked the door wide, the autorifle probing ahead, and moved inside.

BEN SHARON ROUNDED the back end of the large outbuilding and almost onto the muzzle of a SIG autorifle. The other man was just as startled. Sharon immediately dropped to the ground, sweeping the other guy's feet from under him. The man landed hard on his back, Sharon rolling clear and back on his own feet. He angled the big Desert Eagle and pumped a pair of .44 Magnum slugs into the prone figure. Although he was also carrying a 9 mm Uzi, Sharon bent and retrieved the sentry's SIG autorifle. A weapon with a 30 round magazine was too good to pass up.

Sharon tracked across the rear of the outhouse. He heard shots from the distance and knew Bolan had encountered more of Homani's crew. Angling right, Sharon picked up speed. As he reached the end of the outbuilding, the main house facing him, he saw Bolan as the tall American stepped inside the building. Seconds later autofire erupted from inside the house.

BOLAN CROSSED the empty kitchen, reaching the door as an armed figure stepped to the opening at the same moment. The Executioner's fast reflexes gave him the advantage and he slammed the assault rifle into the other guy's face. Blood flared from gouged flesh as the guy stumbled back from the door, his eyes glazed. Bolan hit him with a close burst that cored in and blew out through his spine, leaving a glistening smear on the wall.

A commotion rose from one of the rooms along the passage. At the door Bolan saw a group of white-robed figures milling around in confusion. They were mostly male, but he saw a couple of females. Their confusion was genuine. Bolan aimed the autorifle at the ceiling and triggered a burst that showered the room with plaster dust.

"Out," he yelled. "Get out now."

Bolan stepped back as the room emptied, the robed figures jostling as they crowded past him. He grabbed a man's arm. "Homani? Mullah Homani?"

The man stared at him. Bolan caught him by the throat, pushed him against the wall.

"Homani?"

The man pointed at the floor. "Below," he mumbled in a choked word. Bolan let him go and the guy ran after his departing colleagues.

"In the cellar," a familiar voice said.

It was Sharon. He had followed Bolan into the house.

"Let's find it," Bolan snapped, and headed along the passage. They hit the front section of the house. The main door had been flung open. Outside Bolan caught a glimpse of the robed figures spread across the front area. He slammed the heavy door shut and worked bolts to secure it.

"Here," Sharon said.

Bolan joined him. A short flight of worn stone steps led toward the cellar.

"Go ahead," Sharon said. "I'll check out the rest of the place in case we still have hostiles sneaking about."

"Watch your back."

Sharon nodded. He stayed at the head of the cellar steps as Bolan moved down and through the open door.

CHAPTER THIRTY-FIVE

Bolan felt the chill of the cellar creep over him. It was well lit, fluorescent lights in the ceiling showing him the open area ahead. It was partly filled by packing cases, unused furniture, the universal debris that was on display in a thousand other cellars.

Stone pillars were interspersed at intervals, supports for the house above Bolan's head. At the extreme side of this section, an opening showed where the cellar area branched off. Bolan guess the cellar's dimensions were as generous as the main house. Somewhere he could hear the subdued noise of a generator supplying power to the farm. He could smell diesel oil.

A faint sound alerted him to the presence of others. Bolan followed the noise and arrived at the archway that led through to the extended cellar area. He paused before he stepped through.

Something warned him to be more than cautious.

Bolan waited, close to whitewashed wall. Ahead the new passage was uneven, extra pillars adding a series of alcoves. His wait was rewarded by a flicker of shadow falling on the smooth concrete floor from behind one of the alcoves.

Bolan's rubber-soled combat boots made no discernible sound on the floor as he stepped forward, his eyes fixed on the jutting shadow. He drew level with the alcove, picked up a faint breath as his would-be attacker braced for his move. Bolan feinted, heard the rasp of breath and saw the dark figure lean out, a combat knife catching light as it came at him. Bolan drew back and used the autorifle in a clubbing smash that hammered at the arm holding the knife. The attacker gasped, the blade spinning from numbed fingers, blood starting to bubble from the gashed flesh of his arm. Bolan turned fast, sweeping up the rifle and slugging the guy across the side of his face. The impact bounced the man off the wall. Bolan went in close, hammering at the guy with the solid autorifle onto the torso and head, rolling him along the wall until he stumbled and went down on one knee, head hanging. Blood dripped from him in long strings. He pushed upright, using the wall, his bloody face turning to stare at Bolan.

The man was Ali Asadi.

Recognizing Bolan, the man vented his frustration at the American's interference in the Mahoud affair. His angered scream echoed along the passage.

"No more," he roared. "You interfere no more."

He went for the pistol holstered on his hip. It was a futile gesture.

Bolan triggered the autorifle and punched in a half dozen 5.56 mm slugs that chewed Asadi's insides apart, bloodying his torso and knocking him back along the passage. He hit the floor, writhing and clawing at the air until Bolan ended it with a double tap to his skull, spreading Ali Asadi's brains across the concrete floor.

The Executioner moved along the passage, passing an opening that showed him a deserted shooting range. Next was an open area with padded dojo mats spread across the floor.

Mandelson had been honest in his data. The farm was more than a spiritual retreat. It *was* a training base for Homani's extremist students.

There was a final opening. Light flooded from the room beyond. Bolan edged up to it, glancing inside. The moment his gaze settled on the equipment spread over the benches and on the racks around the walls Bolan knew he was looking at Homani's bomb room. The bench surfaces were covered in antistatic layers to prevent the chance of accidental explosions. A series of vented extraction units kept the air clear of vapors. Even the light fittings were housed behind wired glass.

Five people were in the room.

Homani himself, clad in his somber black robes. His thin hands were clasped together across his stomach. Flanking him were his two dark-suited bodyguards, expressionless, their eyes fixed on Bolan as he eased into the opening, the autorifle covering them.

A few feet away, still in his pristine-white robes was Yusef Masada. When he saw Bolan, he was unable to prevent the anger that burned behind his eyes.

And then there was Raika Mahoud. She refused to look Bolan in the eye after recognizing him. She lowered her head, gazing at her feet.

"A little late for contrition, Raika," Bolan said.

She spoke softly, but Bolan felt the conviction in her words. "I do not recognize your right to challenge me. My choice has been made. My life is here. With Mullah Homani."

"Your father would be hurt to hear you say that. He loves you very much."

"My father no longer exists. The man you know as

Sharif Mahoud is a traitor to our faith. He trails at the heels of the infidels and does their evil bidding. He is a betrayer of all that is holy in our lives."

Bolan had stepped inside the room, his back to the solid wall.

"I have to congratulate you, Homani. Raika *is* a convert. You must be proud. One more for the ranks of the faithful ready to die for you."

"The Western mind is unable to realize the dedication of the true believer. In our faith we do not consider the existence in this life. We are here to serve God. Sacrifice is a joy because it fulfills our purpose. To die in the name of God is to be blessed."

"As long as that sacrifice doesn't include you? I don't see Mullah Homani strapping on an explosive belt and walking into a crowd. I see your faithful doing that while you hide behind closed doors, counting your oil shares."

Homani stiffened in anger. Bolan held the mullah's gaze, reading what lay behind the man's eyes. He knew he had scored. Homani recovered, raising a thin arm and jabbing a bony finger at Bolan.

"This is how the Americans judge us. They fail to understand and fight that ignorance by accusing us of hypocrisy."

"Sharif Mahoud is willing to put his life on the line to procure some kind of peace throughout the region. He uses his faith in the way only a true believer should. Is an end to war wrong? A possibility of relief for all those suffering because of the madness? Deny that, Homani, and *you* are the traitor to your cause."

Homani didn't respond. He was watching Masada. The young man had edged closer to the workbench next to him. Masada stepped up to the bench and reached for the body-wrap explosive device spread out there, his hand dropping onto it, finger curling around the length of cord attached to the detonator.

"Let us show him our faith," Masada said. "Prove our courage."

"Now is not the time, Yusef," Homani said. "Remember our plan."

There was a look on Masada's face that Bolan recognized. The young man was ready to commit right now. The hand holding the detonator cord was shaking.

"Is that the bomb for Sharif Mahoud, Masada? The one you will use to destroy him when Raika introduces you to him?"

Masada stared across the room. His lean face was flushed, glistening with sweat, breath rasping in his throat.

"If you're lucky, Raika's family will be there, too."

Raika looked at Bolan for the first time he had entered the room. "I have no family," she whispered, her voice faltering.

"She looks just like her beautiful mother. Did you know that?"

"Please, no."

"Her younger sister misses her. Amina loves her. She doesn't understand why Raika has gone away." Out the corner of his eye Bolan saw Raika slowly shaking her head. "Amina wants Raika home. She even wants her to bring her boyfriend with her."

Masada was slowly curling his fingers completely around the detonator cord. He reached out with his other hand to draw the bomb to his chest.

"Perhaps you'll get the chance to say goodbye to them before Yusef sets off that bomb, Raika. See the love in Amina's eyes before she's blown apart."

Raika stared at Bolan. Her eyes were glistening with tears.

"You…"

Homani moved forward. "Yusef. Not now."

One of the mullah's bodyguards decided his chance had come and clawed at the pistol holstered under his coat.

Bolan triggered the autorifle, hammering out 5.56 mm slugs one after another. He saw them strike, shredded cloth flecking the air, blood gouting from wounds. His shots were close spaced at the group, striking Homani and his bodyguards.

"Yusef, no," Raika screamed.

Bolan saw her throw herself at Masada as he tensed, his fingers clenched around the detonator cord. As Raika slammed into Masada the pair of them stumbled and slid to the floor.

Bolan about-turned and lunged for the opening, twisting his body around the edge of the wall. As he hit the floor, Bolan felt the instant concussion of the blast, the roar of the explosion filling his head. He dragged himself away from the opening as a rush of flame filled the passage, aware of other explosive material in the work-room. The secondary explosion blew out the protecting wall, and Bolan was picked up and tossed along the passage, helpless in the grip of the blast. His body was pummeled and battered by debris. Heat and dust swirled around him. He lay helpless, choking from the thick smoke that filled the passage, his hearing fading from the concussion.

Half buried beneath the rubble, semiconscious, he passed out before Ben Sharon found him.

CHAPTER THIRTY-SIX

"Damn it, Mack, we were looking in the wrong place. The leak didn't come from the President. It was from Mahoud's family." Brognola took a breath, shaking his head. "How the hell does that happen?"

"Hal, it happens. Raika chose Homani's way. She was young. He would have played on her weaknesses. No different from Yusef Masada, or any of those others at the farm. They wanted to believe and Homani used that need. At least the President knows he doesn't have a leak from the White House. Okay?"

Brognola wasn't entirely satisfied, but he knew when it was time to let something go. After the past week he'd had plenty to chew over, not least the aftermath of the destruction at Homani's retreat.

Bolan and Sharon had been arrested by the French police. Sharon had been locked up. Bolan, concussed and suffering broken ribs and multiple lacerations, had been secured in a hospital under guard. Despite his being semiconscious for the first couple of days, the police insisted he be shackled to the bed. By the time Brognola heard what had happened Bolan was close to being charged with every crime on the books.

Frantic diplomatic maneuvering took place. When it emerged that Homani had been running an indoctrination facility, discovered by the investigating team from French security, and that a plot against Sharif Mahoud and his family had been under way, the French relented a little. There were still the matters of the deaths preceding the strike at the farm. The hits against the Homani bases in Paris. The street battle between Bolan and the pursuit team. The list seemed to become longer as the wrangling continued.

Sharif Mahoud, a well-respected figure in France, presented himself as a witness. His relating of the incidents in Afghanistan and the subsequent harassment of his family in Paris took a lot of the wind out of the French protests. They were aware of his international standing, plus the upcoming peace conference. Mahoud, using his eloquent words and persuasive manner, promised the French security and the government ministers that his revelations at the conference would clear up much of their reservations. It appeared that on the list of individuals he had there were a number of French citizens, some in government posts, who he could link to Homani and the American Hartman.

It was around this juncture that the American President himself made personal telephone contact with French authorities. The U.S. President managed to get his point across concerning the presence in France of Wazir Homani and Ali Asadi. Both active dissidents. Not France's finest example of monitoring illegal activities. In the end, still not completely mollified, and stinging at the American President's subtle reference to the U.S. having to pull France's ass out of the fire once again, the authorities agreed it would be best if the matter was put aside. Bolan and Sharon would return to their respective countries. The French would liaise with the U.S. Embassy and assist in the transfer of Sharif Mahoud to the upcoming peace conference. The promised revelations Mahoud had dangled in front of the French went a long way to appeasing them.

Ben Sharon, after a brief visit to Bolan's hospital to say goodbye, was placed on a plane back to Israel. The Mossad agent had completed his mission and had also furnished his department with additional information from the computer files he and Bolan had obtained.

There was a final meeting between Bolan and Mahoud. The man was still in mourning over the death of Raika. Bolan made it as easy as he could for the man. His respect for Mahoud had grown with each day he had spent with him. Ignoring the pain still plaguing him, Bolan had spoken quietly to Mahoud and Amina.

Alone when they left, Bolan drifted in and out of sleep. He remembered very little about the trip from the hospital to the waiting U.S. military plane that flew him home. After touchdown Bolan was transferred to a private clinic where he was treated like a VIP.

"UPDATE, HAL," Bolan said.

"Aaron and the cyberteam have plenty to work on. Those downloads you sent have exposed a hell of a lot of information about Islamic cells in the Middle East. Some interesting names keep jumping into view. The cell phones you passed along showed calls tying Homani and Asadi to Hartman and his CEO Roger Dane. Corey Mandelson's data has proved valid, too. Okay, the guy was a son of a bitch, but the stuff he detailed is pointing the finger at a bunch of names."

"And?"

Brognola smiled. "Hartman is wriggling under the

spotlight. The information we extracted linking him to less-than-savory individuals and organizations has been snatched up by every security agency on the list. They're practically drooling at what they've been fed. Hartman's legal army is working overtime trying to fend off indictments. He's sinking in the water." Brognola's face became wreathed in a wide smile at the expression.

"Okay, I bite, Hal. Just don't make me laugh. It still hurts."

"I meant to tell you. Hartman's multimillion-dollar motor cruiser, *Crescent Moon,* was sunk yesterday. An explosion below the waterline while she was in Cannes harbor." He shrugged. "No one is claiming responsibility but I think it was a parting gift from the Mossad now that they know Hartman has been supplying rockets to Hamas."

"Hope he's insured."

"French security identified the shooter who took down Mandelson. Jason Decourt. Professional assassin according to their dossier. Decourt was on a Wanted list for a number of killings throughout Europe. There's a lot to sort out of all this, but we'll benefit."

"So how is Mahoud doing?"

"The conference is going well. There won't be any quick fixes from it. Even Mahoud understands that, but he's a long-term guy, Mack. When he passed around printed copies of his information, naming names, there were some of the fastest withdrawals of members ever seen. His revelations caused an uproar, but I think he won himself some brownie points."

Good for Reef, Bolan thought. He was starting to drift again.

"I'll come back later," Brognola said. "You take it easy, big guy." At the door he turned. "The President sends his regards—and his thanks."

"That makes my day," Bolan said.

Brognola paused again. "Leila Mahoud is in the country. She's going to see her son. She said she might drop in to see you."

Bolan raised a hand. He heard the door click shut just before he fell asleep.

IN THE AFTERNOON of the following day Leila Mahoud came into the room. She stood at the side of Bolan's bed. She looked fresh and cool in a slim-fitting pale dress. They made small talk for a while before she sat gently on the edge of his bed.

"It was nice what you said to Amina. Thank you for that. It will help her. When she gets older, perhaps she'll understand."

"She had the right to know how her sister behaved. So did Reef."

"Oh, you mean the truth? Tell me, Matt, what was the truth?" Her stare was unflinching, intense. "I think you and I know what the real truth is. Not the version you delivered to Reef and Amina."

"I did what I had to do," Bolan said.

"Of course."

Her sudden smile caught him off guard. "You understand what I'm saying, Matt. Raika had been behaving oddly for some time. I watched her when she listened to her father. The distance in her eyes. Detached. And there were times she held herself back, almost as if she was about to deny his beliefs. I saw it, but I never took it further, because whatever I might have felt, she was my daughter and that was enough. My excuse, no excuse really, was I had become so immersed in helping Reef that I dismissed her moods. Even when she took herself off for weeks I imagined this boyfriend thing had caused her rebellion. She would phone to say she was fine, with friends. Then she came back and we all traveled to Afghanistan. I misread everything and I regret it so much now. How wrong I was."

"It's easy to blame yourself, Leila. Don't."

"But I understand now. It *was* Raika who was letting Homani know where we were. Her insistence on keeping her cell phone with her at all times, saying she needed to be able to speak to friends. How naive I was. She wasn't calling friends. She was betraying her father, sending text messages to Homani and Asadi, letting them know where they could find Reef. Even when we returned to France she was still doing it. The château. The hotel. I never thought for one moment that was what she was doing."

"We always see the best in those close to us."

"But you saw. You worked it out."

"Almost too late," Bolan said. "At first I thought she was simply against me. A confused young woman in a dangerous situation. I didn't look any deeper. Ben Sharon's photographs made me look closer. Seeing her with Homani and Yusef Masada made the difference. What can I say, Leila? Misjudgment all around."

She fought back the tears, laid a cool hand on Bolan's.

"You are a good man, Matthew Cooper. And a friend to us all."

Before she turned away to leave she leaned over and gently kissed him on the cheek. Then she hurried out of the room, leaving Bolan pleasantly surprised at the show of affection.

He found he was thinking back to the final moments in the room below the farmhouse. When Raika had turned to stare at him, her eyes moist with tears.

For herself?

A moment of doubt over what had happened to her?

The realization at what she had lost and would never have a chance of regaining, regardless of Homani's indoctrination?

The explosion had wiped away any answers. It had destroyed whatever Raika Mahoud had been, leaving Bolan with the doubt.

He might have given it some thought, but the door to his room opened and Barbara Price and Carl Lyons burst in, and Mack Bolan found he had enough on his hands with the living.

The dead would have to wait.

There was no rush.

They had an eternity stretching before them.

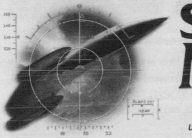

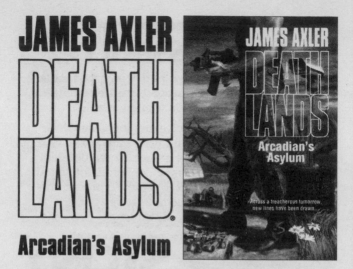